WITHDRAW

THE SEARCH

IRIS JOHANSEN

THE SEARCH

WHEELER
PUBLISHING, INC.
ROCKLAND, MA

★ AN AMERICAN COMPANY ★

Copyright © 2000 by I.J. Enterprises
Published in Large Print by arrangement with Bantam Books, a division of Random House, Inc., in the United States and Canada.

Wheeler Large Print Book Series.

Set in 16 pt Plantin.

Library of Congress Cataloging-in-Publication Data

Johansen, Iris.
   The search / Iris Johansen.
      p. (large print) cm.(Wheeler large print book series)
   ISBN 1-58724-052-1 (hardcover)
   1. Search and rescue operations—Fiction. 2. Search dogs—Fiction.
3. Arizona—Fiction. 4. Large type books. I. Title.

[PS3560.O275 S43 2001]
813'.54—dc21

2001026367
CIP

Many thanks to Sergeant John Hall and Danny Henderson, Technical Rescue Experts with the Clayton County Fire Department, and Captain Timothy Dorn, Commander, Maricopa County Sheriff's Office, for all their help.

My deep appreciation to Adele Morris, Shirley Hammond, and Bev Peabody of California Rescue Dog Association. Each was invaluable to my story with her rich store of information.

My gratitude to all search and rescue personnel who risk their lives so often to help those in need—and to all the Montys who work with search and rescue and offer their labor, love, and sometimes their lives without question.

1

Barat, Turkey
June 11

"Get out of there, Sarah," Boyd yelled from outside the house. "That wall is going to tumble any minute."

"Monty's found something." Sarah carefully moved over to the pile of rubble where the golden retriever was standing. "Be still, boy. Be very still."

Child?

"How do I know?" Monty always hoped it would be a child. He loved kids and all these lost and hurt children nearly killed him. They nearly killed her too, Sarah thought wearily. Finding the children and the old people was always the most painful. So few survived these catastrophes. The earth trembled and the walls fell and life was snuffed out as if it had never been.

Out.

"You're sure?"

Out.

"Okay." She absently patted Monty's head as she gazed at the rubble. The second story of the small house had caved in, and chances

1

of anyone being alive beneath the wreckage were minimal. She could hear no groans or weeping. It wouldn't be responsible of her to bring anyone else from the search and rescue team into the building. She should get out herself.

Child?

What the hell? Stop wasting time. She knew she wasn't going to leave until she investigated more closely. She reached for a stool and tossed it aside. "Go to Boyd, Monty."

The retriever sat down and looked at her.

"I keep telling you that you're supposed to be a professional. That means you obey orders, dammit."

Wait.

She tossed a cushion to one side and tugged at the easy chair. Jesus, it was heavy. "You can't help me now."

Wait.

"Get out of there, Sarah," Boyd yelled. "That's an order. It's been four days. You know you probably won't find anyone alive."

"We found that man in Tegucigalpa alive after twelve days. Call Monty, will you, Boyd?"

"Monty!"

Monty didn't move. She hadn't thought he would, but there was always a chance. "Stupid dog."

Wait.

"If you're going to stay there, I'm coming in to help you," Boyd said.

"No, I'll be out in a minute." Sarah glanced warily at the south wall, then tugged at the mattress until she got it to one side. "I'm just looking around."

"I'll give you three minutes."

Three minutes.

She pulled frantically at the carved headboard.

Monty whined.

"Shh." She finally heaved the headboard to one side.

And then she saw the hand.

Such a small, delicate hand, clutching a rosary...

"A survivor?" Boyd asked as Sarah walked out of the house. "Do we need to send in a team?"

She numbly shook her head. "Dead. A teenage girl. Two days, maybe. Don't risk anyone's neck. Just mark the site." She snapped on Monty's leash. "I'm going back to the trailer. I've got to get Monty out of here. You know how upset he gets. I'll be back in a couple of hours."

"Yeah, it's only your dog that's upset." Boyd's tone dripped sarcasm. "That's why you're shaking like a leaf."

"I'm fine."

"I don't want to see you take a step out of that trailer until tomorrow morning. You've gone without sleep for thirty-six hours. You know exhausted workers are a hazard to themselves and the people they're trying to help. You were incredibly stupid to run that risk. You're usually smarter than that."

3

"Monty was sure there was someone—" Why was she arguing? He was right. The only way to stay alive in situations like this was to stick to the rules and not act on impulse. She should have gone by the book. "I'm sorry, Boyd."

"You should be." He scowled. "You're one of my best people, and I won't have you thrown off the team because you're thinking with your heart instead of your head. You endangered not only yourself but your dog. What would you have done if that wall had fallen and killed Monty?"

"It wouldn't have killed Monty. I'd have thrown myself on top of him and let you dig the wall off me." She smiled faintly. "I know who's important around here."

"Very funny." He shook his head. "Except you're not joking."

"No." She rubbed her eyes. "She had a rosary in her hand, Boyd. She must have grabbed it when the quake started. But it didn't help her, did it?"

"I guess not."

"She couldn't have been over sixteen, and she was pregnant."

"Shit."

"Yeah." She gently tugged on Monty's leash. "We'll be back in a little while."

"You're not listening. I'm in charge of this search, Sarah. I want you to rest. We've probably found all the live ones. I'm expecting the order to pull out tomorrow. The Russian team can finish searching for the dead."

4

"All the more reason to work harder until the order comes. None of the Russians' dogs has Monty's nose. You know he's incredible."

"You're not so bad yourself. Do you know the other members of the team are making bets on whether or not you can actually read that dog's mind?"

"That's pretty dumb. They're all close to their own dogs. They know that when you live with an animal, you get to learn how to read them."

"Not like you."

"Why are we talking about this? The important thing is Monty is unique. He's found survivors before when everyone had given up hope. He may find more today."

"It's not likely."

She walked away.

"I mean it, Sarah."

She glanced back over her shoulder. "And how long has it been since you slept, Boyd?"

"That's none of your damn business."

"Do as I say and not as I do? I'll see you in a couple of hours." She could hear him swearing behind her as she picked her way through the rubble toward the line of mobile homes at the bottom of the hill. Boyd Medford was a good guy, a fine team leader, and everything he said made sense. But there were times when she couldn't be sensible. Too many dead. Too few survivors. Oh, God, too many bodies...

The rosary...

5

Did that poor girl have time to pray for her own life and the life of her child before she had been crushed? Probably not. Earthquakes took only a heartbeat to destroy. Maybe she should hope that death had come quickly and the girl had not suffered.

Monty pressed against her legs. *Sad.*

"Me too." She opened the door of the mobile home for Monty. "It happens. Maybe next time it won't be that way."

Sad.

She filled up Monty's water dish. "Drink, boy."

Sad. He lay down in front of the metal dish.

He'd drink soon, but she'd wait for an hour or two before she tried to feed him. He was too upset to eat. He never got used to finding the dead.

Neither did she.

She sat down on the floor beside Monty and put her arms around him. "It will be okay," she whispered. "Maybe next time we'll find a little boy alive like we did yesterday." Was it yesterday? The days blurred together when they were on a search. "Remember the child, Monty?"

Child.

"He's alive because of you. That's why we have to go on. Even if it hurts." Jesus, it did hurt. It hurt seeing Monty this upset. It hurt remembering that girl clutching the rosary. It hurt knowing there would probably not be another person found alive.

But probably was not certainly. There was always hope as long as you kept trying.

She closed her eyes. She was tired and all her muscles ached. So what? She'd have time for a long rest later. All she needed right now was a few hours of sleep and she'd be ready to go on. "Come on, let's take a nap." She stretched out beside the retriever. "Then we'll go see if we can find anyone else alive in this hellhole."

Monty was whining softly as he put his head on his paws.

"Shh." She buried her face in his fur. "It's okay." It wasn't okay. Death was never okay. "We're together. We're doing our job. We just have to get through the next few days. Then we'll be back at the ranch." She began stroking his head. "You'll like that, won't you?"

Sad.

He was hurting, but it wasn't as bad as usual. Sometimes isolated cases were worse for him. It wasn't that he became calloused to the massive loss of life he encountered in major disasters. It was just that they were working so constantly, the reaction was delayed. He'd be ready to go again in a few hours.

But would she?

She'd be fine. Just as she'd told Boyd. The last few days were always the worst. Hope was dimming, desperation growing, and the sadness lay in your heart and mind until you thought you couldn't bear it.

But she always did bear it. You had to bear it because there was always a chance someone was out there waiting. Someone who would be lost if she and Monty didn't find her.

Monty rolled over and lay on his side. *Sleep.*

"Yes, that's what we should do." Sleep, friend, and so will I. Let the memory of rosaries and unborn children fade away. Let death go. Let hope come back. "Just a little nap..."

Santo Camaro, Colombia
June 12

"How many dead?" Logan asked.

"Four." Castleton's lips tightened grimly. "And two men are in the local hospital in serious condition. Can we leave now? The stench of this place makes me want to throw up. I feel guilty as hell. I'm the one who hired Bassett for this job. I liked him."

"In a minute." Logan's gaze wandered around the scorched ruins that had once been a state-of-the-art facility. It had been only three days, but the jungle was already reclaiming its own. Grass sprouted among the fallen timbers, vines reached toward the site in a macabre embrace from nearby trees. "Were you able to recover any of Bassett's work?"

"No."

Logan looked down at the dark red carnelian scarab in his hand. "And Rudzak sent this to me this morning?"

"I guess it was Rudzak. It was on my doorstep with your name on it."

8

"It was Rudzak."

Castleton's gaze shifted from the scarab to Logan's face. "Bassett has a wife and kid. What are you going to tell them?"

"Nothing."

"What do you mean, nothing? You have to tell them what happened to Bassett."

"And what am I supposed to tell them? We don't know what happened to him. Not yet." He turned away and headed back toward the jeep.

"Rudzak's going to kill him," Castleton said, following Logan.

"Maybe."

"You know it."

"I think he'll try to make a deal first."

"Ransom?"

"Possibly. He wants something, or he wouldn't have bothered to take Bassett."

"And you're going to deal with that bastard? After what he did to your people?"

"I'll deal with the devil himself if it will get me what I want."

It was the answer Castleton expected. John Logan had not gotten to be one of the foremost economic forces in the world by avoiding confrontation. He had made billions with his computer company and other enterprises before he'd reached forty.

And he had risked the lives of several scientists to realize the gigantic rewards this project offered. Some people would say that no man with a conscience would have set up this facility when he knew what the consequences might—

9

"Say it." Logan was staring at him. "Let it out."

"You shouldn't have done it."

"Everyone in this facility chose to be here. I never lied to them about what they were facing. They believed it was worth it."

"I wonder how they felt when the bullets hit them. Do you think they still thought it was worth it?"

Logan didn't flinch. "Who the hell knows what's important enough to die for? Do you want out, Castleton?"

Yes, he wanted out. The situation was becoming too deadly and complicated. He didn't deal well with either, and he cursed the day he'd become involved in it. "Are you firing me?"

"No way. I need you. You know how things work down here. That's why I hired you in the first place. But I'll understand if you want out. I'll pay you and let you walk away."

"Let me?"

"I could find a way to keep you on the job," Logan said wearily. "There's always a way to do anything you want to do. You just have to decide how far you want to commit yourself. But you've done a good job for me and I'm not willing to force you to stay on. I'll try to find someone else."

"No one could force me to do anything I don't want to do."

"Have it your way." Logan got into the jeep. "Take me back to the airport. I've got to get busy. Am I going to have trouble with the local police?"

"You know better than that. These hills are deep in drug country. It's not safe to ask questions. The police just look the other way." He smiled bitterly as he started the jeep. "Isn't that why you built the facility here?"

"Yes."

"And they won't help you get Bassett away from Rudzak. He's a dead man."

"If he's not dead now, I'll get him back."

"How? Money?"

"Whatever it takes."

"It's impossible. Even if you pay a ransom, Rudzak may kill him anyway. You can't expect to—"

"I'll get him back." Logan's voice suddenly vibrated with harshness. "Listen to me, Castleton. You may think I'm a son of a bitch, but I don't shrug off my responsibilities. Those were my employees who died and I want the man who did it. And if you think I'm going to let him kill or use Bassett to get at me, you're wrong. I'll find him."

"In the middle of the jungle?"

"In the middle of hell." Logan's voice was flint sharp. "Now you've been telling me how sorry you are and how guilty I should feel. Well, I don't have time for guilt. I've always found it counterproductive. You do what you have to do, but don't tell me anything's impossible until you've tried and failed and tried again. I won't buy it."

"You don't have to buy it. I'm not asking you to—" His gaze narrowed on Logan's face. "You're trying to manipulate me."

11

"Am I?"

"You know damn well you are."

"Smart man. You should have expected it. I'm just as ruthless as you think I am, and I told you I needed you."

Castleton was silent for a moment. "Do you really think you have a chance of saving Bassett?"

"If he's alive, I'll bring him back. Will you help me?"

"What do you want me to do?"

"What you've been doing all along. Grease palms and take care of my people. By the way, I want them out of that hospital and on their way home as soon as possible. They're too vulnerable here."

"I was going to take care of that for you anyway."

"And keep your ears open and your mouth shut. If I'm not in the area, Rudzak will probably contact you first." He smiled crookedly. "Don't worry, I'm not going to ask you to put your neck on the block. You're much too valuable to me in other ways."

"I'm not a coward, Logan."

"No, but this is out of your area of expertise. I always get the right person for the right job. I assure you I wouldn't hesitate to rope you into it if I thought it necessary."

Castleton believed him. He had never seen Logan like this. Most of the time he kept that streak of hard ruthlessness buried beneath a layer of easy charisma. He suddenly recalled the many stories about Logan's shady associations in the early years he had spent in Asia. Gazing at Logan now, he could believe there was more truth than fiction in those wild tales of smuggling and violent power struggles with local gangs who had tried to sell him "protection."

"Well?"

"Okay." Castleton moistened his lips. "I'll stay."

"Good."

"But not because of anything you've said. I just feel guilty as hell that I was in town and not here when it happened. Maybe I could have done something, anything to prevent—"

"Don't be an idiot. You'd have been dead too. Now, do you know of any contact Rudzak might have that we can tap?"

"The talk is there's a dealer named Ricardo Sanchez in Bogotá who's been acting as a go-between for the Mendez cartel and Rudzak."

"Find him. Do anything you have to do. I want to know where Rudzak's camp is located."

"I'm not a thug, Logan."

"Then would it hurt your delicate sense of ethics to hire a thug?"

"You don't have to be sarcastic."

"No, I don't," he said wearily. "If I weren't pressed for time, I'd go to Bogotá and pressure Sanchez myself. Never mind, I have a man who can find out what I need to know."

"I hope you succeed."

"So do I. But even if Sanchez proves useless, I'll still find Bassett."

Castleton shook his head. "No one around

here is going to tell you where he is or go into that jungle to look for him."

"Then I'll find him on my own."

"How?"

"I know someone who might be able to help me."

"The right person for the right job?"

"Exactly."

"Then God help him."

"It's not a man." Logan glanced back over his shoulder at the ruins. "It's a woman."

Logan called Margaret Wilson, his personal assistant, the minute his jet was airborne out of Santo Camaro. "Pull the file on Sarah Patrick."

"Patrick?" Logan could visualize Margaret mentally going over the files in her head. "Oh, the dog lady. I did that research on her about six months ago, didn't I? I thought you'd gotten what you needed from her."

"I did. Something else has come up."

"The same lever won't do?"

"Maybe. But this situation has complications. I need to review the file because I'll probably have to use everything we know about her. Not just how to make her jump when I whistle."

"I don't think Sarah Patrick is going to jump when anyone whistles," Margaret said coolly. "And I'd like to be around when you pucker your lips, John. I have an idea that you got lucky the last time. Serve you right if you go around—"

14

"Lay off me, Margaret," he said with a sigh. "I'm not up to defending myself right now."

"Why not?" She paused. "Is Bassett dead?"

"No, I don't think so. He was alive when they took him."

"Shit."

"I need that file, Margaret."

"Five minutes. Do you want a fax or should I give you the information over the phone?"

"Call me back." Logan hung up, leaned back in his chair, and closed his eyes.

Sarah Patrick.

Her image was there before him: short dark hair streaked by sunlight, high cheekbones, olive skin, and a lean, athletic body. Features more interesting than pretty and a wit as sharp as her tongue.

That sharpness had stung him innumerable times during the time in Phoenix. Sarah was not one to forgive and forget. But the sharpness had been for him only. She had become good friends with Eve Duncan and Joe Quinn after Logan pressured Sarah into working with Eve. The three were still good friends, according to Eve. She had called him last month and told him that Sarah had visited them in Atlanta and had—

His phone rang.

"Sarah Elizabeth Patrick," Margaret said. "Twenty-eight. Half Apache Indian, half Irish. Grew up in Chicago, except the summers she spent with her father on the reservation. Mother and father both deceased.

15

The father died when Sarah was a child, her mother five years ago. High IQ. She studied veterinary medicine at Arizona State University. Inherited a small ranch from her grandfather in the foothills of the mountains outside Phoenix at about the same time the mother died. She still lives there. Oh, you know that. You visited her ranch. She's something of a loner but got along well with students and professors. After school, she started working with the K9 training unit of ATF. She can do anything with animals. She's affiliated with a volunteer search and rescue group based in Tucson, and evidently ATF has given her permission to work with them on both man-made and natural disasters. She and her dog, Monty, have also been lent out to several police departments to find cadavers and also to detect explosives. Monty is something of a wonder dog."

"I know."

"That's right, he found that body in Phoenix." She hesitated. "You know, I think I'd like her, John. Those search and rescue people are pretty wonderful. When I was watching the television coverage of the Oklahoma City bombing, I wanted to give every one of those guys a medal. Or my firstborn child."

"You don't have a child."

"Whatever." She paused. "She doesn't deserve to be pulled into this thing with Bassett."

"Bassett didn't deserve what happened to him either."

"He made a commitment and a choice."

"She can always tell me no."

"You won't let her. It means too much to you."

"Then why are you trying to argue me out of it?"

"I don't know. Yes, I do. Did I mention that Sarah Patrick was one of those rescue workers at Oklahoma City? Maybe this is my try at giving her my firstborn child."

"She doesn't need it. She has her dog."

"And you're not going to listen to me."

"I'm listening. I wouldn't dare do anything else."

"Bull. I'm not asking you to give her a medal. Just give her an out."

"Where is she now?"

"On her way home from Barat. She's been there five days. Earthquake."

"I've not been totally in my own world, Margaret. I heard about the earthquake before I left Monterey."

"But it didn't rock you like the news about Bassett. So what do I do? Do you want me to phone her? Set up a meeting?"

"She'd tell you to go to hell. Since I'm a true gentleman and want to spare you that indignity, I'll take care of it myself."

"You're afraid I'll bond with her and we'd gang up on you."

"You guessed it."

"Okay, then where can I reach you? Are you flying direct to Phoenix?"

"No, I'm going to Atlanta."

Silence. "Eve?"

"Who else?"

"Oh."

"I believe I have you speechless. What an accomplishment. I'll take pity on you. No, I'm not going in sentimental pursuit of a lost love. Eve and I are friends now."

"Heaven forbid anyone would mistake you for being sentimental. You don't have to explain to me about—"

"No, but you'd die of curiosity and then I'd have to break in a new personal assistant. Such a bore."

"I'm not nosy. Anyone would be curious," she said tartly. "After all, you spent a year with her. I thought you might—"

"You can reach me in Atlanta at the Ritz Carlton in Buckhead."

"If you're not going directly to see Sarah Patrick, I'll keep tabs on her."

"That's not necessary. I'll see her in Atlanta."

"No, she's booked back to Phoenix."

"She'll change her plans. By the way, I'm calling Sean Galen after I hang up. If he needs funds, give him—"

"Carte blanche," Margaret finished for him. "As usual. I thought you'd pull him into any rescue attempt. Is he to go directly to Santo Camaro?"

"No, I'm sending him to Bogotá on a fact-finding mission."

Margaret made a distinctly skeptical sound. "Pretty words. Who's he going to beat up?"

"Maybe no one. I just need him to find someone and ask a few questions."

"Yeah, sure."

"If Castleton calls, I want to hear from him immediately. He has my digital phone number, but he's too cautious for my taste. He may try to reach me on it only in case of emergencies. But as far as I'm concerned, everything is an emergency at this point."

"No problem."

"Wrong. I see nothing but problems looming. I'll keep in touch." He hung up.

He should have known Margaret would champion Sarah Patrick. Margaret was an ardent feminist who admired tough, smart women who boldly ran their own lives and careers. She had liked Eve Duncan for that same reason. Eve was a top forensic sculptor who had overcome tremendous odds in both her personal and professional life. A very special woman...

He hadn't seen her in almost six months. Had he made the transition from lover to friend as he'd told Margaret? Who knew? He had felt something for Eve he'd never felt for any other woman, and he'd tried to analyze it in these last months. Respect, pity, passion...Hell, maybe all those emotions had been present. She had certainly caught his imagination from the moment he had met her.

No, he wasn't being honest. He had loved Eve. What was love but respect, pity, passion, and a hundred other emotions? Joe Quinn had said Logan didn't love her enough and deserved to lose her. Well, he had lost her, so maybe the bastard was right. Maybe he'd never make a total commitment to a woman. Totality was for the young and the daring.

Christ, that sounded like a soap opera.

Okay, forget personal problems. Eve was going to marry Joe Quinn, a fact that he'd accepted months ago. His commitment now was to Bassett, and he had to concentrate all his efforts on bringing him back.

That's where Sarah Patrick came in.

He could force her to help him as he'd done the last time, but he'd prefer not to do that. Was there anything else in her background he could use to manipulate her?

He had time to think about it. He should have at least a day to decide what to say to her.

It might take every minute of that time, he thought ruefully. Sarah was tough as nails and Margaret was probably right. This time when he tried to get her to jump when he whistled, there was every chance the situation would explode.

And the situation was explosive enough without Sarah. He had been uneasy ever since he had left Santo Camaro. His instincts told him that something was not as it should be, and he trusted his instincts. What the hell was bothering him?

He was filled with anger and sadness and the usual adrenaline-charged eagerness to jump into the fray—emotions that were getting in the way. So put those emotions on hold. He had to clear his head and analyze Rudzak's opening move. Why had Rudzak taken Bassett? Ransom or revenge was the obvious answer, but Rudzak was seldom obvious.

He pulled the scarab from his pocket, the one Rudzak had sent him via Castleton. His thumb rubbed its carved surface. The scarab was from such a long time ago, a time of pain and torment and regret.... Rudzak had meant to send a message with it, but what did the message have to do with Bassett?

He leaned back in his chair. Think. Play the scenario out. Put everything together before you call Galen.

The shrill howl echoed eerily in the night.

Sarah stopped at the top of the hill, her breathing labored from the hard uphill run.

Another howl, more mournful than the first.

A wolf, Sarah thought. Probably one of the Mexican gray wolves that had been recently released in western Arizona. There had been stories of a few migrating to this area, much to the anger of the local ranchers. That howl had sounded very close. She stared at the crags spiking the mountain behind her.

Nothing. The night was clear and still and the wolf was probably farther away than he sounded.

Beautiful. Monty was staring at the mountain.

"You wouldn't think so if you ran across one of those wolves, Monty. They have no manners. Ask the ranchers around here."

Another howl echoed through the night.

Monty's head lifted. *Beautiful. Free.*

Dogs were supposed to be descended from wolves, but she had never noticed any savage qualities in Monty. No animal could be more gentle or loving. Yet was he feeling some buried instinct as he listened to that wolf? The idea made her uneasy, and she dismissed it immediately. "I think it's time we went back to the cabin. You're getting moonstruck." She started at a run down the path toward the cabin in the valley below.

Clean wind.

Clean air.

Firm earth.

Silence that had nothing to do with death or sorrow.

God, it was good to be home.

Good.

"You bet. Beat you to the cabin."

She didn't, of course. Monty had already jumped through his dog door and was lapping at the water in his dish when she threw open the front door. "You're supposed to be tired from that job in Barat. Give me a break."

Monty gave her a scornful look and then leisurely walked over to his rug in front of the fireplace.

"Okay, don't give me a break. But remember who pays for the groceries."

Monty yawned and stretched out.

The fire was welcoming and her easy chair beckoned. She would like to stretch out herself.

She reluctantly glanced at the blinking red

light on her answering machine. She had ignored it when she'd arrived at the cabin two hours before and was tempted to do the same thing now.

Retrieve the messages or take a shower and then curl up in front of the fire? She knew what she wanted to do. Close the world out and go back to the routine with Monty that soothed and sustained them during these off periods. Even the telephone was an intrusion when all she needed was rest, exercise, and no more mental stress than was involved in reading a good book.

But that red light wouldn't stop blinking. She might as well get it over with.

She crossed the room. Two messages.

She punched the button.

"Todd Madden. Welcome back, Sarah."

Shit. She didn't need this.

Her hands clenched into fists as she heard Madden's smooth, faintly mocking tone. "I hear you did a magnificent job. The team earned grateful praise from the Turkish government, not to mention nice coverage by CNN. I think we may have to bring you and Monty up to Washington for a few interviews."

"The hell you will, you asshole," she muttered.

"I can almost see your expression. You're so predictable. Unfortunately, Boyd's mandatory report to ATF on you mentioned that you disobeyed orders on one occasion. He was obviously trying to protect you, but he had to do his job. Are you becoming unstable, Sarah? You know we can't permit instability at ATF. And you know the consequences of your expulsion from ATF." He paused. "But I'm sure you can persuade me that this was just an isolated incident. Come up to Washington for those interviews and we'll talk about it."

Slimy bastard.

"Call me and tell me when you'll arrive. No more than two days, I think. We don't want to be old news." He hung up.

She closed her eyes as waves of rage poured through her. Damn him. Damn him.

She drew a deep breath and tried to control herself. Madden would love to know that he had upset her. He preferred cowed obedience and he didn't like it when she refused to give it to him. He might have the upper hand, but she had let him know what she thought of him any number of times in language that was both abusive and explicit.

Screw him. There wasn't any question she'd have to go to Washington, but she wouldn't call him back and she'd take at least a three-day rest before she left the ranch.

She punched the button for the second message.

"It's Eve, Sarah. We've finally got it. It's confirmed. We'll wait for you. Please come right away." Eve hung up.

So much for rest, she thought resignedly. She would never phone Eve to ask her to wait a day or two. Eve had waited too long already.

"Looks like we have another plane trip

tomorrow, Monty. We have to go see Eve in Atlanta."

"I'm here," Logan said as soon as Eve picked up the phone. "I've checked in at the Ritz Carlton in Buckhead."

"Thanks for coming, Logan. I wasn't sure you would."

"I always told you I'd come when you called." He hesitated before asking, "How's Quinn?"

"Wonderful. He's very good to me."

"That's no great chore. Who could help it? I'll see you tomorrow morning."

"You could come to the cottage tonight."

"No, I'm here to support you, not irritate Quinn. Take care of yourself." He hung up.

She had sounded calm and there was a ring of truth in her words when she spoke about Joe Quinn. It was clear all was going well in that quarter. Was he disappointed? It surprised him that he felt a tinge of regret but no pain. Well, you got over everything in time, and he had never really felt that Eve belonged to him even when they were living together. Their bond had been fragile, and Quinn had no trouble barging in and—

His phone rang.

Margaret?

"Hello, Logan, it's been a long time."

Logan's hand tightened on the receiver. "Hello, Rudzak."

"You don't sound surprised to hear from me."

"Why should I be surprised? I knew it was only a matter of time."

"You don't know the meaning of time. Neither did I until I lived in that hell you threw me into. It was like being buried alive. Every minute was a decade. Did you know my hair turned white in that prison? I'm younger than you and I look twenty years older."

"How do you know how I look?"

"Oh, I've kept tabs on you. I saw you once on the street and several times on television in the last two years. You've done well for yourself. You're a very big man."

"Where's Bassett?"

"I don't want to talk about Bassett. I want to talk about you...and me. I've waited a long time for this moment, and I'm savoring it."

"I'm not. Talk about Bassett or I'll hang up."

"No, you won't. You'll stay on the line as long as I want to talk to you because you're afraid of what will happen to Bassett if you don't. You haven't changed. You still have that streak of softness. I'm glad you're not completely hard. It's going to make it easier for me."

"Is Bassett alive?"

"At present. Do you believe me?"

26

"No, I want to hear his voice."

"Not now. Bassett is such a small part of what's between us. Did you know the first thing I did after I got out of prison was visit Chen Li's grave?"

"This isn't about Chen Li. This is about Bassett."

"It's about Chen Li. Everything is about Chen Li. You allowed her to be buried in that disgustingly simple grave like a thousand others in that cemetery. How could you do that?"

"She was buried with quiet dignity and grace. The way she lived."

"The way you made her live. She was a queen and you made her common."

"Don't talk about her."

"Why not? What can you do to me that you haven't done? Am I making you feel guilty? You are guilty."

"And you're a crazy son of a bitch."

"I wasn't crazy when I went into that prison. If I'm crazy now, it's because of you. You knew what I did was right and you let me rot in that cell. But I'm not insane, and when this is over I'll be able to live again. Do you know why I hit that research facility?"

"You knew it was important to me."

"No, that wasn't the reason. Think about it. It will come to you. I'll even help you along. Did you get the scarab?"

"I got it."

"Good. I thought it was a fitting signature to Santo Camaro. It was the first Egyptian piece I gave to Chen Li. It wasn't very expensive or important, but she didn't care. I was able to give her much nicer pieces later."

"That you stole and murdered to get. Do you think she would have accepted them if she'd known how many people you killed to get those artifacts?"

"But she didn't know and those people didn't matter. She was the only one who mattered. She deserves the best. I'll always give her the best."

"You're talking about her as if she's still alive."

"She'll always be alive to me. Every day in that prison she was with me. She kept me sane. I talked to her and told her how much I hated you and how I was going to hurt you."

"You can't hurt me, Rudzak."

"Oh, but I can." His voice lowered to a silken murmur. "I may be white-haired, but Chen Li would still think I'm handsome. I remember how she would stroke my face and tell me how beautiful I was, how kind and—"

"Shut up."

Rudzak chuckled. "You see, it's easy to hurt you. I'll be calling you again. I've gotten a great deal of satisfaction out of this conversation." He hung up.

Bastard.

Keep calm. The anger pouring through him was counterproductive. Rudzak would enjoy knowing how that jab had pierced his defenses. He did know. Logan had been caught unprepared and let Rudzak see his rage and pain.

28

You are guilty.

Chen Li.

Don't think of her. Think of Bassett and the problems Rudzak was causing now.

Don't think of Chen Li.

Rudzak pressed the disconnect on the phone and looked down at the tiny round box in his other hand. He wiped the raindrops from the lid. It was a lovely thing, studded with ivory and lapis lazuli. He'd been told that it had once belonged to a princess of Egypt, but he'd embroidered the tale for Chen Li when he gave it to her.

"This belonged to Meretaten, the daughter of Nefertiti. She was supposed to be even lovelier and more clever than her mother."

"I never heard of her." Chen Li held the box up to the window to see the sunlight glitter on the blue stones. "I love it, Martin. Where did you get it?"

"A collector in Cairo."

"It must have cost the earth."

"Not so much. I made a good deal."

She chuckled. "That's what you always say."

He smiled. "I told him it was joining the collection of a woman who should have been born a queen in the time of the pharaohs. There were no rules then but the ones they made for themselves."

A shadow crossed her face. Things had been going so well that he had moved too fast. He pretended to misunderstand the withdrawal. "You were just being polite? You don't really like it?"

She walked into his arms. "I love it. I always love everything you give me."

She leaned back and looked up at him. Her eyes were night dark and he could see himself mirrored in them. His reflection was always better, almost godlike when he saw himself in Chen Li's eyes.

She was gazing at him uncertainly. "Martin?"

Don't scare her. She was closer to him than ever and there would soon come a moment when she would be his. Just don't scare her.

He lifted her hand to his lips. "Happy birthday, Chen Li."

One of her last birthdays.

He could feel warm tears blend with the rain on his cheeks.

"Rudzak." He turned to see Carl Duggan coming toward him. "I've set the timer. We've got to be out of here before someone trips it."

"In a minute. I want to leave Logan a present." He carefully placed the box behind a boulder where it would be sheltered from the blast. He whispered, "Happy birthday, Chen Li."

Rest in peace, Bonnie Duncan.

The minister's words echoed in Sarah's mind even as the casket was lowered into the grave. It wasn't only Bonnie who was at peace now, she thought as she looked at Eve Duncan, who stood between Joe Quinn and Eve's adopted daughter, Jane MacGuire. After all these years of searching for the remains of her child who had been murdered over a decade

30

ago, Eve had brought Bonnie home. The DNA report that had just come through had confirmed these bones were her daughter's.

Tears were running down Eve's mother's face, but Eve was not weeping. Her expression reflected peace, sadness, and completion. She had wept her tears for Bonnie long ago. Her daughter was home now.

But Sarah felt tears sting her own eyes as she tossed the rose in her hand on top of the casket.

Good-bye, Bonnie Duncan.

"I think we should leave the family alone to say their good-byes," John Logan said in a low voice. "Let's go back to the cottage and wait for them."

Sarah hadn't been aware that he had moved to stand beside her. She instinctively shifted away from him.

Logan shook his head. "I know how you feel about me, but this isn't the time to burden Eve with it. We've got to help her get through this."

He was right. She hadn't been pleased when she had seen him drive up to the cottage a few hours before it was time to go to the burial site, but she couldn't fault his behavior toward Eve and Joe. He had been both sympathetic and supportive. And he was also right about leaving the family alone now. She turned away from the grave and started the short walk around the lake toward the cottage. It was pretty here, she thought. Eve had chosen a lovely spot on a small hill overlooking the lake to bury her daughter.

"Where's Monty?" Logan asked as he caught up with her.

"I left him in the cottage. Being at the grave site would have upset him."

"Ah, yes, I'd forgotten what a sensitive canine your Monty is."

"More sensitive than some people."

"Ouch." He grimaced. "I didn't mean to slam your dog. I'm actually trying to be pleasant."

"Are you?"

"And evidently not succeeding."

"Right."

"I'll start again. Eve told me that it was you and Monty who found Bonnie. She said the two of you must have gone over every foot of that national park until you discovered where that murderer buried her."

"We did. But I almost gave up."

"But you didn't."

"Eve's my friend."

"Then don't you think you could forgive my rather unscrupulous methods of bringing the two of you together?"

"No," she said coldly. "I don't like being forced to do anything. You're as bad as Madden. Always trying to manipulate everyone and every situation."

"I'm not quite as black as you're painting me. I do have a few virtues."

She was silent.

"I'm patient. I'm responsible. I can be a good friend. Ask Eve."

"I'm not interested. Why are you making this futile attempt to convince me you're a decent human being?" Her eyes narrowed. "You're up to something."

"Why should I be—" He shrugged. "Yes, I'm up to something, besides failing to convince you that I'm anything but a son of a bitch. Too bad. It would have made it easier on both of us."

"Why the hell are you here?"

"I'm here for the same reason you're here. I wanted to support Eve when she needed her friends."

"You weren't her friend. You were her lover and it won't do you any good to come here and try to lure her away from Joe. She loves him and you're past history, Logan."

"I know, but thanks for reminding me. I can see it's only your dog that has any sensitivity. I'm not here to stir up old embers. Is it too hard to believe that I want only the best for Eve?"

"I don't have to believe or disbelieve you." Her pace quickened. "As I said, I don't care. It doesn't matter if you—"

"Sarah!"

She turned to see Jane MacGuire running down the hill toward them, her red hair gleaming in the sunlight. The ten-year-old's expression was pale and strained as she stopped beside Sarah. "Hi, can I walk back with you?"

"Sure. But I thought you'd want to wait for Eve."

She shook her head. "She doesn't need me. She has Joe." She looked straight ahead. "Neither of them wants me there right now."

Sarah could see a problem looming. "You're

part of Eve's family. She always wants you with her."

"Not now. I don't belong here. It's Bonnie's time." She shifted her glance to Logan. "You knew it. That's why you took Sarah away."

Logan nodded. "At least someone appreciates my sensitivity. But Sarah is right. You're part of the family."

Jane's lips tightened. "You're trying to make me feel better. I don't need your pity. I know Joe and Eve care about me, but I'm not Bonnie. I'll never be Bonnie to them. So don't tell me they want me there when they're saying good-bye to her. Can't you see how hard it is for them having me here right now? All they want to think about is Bonnie, but they have to try to make me feel all cozy and wanted because they don't want to hurt me."

"Talk to them," Sarah said gently.

"No." Jane looked away from them and repeated, "It's Bonnie's time." She changed the subject. "May I go on ahead and take Monty out for a walk?"

"I think that would be a very good idea."

Sarah frowned, troubled, as she watched Jane run down the path toward the cottage.

"Will Monty go with her?" Logan asked.

She nodded. "He adores her. They got to know each other very well in Phoenix."

"You like her too. She's not the easiest kid to get to know."

"She may look like a kid, but she's more grown-up than most adults. That's what happens when you're raised in foster homes and on the streets." She nibbled at her lower lip. "She's right, isn't she? Having her here is going to be a strain on Eve and Joe."

"Probably. It seems Jane has good instincts." He was studying her face. "What are you thinking?"

"None of your business." They had reached the porch of the cottage. "Are you leaving now?"

"Not yet. I thought I'd leave for the airport after lunch. You're on the three o'clock flight, aren't you?"

"How do you know that?"

"Eve told me on the phone. She said they picked you up at the airport. Could I give you a lift?"

"Joe's going to drive me."

"But shouldn't he stay with Eve? It won't hurt you to occupy the same car with me. It's only an hour's drive."

It wouldn't hurt her, but she didn't want any favors from him.

It was as if he'd read her mind. "I'm not doing you any favors, Sarah. Considering your opinion of me, you should know better."

No, she could see Logan doing favors for Eve but not for her. Why should he? She didn't know why he had made the attempt to bridge the gulf between them, but it wasn't because he regretted what he had done. Logan never looked back after he had made a decision.

"Eve needs Joe right now," Logan said. "We both know it."

"And does that sting, Logan?"

"Would you feel sorry for me if it did?"

"Hell, no."

"I didn't think so. So do I take you to the airport?"

She shrugged. "Okay. I should leave by one."

He nodded. "I'll be ready. But shouldn't you be there earlier to board Monty in the cargo?"

"Monty always travels in the cabin with me."

"I thought only small animals or dogs for the blind were permitted in the cabin."

"He has special ATF clearance."

He smiled. "And if he didn't, you'd probably insist on traveling in the baggage with him."

"You've got it." Sarah opened the front door. "I'm going to start making sandwiches and coffee. There's Reverend Watson coming down the path. Why don't you make yourself useful, say something charming and send him on his way?"

"I'm surprised you think I'm capable of being charming."

Oh, he had never tried it on her, but she had seen him work that charisma. It was probably one of the more potent weapons in his arsenal. "Why should it surprise you?" As she entered the cottage, she glanced at him over her shoulder. "I understand that most of Germany's population thought Hitler was charming."

"Thanks for coming, Sarah." Eve sat down in the porch swing and looked out at the lake. "I know you're tired. But it meant a lot for me to have you here."

"Don't be silly. I wanted to come."

"I think Bonnie would have liked you to be here. After all, you did find her."

"We were lucky."

"Don't give me that. You worked your butt off."

"That doesn't always mean that Monty and I find what we're looking for." She studied Eve's face. "Is everything okay with you?"

"It will be soon. It feels very strange right now." Her gaze moved to the hill across the lake. "She's home now. That means everything. Even though she never really left me."

Sarah nodded. "Memories can be very precious."

"Yes." She smiled faintly. "But that's not exactly what I meant." She changed the subject. "I'm worried about Jane."

"I thought you would be."

"Most of the time I think she's happy with us. She knows we love her." She sighed. "But Jane's not easy."

"The situation's not easy." Sarah paused. "How would you feel about Jane spending a few weeks with me at my cabin?"

Eve didn't speak for a moment. "Why?"

"A change will be good for her. She loves Monty and she likes me. I'd take good care of her."

"I know you would." She frowned slightly. "Has she talked to you about Bonnie?"

"The important question is if she's spoken to you about her."

"Not since you found Bonnie. I tried a

37

couple of times, but she shuts me out. I've been hoping that time— I don't know. It's hard for me to think right now."

"It's a period of adjustment for all of you. You've been obsessed for years with the thought of bringing Bonnie home. I know you're happy that she's here now, but it will be—"

"Jane thinks she's second best," Eve interrupted. "I tried to tell her how different— She won't accept it. She's not resentful, but I can't talk her out of it."

"With her lousy childhood, it's possible you may never be able to convince her. But that doesn't mean you can't have a good life together."

"Don't tell me that. I want her to feel special. Everyone should feel special."

"Jane *is* special. She's tough and independent and smart as a whip. So smart she knows that you're confused and sad right now and she can't help you. It hurts her. Send her to me for a while, Eve."

"I'll think about it." Eve tried to smile. "I never thought I'd have this kind of problem adjusting when I found Bonnie. It's not that I'm not relieved, it's just..."

"You've lived your life a certain way because Bonnie was lost. Now she's found."

Eve nodded. "It will take a little time, but God, I'm lucky, Sarah. I've got Joe. Everything will fall into place as long as I have Joe." She reached over and took Sarah's hand. "And friends like you and Logan."

"Speaking of Logan, it's time I left for the airport. Where is he?"

"He walked down to the lake."

"Alone?"

Eve nodded. "Which is just as well. He and Joe are still not too friendly."

Sarah grinned. "Because you're such a femme fatale."

"Yeah, sure." She straightened her glasses and got to her feet. "Let's go find Jane and Monty. You'll have to pry her away from him."

"It won't be so bad if you tell her that she'll see him soon."

"I said I'd think about it." She made a face. "You're obstinate as hell, Sarah. What makes you so sure you're the best thing for Jane right now? If you get a call, you and Monty will be trekking off to some outlandish part of the world. What would you do with her?"

Sarah shrugged. "We'd make out."

Eve shook her head. "For that matter, what would you do if you had a child of your own? Talk about adjustments."

"I'd deal with the problem when I had to face it."

"Kids are more demanding than dogs."

"That's why I stick to dogs. I'm happy living just as I am. Can you imagine me with a husband and a bunch of kids?"

"No, not really. But it must be a lonely life."

"Why? I have Monty and my friends in the unit."

"Who you never see unless you're on some rescue mission."

"It's enough."

"Why is it enough? Why won't you get close to anyone?"

She smiled. "Eve, stop trying to make me into some kind of scarred drama queen. I'm not like you. I've no dark, brooding past. I'm just a normal woman who happens to be a little more selfish than most people. My life suits me just fine."

"And I'm to mind my own business."

"Do what you like. But you surprise me. You were once one of the most isolated women on the planet, and you think *my* lack of social interaction is a problem."

"Touché." Eve smiled. "I guess I just want everyone to be as happy as I've been lately."

"I'm happy as a clam." She tilted her head. "You know, I've always wondered about that phrase. How does anyone know how happy a clam is? And why should a clam be particularly happy?" She chuckled. "Okay, I'm as happy as Monty when he's getting his belly rubbed. It doesn't get any better than that."

Fifteen minutes to one. It was almost time to go.

Logan started back toward the cottage. He could see the shadowy figures of Sarah and Monty silhouetted in the windows. They looked like two fantasy figures on the cover of a novel.

But there was nothing fanciful about Sarah Patrick. Damn, she was hardheaded. She would neither forgive nor forget, and she was tying his hands. He had only another hour to find a way to get her help on a voluntary basis; after that he'd have to—

His digital phone rang.

"I've heard from Rudzak," Castleton said. "He wants to deal."

Logan's hand tightened on the phone. "Did you talk to Bassett?"

"Not yet. He says that all you have to do is come up with fifty thousand dollars and he'll let you talk to Bassett. I'm to leave the money at a drop near the research facility."

"And how much cash to release him?"

"He wants to negotiate that with you personally."

Logan had expected that. "Have you found out anything more about Rudzak's location?"

"I told you that you'd have to take care of that. I gave you a lead. Hasn't your man found Sanchez yet?"

"He's working on it, but it wouldn't hurt if he had help."

"Dammit, I'm doing everything I can on this end. When are you coming?"

"I'm leaving this afternoon."

"And what do I do about the money?"

"Give it to him. I've told Margaret to give you anything you need."

"It could be a bluff. Bassett could be dead."

"Give it to him."

"What if he doesn't let you talk to Bassett?"

"We'll worry about that when it happens."

Castleton paused. "I gave him your number when he asked me for it. I hope you don't mind."

"No, you did the right thing. If he wants to talk to me, make it easy. I want to keep on with the dialogue. The more we're in contact, the better our chance of finding out something."

"I think he's killed him, Logan. What if he's dead?"

"Then Rudzak will be dead too."

He hung up and shoved the phone into his pocket. He needed to get down to Santo Camaro. He had learned long ago that you played by the rules of the game in progress and this game was shaping up to be very nasty.

His gaze went back to Sarah and Monty waiting on the porch. Too bad. He had no more time. He took out his phone again and quickly dialed a number.

"Take care of yourself." Logan brushed a kiss on Eve's forehead before he got into the car. "If you need me for anything, give me a call."

"I'm fine." She looked at Sarah, who was sitting in the passenger seat. "I'll let you know about Jane."

"I have to fly straight from here to Washington, but that should take only a couple of days. After that I'll be at the cabin."

Eve waved and stepped back as Logan started the car.

Sarah turned her head and saw Eve still standing there, watching them as they started down the gravel road. For a moment she looked very lonely, but then Joe came out of the cottage and stood behind her with his hands on her shoulders. No, Eve wasn't lonely. She had Joe and her mother and Jane. She would never have to be lonely again unless she wanted to be. But wasn't that true of everyone? You made choices, and to be alone was one of them.

What was she thinking? She wasn't alone. As she had told Eve, she had Monty and a job that fulfilled her. She didn't want anything or anyone else.

"What did she mean about letting you know about Jane?" Logan asked.

"I may have Jane visit me for a few weeks."

"When?"

"As soon as possible."

"No."

She turned to stare at him. "What?"

"Not now."

"What the hell are you talking about? Now is when Eve needs my help. The sooner the—Why am I even talking to you about it? It's none of your business."

"It's my business. I need your help. And I need it now."

The arrogance of the bastard. "Go jump in the lake, Logan."

"I'll pay you anything you want. Name your price."

"You don't have enough money."

His lips tightened. "I was afraid you'd say that. Sorry. I can't let you walk away from this job, Sarah. It's too important."

"To you. I don't give a damn about what you need, Logan."

"I know. That's why I called Todd Madden and asked him to arrange for ATF to lend you to me."

She stared at him, stunned. "What?"

"You heard me."

"My God, you're doing it again."

"I tried to avoid it." He shrugged. "But I couldn't get through to you. You're still holding a grudge."

"And you wouldn't? I can't see you being railroaded and then forgiving and forgetting."

"I'm not saying I don't understand, I'm just explaining why I had to call Madden. He told me to tell you to forget about that press conference for the time being. You and Monty belong to me for as long as I need you."

Her surprise was turning to fury. "The hell we do."

"Madden assured me you'd do whatever I asked."

"And what did you promise him?"

"My gratitude. And all the influence that goes with it. Your Senator Madden is very ambitious, isn't he? Is he eyeing a cabinet post?"

"I can't believe he canceled the press conference. He likes to see his face in the newspapers too much."

"Oh, I had to be very persuasive."

"You son of a bitch."

"I was worried that you'd turn me down in spite of Madden's orders, but he said there was no way you'd refuse him." His gaze narrowed on her face. "He has something on you, doesn't he? Some kind of hold?"

"What do you care? It was nothing to you how Madden got me to do what you wanted the last time. All you wanted was results. That's all you care about now." She was shaking with anger. "Is that why you came here?"

"I came here because Eve wanted me to be here. The same reason you came."

"But you knew I'd be here. Two birds with one stone."

"Yes, I knew you'd be here."

"And what do you want me to do? Find another corpse for you?"

"I don't think he's dead." He smiled crookedly. "I know how you hate using Monty as a cadaver dog. You should be pleased that I'm asking you and Monty to work on rescuing a real live person."

"Pleased?"

"Wrong word. I'm trying to put a tolerable light on a bad situation."

"It's not tolerable."

"It will have to be."

"Screw you." She took out her phone and dialed Madden's number. "What the devil are you doing to me?" she asked as soon as he answered.

"Now, Sarah, it's for the best."

"Whose best, damn you?"

"Logan tells me the job is very important and it may not be all that long."

"Did it occur to you that Monty and I just came back from a job that wore us down to the bone? We need to rest."

"You need to do what I tell you to do. I'm sure Logan will take care of you. Let me know when you're available again." He hung up.

Her hand clenched the phone so tightly, her knuckles turned white. Bastards. They were both bastards.

"Satisfied?" Logan asked.

"I'd like to castrate him." She glared at him. "And you too."

He flinched. "I gather he verified what I told you. Now, shall I tell you about the job?"

She tried to control herself. A long time ago she had accepted the fact that she couldn't beat Madden. The card he was holding was too high. But, dear God, she hated the idea of being under Logan's thumb. She wanted to pound someone. No, not someone. Logan.

Monty whimpered in the backseat and she reached over to stroke him. "It's okay, boy. It's okay."

"It's not okay, but you'll do it," Logan said. "Right?"

"Damn you."

Monty whimpered again.

"Shh."

"He senses that you're upset." Logan smiled. "I remember how close you are. He's a good dog."

"I should have him go for your throat. Do you know how tired he is?"

"Monty doesn't impress me as being a very vicious guard dog."

"He makes an exception when he thinks I'm in danger."

"But you're not in danger yet."

Her gaze flew to his face. "Yet?"

His smile faded. "There are a few problems with this job, but I'll try to keep you both safe."

"Just what do you want me to do?"

"I need you and Monty to find one of my employees who has been kidnapped. One of my research facilities in Colombia was attacked and four of my employees killed. Tom Bassett was taken hostage."

"Do you know who kidnapped him?"

"Martin Rudzak. He's a very nasty fellow."

"How nasty?"

"About as nasty as they get. He dabbles in everything from drug running to terrorism."

"Terrorism? Why is he targeting you?"

"We had a run-in several years ago when I was in Japan. He doesn't like me very much."

"Then he should have kidnapped you."

"I'm sure you'd prefer that, but there are reasons why he picked Bassett."

"And you're not going to tell me."

"Not at the moment."

"I don't track criminals, Logan."

"You work for ATF."

"These days my primary job is search and rescue."

"You'd be rescuing Bassett."

47

"Just pay the ransom. You've got plenty of money."

"The percentages are high that after I pay it, Bassett will be killed anyway. I need to find him and get him away."

"And how am I supposed to find him? Do you know the specific locality?"

"Not yet. Somewhere in the jungle near Santo Camaro, Colombia."

Her eyes widened. "South America?"

"Last time I checked."

"You want me to go to South America? You want me to wander around the jungle until I find—"

"I have someone working on pinpointing Rudzak's location. I'm hoping to have more information by the time we reach Colombia."

"And when will that be?"

"My plane is waiting at the Atlanta airport now."

"And you think I'll hop on the plane and go meekly with you."

"Not meekly. Never meekly."

She drew a deep breath. "You're not only risking my neck, you're risking Monty. If those scumbags see Monty trying to track them, the first thing they'll do is shoot him."

"I'll be very careful with both of you. I'll do everything I can to keep you safe."

"And you expect me to trust you?"

He shook his head. "No, but it doesn't make it less true."

"I'll never trust you. You're a user, just like Madden. I'm the one who'll keep Monty safe. You don't care about anyone or—" She broke off. Why was she arguing? She knew she didn't have a choice. He and Madden had backed her into a corner. "How long?"

"I don't know."

She closed her eyes as the anger and frustration poured through her. "I'll do the job. I'll find your man." Her eyes opened and she added with soft venom, "But then I'll find a way to get you. And if you get my dog killed, you'll wish you'd never been born."

"I believe you." He pulled off the freeway into the lane leading to the airport. "You know, even using Madden as a lever, I wasn't sure you'd go with me. Whatever Madden has on you must be pretty powerful stuff. You wouldn't care to tell me what it is?"

"Go to hell, Logan."

"It's been over an hour since we took off," Logan said. "It would be nice if you said a word or two. Maybe even three."

"We've said everything that needed to be said and I don't feel like being nice."

"Would you like something to eat?" Logan asked.

"No."

"What about Monty? Do you suppose he might be hungry?"

"Monty eats only twice a day. I fed him at the cottage." Sarah curled up in the wide leather chair and stared out the window. "And you don't have to be concerned about Monty. I always take care of him."

"That's obvious. I just thought I'd play the gracious host and offer."

"Offer us food and then put our lives on the line?"

"I can do only what I can," he said wearily. "I told you I'd try to keep you safe."

"Trying isn't good enough." She reached down and stroked Monty's head, then said through gritted teeth, "Do you know how this makes me feel? It's not only you who's responsible for putting Monty in danger. He's my dog. The bottom line is always me. He never says no, so if I make the wrong decision, I have to bear the blame."

"Even if I blackmailed you into it?"

"That makes you a bastard, but I'm the one who makes the final decision."

He was silent a moment. "You find the camp and you're done. You won't be within a mile of any firepower. Nothing will happen to you or Monty."

"I know," she said sarcastically. "You'll try to keep us safe."

"No. It won't happen. I promise you."

She turned to look at him.

"You don't believe me?"

"Should I?"

"I suppose not. Sometimes fate takes a hand and there's nothing anyone can do to change what happens. But if I'm still alive when we get out of that jungle, you and Monty will be too." He grimaced. "I assure you that's not a promise that's easy for me to make. I have a keen sense of self-preservation." He stood up. "I'm going to the cockpit to talk to our pilot. You might make a list of your needs on this job, and I'll call my assistant and have her make sure they're waiting for you in Santo Camaro. There's a pad and pencil in the drawer of the table next to you. I won't be gone more than fifteen or twenty minutes, but then, I'm sure you won't miss me."

"No, I won't." She watched him walk down the aisle before she reached for the pad and pencil and started making her list. Why had he tried so hard to convince her he'd protect her and Monty? They were nothing to him. Just tools to get him what he wanted. Yet for a moment she had believed him. She had faced crooked bureaucrats and power figures in disaster sites around the world, and she could recognize sincerity when she saw it.

Or could she? Logan had learned manipulation in a hundred corporate boardrooms. Maybe he was a little out of her league.

Bull. Either she trusted her judgment or she didn't. Was Logan a complete son of a bitch or was there a trace of softness that she could exploit?

She finished her list, then closed her eyes. She didn't want to exploit anyone or anything. She just wished she could go home and forget about Logan and Madden and everything connected with them.

"Coffee?"

She opened her eyes to see Logan holding a cup out to her.

He smiled faintly. "It's only coffee. It's not like eating at your enemy's table. Besides, you should really take me for all you can get. Food, drink, money." He looked down at Monty. "Isn't that right, boy?"

Monty's tail thumped, and he rolled over on his back.

Logan reached down and scratched his belly. Monty gave a soft woo-woo from the back of his throat.

Good.

"Traitor," she muttered.

Nice.

"The hell he is."

Logan raised his brows. "Am I missing something?"

"You're not going to convince me you're a great guy just by petting my dog."

"But he likes me."

"Don't flatter yourself. He likes everyone. He's a golden retriever, for God's sake. They're known for being affectionate...even with someone who doesn't deserve it."

Nice.

She looked down at Monty in disgust. No discrimination.

"Why do I feel out of the loop here?" Logan thrust the cup at her. "The reports I had on you said that you could almost read that dog's mind. I'm beginning to think he may be able to read yours too. Drink your coffee while I go get your familiar a bowl of water."

Before she could argue, he was strolling back to the galley.

Monty wriggled over onto his belly. *Nice.*

She ignored him as she took a sip of the coffee. She had been tempted to refuse, but she was so tired she could scarcely think, and what he said made sense. Why shouldn't she use him as he was using her? She suddenly stiffened as a thought occurred to her. *My God, why not? Why sit there feeling sorry for herself when she had a chance to*—

"Good. I was afraid you'd pour that coffee on the floor." Logan set a delicate china bowl down before Monty. "I'm glad you're being sensible."

"And being sensible is doing what you want me to do?" She took another drink of coffee. "I wanted this coffee, so I took it. I'm not into futile gestures."

"Why isn't Monty drinking?"

"He won't take food or drink from anyone but me." She reached down, touched the rim of the bowl, and Monty started thirstily lapping up the water. "That's fine china. Monty may break it. He has a tendency to push his bowl around when it's empty."

"It's all I had and he deserves the best."

"Yes, he does. Screw your china." She looked around the luxurious interior of the jet. "This is beautiful. I've never seen one like it."

"I like to be comfortable. I do a lot of traveling and there's nothing worse than being tired and irritable when I get off a plane. One mistake in protocol or financial misstep and the entire trip could be blown." He sat down beside her. "And do you see the inside of a lot of corporate jets?"

"A few. The government seldom pays for transporting search and rescue groups, and the current administration has given us zilch." Her lips twisted. "Though they're very willing to take advantage of any publicity we generate. We rely heavily on corporations to give us a ride when we need it."

"I'm surprised. Billions of dollars in foreign aid and not a dime to search and rescue?"

"We get along." She shrugged. "It's probably better that the government doesn't get involved. We'd probably have to fill out requests in triplicate and deal with strings attached."

He was silent a moment. "Like the ones Madden has you dancing on?"

She stiffened. "You don't have an aversion to pulling the strings yourself. You're both into power trips."

He quickly changed the subject. "You have a job with ATF, don't you? Don't they foot the bill to send you and Monty to disaster sites?"

"Only when there are explosives involved. ATF doesn't have search and rescue missions."

"Then why did you take the job?"

"I had to live." She glanced out the window. "And after the first year I was only loosely affiliated with ATF. Monty and I were permitted to go with volunteer search and rescue groups when we weren't being loaned out to police departments to use in particularly difficult cases."

"Cadaver searches?"

"Yes."

"Why did you do it? You hate them. I had to twist your arm to get you to help Eve."

"I did what I had to do."

He studied her closed expression with narrowed eyes. "And why would you have to do it? Why not just quit?"

"I told you, I had to live."

"I don't think that's the reason." He said thoughtfully, "You live simply and seem to enjoy it. I offered you any amount you wanted for this job. So it's not money. Blackmail? Now, what kind of crime could you have committed to put you under Madden's thumb?"

She stared him directly in the eyes. "I murdered a manipulating bastard who pried into my business."

He chuckled. "Sorry, I'm cursed with an inquiring mind. You're an interesting enigma, Sarah. The temptation to solve you is almost irresistible."

"Because you think you may need another hold on me?"

His smile faded. "No."

"Bullshit. You're thinking all the time, weighing advantages and disadvantages, bad moves, good moves. This was a bad move, Logan."

"It was the only one I had."

"There are always choices. You chose Monty and me. It may be the worst choice you've ever made. Because if anything happens to Monty, I'll hunt you down and tear you limb from limb." She finished her coffee in one swallow. "I've been sitting here, doing some thinking myself. For some reason you want my willing cooperation to find this Bassett. I don't know why. Maybe you're smart enough to realize that working smoothly together as a team will increase the chances of getting him out."

"Perish the thought that I might dislike using force."

"That never occurred to me. You're a user, like Madden. If force was needed, you'd be there with your little hatchet." Her lips tightened. "Well, I'm tired of being used. It's not going to happen again. Not by you and not by Madden."

"Really."

"You want cooperation, I'll give you cooperation. I'll get your man out, but I want a payoff."

"I told you I'd give you any amount you wanted."

"I want Madden out of my life."

He was silent a moment. "I've no doubt he's very unpleasant, but I hope you don't want me to take a contract out on him. That could be very awkward."

"What if I said I did?" she asked, curious.

"I'd have to think about it."

Her eyes widened with shock as she realized

he wasn't ruling out the possibility. "Don't be stupid. I just want him out of my life with no holds on me."

"That's a great relief. You wouldn't care to confide what hold he has on you?"

She didn't answer.

"I didn't think so. You don't trust me. You're afraid I'll just take over the reins from Madden. Did it occur to you that you'll still run that risk?"

"It occurred to me. That's part of the deal. I'm free of both of you."

"Then it seems you trust me more than you do Madden."

"Eve trusts you. You might keep your word. And once this job is over, you won't have any other use for me. You can afford to let me go."

"True. But I can hardly help you if I go at it blind."

"I'll tell you when you need to know."

"And why do you think I can help you?"

"I don't have the kind of clout I need to get away from him or I'd have done it years ago. Is it a deal?"

Logan slowly nodded. "As long as you give me your best effort, Madden's out of your life whether we get my man out or not. You have my word on it."

She felt a flicker of surprise.

"I'm not quite the bastard you think me," Logan said roughly. "Ask Eve. As you said, she trusts me."

"She's prejudiced. You were lovers. You

probably behaved differently with her than you do with other people."

"Yeah, I made a really big effort to treat her like a human being. It was a great strain on me." He stood up. "I need to go and make some telephone calls. Why don't you stretch out on the couch and try to sleep? We're going to hit the ground running when we reach Santo Camaro." He picked up the list on the table. "Is this all you need?"

"That's it."

"I'll see that you get it," he said, and strode down the aisle.

She had made him angry and his response had been uncharacteristically vulnerable. Maybe he wasn't quite the steely man she had thought. But it didn't matter how hard or soft he was as long as he could get Madden out of her life.

A life without the threat of Madden...

The thought brought an unbelievable surge of relief. For years she had lived without hope, and suddenly the possibility was there before her. Win or lose, Madden would be out of her life if she just did her job. Logan had given his word.

Monty whined softly and put his head on her knee, sensing her excitement.

"We've got a chance, boy," she whispered. "If he's not lying, we may be able to come out of this with something pretty good."

Nice.

"He's not nice, but it doesn't matter if he keeps his word."

Nice.

Stubborn dog. She got up and moved over to the couch. "Come on, we have to get some sleep. We want to be in top form and get through this fast and get home."

Monty settled on the floor in front of the couch, but his gaze went to the back of the cabin, where Logan had disappeared.

Nice...

"Then you've got her?" Margaret asked after Logan had rattled off Sarah's list to her. "I was hoping maybe you'd strike out."

"I know you were. You made that pretty clear," Logan said. "Find out everything you can about Todd Madden. I want a complete report."

"How complete?"

"I want to know the name of every kid he mugged in kindergarten."

"Oh, that kind of report. I gather we're no longer playing on the same team with him?"

"He's on the funding committee for ATF, but I don't think that's how he's pulling Sarah Patrick's strings. It's something else."

"You've got her. What difference does it make?"

"It makes a difference. Any messages?"

"Galen called from Bogotá. He said it's not urgent, but he wants you to phone him."

"As soon as I hang up. Did he mention any problems?"

"No, he said to tell you the team was in

place." She paused and then added grudgingly, "You know, I really like him."

"And that surprises you? Oh, yes, it would. You're not supposed to like men like Galen. It violates your code."

"Yes, it does, but Galen is...different."

"That's indisputable. Nothing from Castleton?"

"No. And it may take a while to get the dirt on Madden. He's a politician and they bury their skeletons pretty deep."

"Just get it."

"How's the pooch?"

"Easier than Sarah."

"Well, you can hardly blame her for—"

"I'll call you when we get to Santo Camaro." He ended the call and dialed Galen's number.

"What's happening?"

"No greeting? No small talk?" Galen drawled. "After all those years in Tokyo, I'd think you'd have learned some manners."

"Do you have a location?"

"Have I ever failed you? I got a general location, but Sanchez says Rudzak moves camp every few days. And he's going to set up a decoy camp as bait."

"We have to find the main camp now. We can't afford any extra time. We have to get in and out fast or we'll have a dead hostage. You're sure you got the truth from Sanchez?"

"I'm truly hurt. Not only a lack of manners, but doubt? I admit Sanchez was stubborn, but eventually his good sense prevailed."

"Money?"

"No. Sanchez already makes a tremendous amount in the drug trade. There's millions floating around down here. I had to convince the scumbag he'd be safer running from Rudzak than from me. Can you imagine, he wasn't taking me seriously?"

"I'm sure that didn't last long."

"Almost thirty minutes."

"You're slipping."

"Now insults?" He made a *tsk-tsk* sound. "And while I was at it, I did that little research project you heaped on me."

"And?"

"Confirmed."

Logan's hand tightened on the phone. "Son of a bitch."

"Do you want me to take care of it?"

"No, I'll do it myself." Dammit, he had known it. "But I can't have Sanchez ratting to Rudzak."

"He won't. I sent him out of the country with a suitcase of Rudzak's money he was laundering. He's neatly boxed."

"Good," Logan said. "We'll be arriving in Santo Camaro shortly."

"I'm already on my way. I should be there in about an hour, and I'll contact Castleton to pick you up at the airport."

Logan hung up. Everything was in motion. As usual, Galen had succeeded and had the information he needed. Logan had Sarah and Monty in hand and had found a way to get Sarah to voluntarily work with him.

Yeah, sure. Actually Sarah had taken control. She'd turned a situation that made her a victim to one in which she had control. How many times had she had to do that with her life on the line?

Christ, what was he doing? He had made his decision and it was no time for regrets. He shoved his phone in his pocket, left his office, and started back up the aisle toward the cockpit.

Sarah was asleep on the couch and didn't stir as he stopped beside her. Monty opened one eye and his tail thumped lazily.

"Shh."

But Sarah didn't wake, and even in slumber she was curled up in a defensive position, her muscles locked and stiff.

Search and rescue. What made anyone embrace a career that involved not only danger but constant despair? All the dossiers and reports in the world never really told you what made a person tick. Logan knew Sarah was strong, smart, streetwise, and had a wicked sense of humor with everyone but him. But he was beginning to realize that there might be a whole lot more beneath that tough facade. What kind of woman was Sarah Patrick?

Well, he was not likely to find out. She was wary and he had established himself firmly in the enemy camp. What the hell. It didn't matter. He didn't have to know her. It was better if he didn't. He had learned a long time ago that it was dangerous to get close to people in dangerous situations. It hurt too much if you lost them.

Chen Li.

He shunted the thought back into the darkness, where it belonged. He had been younger, less experienced then. This situation didn't have to end as that one had. Sarah Patrick wasn't Chen Li.

He could keep Sarah alive.

Santo Camaro

"This is Sarah Patrick," Logan told Castleton at the airport. "Ron Castleton. He works for me."

"Don't we all," she murmured. She gestured and Monty jumped into Castleton's car. "How do you do, Mr. Castleton. This is Monty. I don't have any health papers for him. Are we going to have any trouble with the authorities?"

Castleton was staring wide-eyed at the dog. "What's happening here? If I'd had any warning, I could have—"

"We won't need papers," Logan said. "We'll be in and out before anyone knows we've arrived."

"And what if we aren't?"

"I'll take care of it." Logan got into the front passenger seat. "Have you heard from Galen?"

"He's at the facility. He said you'd want to start out right away."

"He's right." He looked at the sky, which was already darkening to twilight. "But we should probably wait until morning. Did you hear any more from Rudzak?"

"Not since I left the money where he told me." He glanced sideways at Logan. "But he has informants everywhere. He's probably got someone watching us now."

"Then let's get moving."

Castleton started the car. "The dog's a dead giveaway. He'll know you're trying to find Bassett. He has contacts who can trace—"

"That's why we have to move quickly."

"Did you get the supplies on the list I made out?" Sarah asked.

Castleton frowned. "What supplies? I didn't receive any list."

"Galen has the supplies, Sarah," Logan said. "I had Margaret call him while he was on the road and give him your list."

"I don't like bringing a woman into this." Castleton looked over his shoulder at Sarah. "Has Logan explained how dangerous this situation is? I hope you know what you're getting into."

She didn't really know anything, dammit. "Thanks for your concern, but we'll be okay." Although Castleton wasn't making her feel any better. And the heat...it was going to make the search twice as difficult. It was hard to breathe and Monty was already panting. She reached down and stroked Monty's head. "I think it's time for a clip, boy."

"We don't have time," Logan said.

"I'm not suggesting taking him to a groomer. I'll do it myself." Her lips thinned. "I won't take him into the jungle until he's more comfortable. He's a long-haired dog and we don't know how much time this search will take."

"If it takes enough time for the heat to cause him a problem, then we're in trouble."

"It's causing him trouble now. I'm clipping him."

Logan opened his mouth to protest and then thought better of it. "Okay, we'll work around it."

"You bet we will." She looked out the window. They'd turned onto a bumpy dirt road and the jungle foliage was crawling over the road, encroaching on both sides of the car. It was not only the weather that was oppressive. "Who is this Galen? Another employee?"

Logan nodded. "Sort of a freelance agent."

"Sort of?"

"We're here." Castleton turned a curve in the road and then screeched to a halt to avoid hitting the man standing in the middle of the road. "What the hell! Are you crazy, Galen?"

"That's been debated for decades." He grinned at Logan. "What am I going to do with you? You're always late. I have dinner on the table."

"You almost caused me to run off the road." Castleton turned off the ignition. "I wasn't expecting you to—"

"I didn't think there'd be any real danger. This is private property and you're the cautious type, Castleton. I knew you'd be meandering along at a snail's pace." He opened the back door of the car and gave a low whistle as he saw Monty on the floor. "Ah, the recipient of the dog biscuits in my backpack. I admit I'm a little disappointed. I thought they might be for you, Logan. I was hoping you'd acquired more adventurous tastes. Remember when you refused to eat those delicious grubs in that Maori settlement in—"

"This is Sean Galen," Logan interrupted. "Sarah Patrick and her dog, Monty."

"Delighted." Galen smiled as he helped her out of the car. He was in his mid-to late thirties, a little over medium height, with a lithe and athletic body. His dark hair was cut close, but it persisted in curling and his eyes were as dark and irrepressible as his hair. Energy emanated from him in waves. "Do you like ham and macaroni casserole?"

British? He had a faint cockney accent. "Yes."

"Good. That's what's for dinner." He glanced down at Monty. "I might sneak some to you too. That dog food and vitamins I brought don't look awe-inspiring."

"So much for adventurous dining," Logan murmured.

"Well, I didn't know about the lady, but Castleton didn't impress me as being anything but a meat-and-potatoes man." He strode off to the side of the road. "This way. I set up camp some distance from those ruins. They depressed me."

For the first time, Sarah's gaze turned to the burned-out facility a few hundred yards ahead. She had been so filled with anger, worry, and resentment, she hadn't really thought about the people who had lived and died here. All those promising lives cut off by assassins' bullets...

"See? The lady's getting depressed too," Galen said. "Come on, Castleton. You can help me dish up."

"I have to get back to town."

"After dinner. Do you want to hurt my feelings?"

"I should..." Castleton shrugged and then followed Galen into the brush.

She stood looking after them for a moment. She felt as if she were being swept away and she wasn't sure she liked it.

"It's okay." Logan took her elbow. "He won't poison you. Galen's actually a gourmet cook."

"In the middle of the jungle?"

"In the middle of a hurricane. He adapts to any situation."

"I wasn't afraid of his poisoning me. He just surprised me."

"I can understand the feeling." He pushed her gently toward the side of the road. "He's surprised me a few times."

They were obviously old and good friends. "The grubs?"

"He didn't tell you I actually ate the damn things. He backed me in a corner where I had to do it or insult the Maoris."

"Just what are grubs?"

"Larvae. And they look disgustingly like worms."

"I thought so." She smiled. "I think I'm beginning to like your Mr. Galen."

"I thought that story would endear him to you." He was silent a moment. "You can trust him, Sarah. If anything happens to me, do what he says and he'll get you out."

She felt a chill she tried to ignore. "I'm not used to trusting anyone else to take care of me. Just what does he do for you?"

"I suppose you might call him a problem solver."

"Problems like this?"

"It's his specialty. So don't feel bad about letting him take over if things get rough."

"Do you let him take over?"

"Hell, yes."

She gazed at him skeptically. "I can't see you trusting anyone but yourself."

"I learned a long time ago how to delegate." He smiled. "Why else would I have gone after you?"

"I don't see you stepping aside and turning me loose to do my job."

"In spite of what you think of me, I can't shrug off responsibility."

"How long have you known Galen?"

"Fifteen years or so. I met him when I was in Japan. He was fresh out of the service and working for a local businessman."

"So you hired him away?"

"At that point in my life I couldn't afford him. I was struggling to keep a fledgling business afloat. We became involved in several projects together in the next few years. Then, when I began having personal problems, he helped me out."

What kind of personal problems? she wondered. She wasn't about to ask. She didn't want to know anything about his personal life. She just wanted to do the job and walk away. "And he's worked for you ever since?"

"On occasion." They had come into the clearing where Galen had set up camp. To her amazement, there was a table beside the fire with a damask tablecloth and colorful china. "What the hell?"

Galen looked up and grinned. "My mum always told me that you should never use a picnic as an excuse for ignoring the finer things in life."

"And you think this job is going to be a picnic?"

"It depends on how you look at it."

"How do you intend to transport all this stuff?"

"I don't. It's disposable. Isn't everything?"

"No."

He raised his brows. "Good. It's refreshing to meet someone who's not a cynic." He carefully dished up the macaroni. "Tell me, Logan, do these squiggly bits of pasta remind you of grubs?"

The casserole was excellent and the coffee Galen served afterward was even better. "I'm sorry, there's no dessert. Next time perhaps." He lifted a brow. "Are you going to wash up, Castleton? It's only fair."

Castleton got to his feet. "I have to get

back to town. I've got to make final arrange-
ments to get our people out of the hospital.
Thanks for the meal. It was really very good."

Galen made a face. "Words of praise don't
get those dishes done."

Logan stood up. "I'll walk you to the car,
Castleton. There's something I want you to
do for me."

"Sure." Castleton turned to Sarah. "Take
care of yourself. Good luck."

"Thank you."

She watched Castleton and Logan stroll
across the glade and into the trees, then she
stood up and began stacking the plates.

"Sit down and have another cup of coffee,"
Galen said. "I was joking."

"I'm not. Fair is fair."

"Right. And you said you have to clip the
pup." He nodded at Monty. "That's going to
be quite a job with all that golden fluff. I
want you to get some sleep tonight."

"It won't take that long. Monty's very
good."

"Clip the pup," he said firmly as he took the
dishes from her. "You might break my fine
china."

"It's plastic."

"Oh, you noticed? The catalogue swore no
one would be able to tell the difference."

She smiled. "They took you, Galen."

"The story of my life. Do you want me to
get your clippers for you? They're in a backpack, along with all your supplies."

She wasn't going to win this one. In spite

70

of Galen's easygoing manner, it was clear he also had a streak of iron. "I'll get them."

"That was quite a list you gave Logan."

She knelt and rummaged in the backpack. "I had to leave without my equipment. You got all the bottled water? I can't have Monty getting sick."

"So the water is all for Monty?"

"Most of it. I can get along on less than he can." She sat down beside Monty. "Come on, boy. Let's get this stuff off you."

He sighed and rolled over on his stomach.

Galen chuckled. "You're right, he's good with it. Nice dog."

"Do you have any pets?"

He shook his head. "I'm on the move too much. I had a parrot once, but I gave him away. He was abusive and my ego couldn't take it. Now, your Monty would never be abusive."

"Don't count on it."

"Well, not verbally. He might lift his leg on something he shouldn't."

She nodded. "He always makes his dis-pleasure known."

"But you're obviously soul mates. How long have you had him?"

"Four years. He was a year old when I saw him at the ATF training school." She smiled reminiscently. "He'd just flunked out of guide dog school and ATF picked him up."

"He flunked out?"

"Not because he wasn't smart enough," she said defensively. "He would just get dis-tracted and that could have been a danger."

"Attention deficit disorder?"

"It's his nose. He was only a puppy and his sense of smell is probably the keenest ATF has ever run across. When he's constantly bombarded with scents, it's natural that he'd become distracted."

He held up his hands. "I didn't mean to insult your dog. I have too much respect for dogs. I've seen them work during combat conditions and I'd rather have one of them as a buddy than anyone on two legs."

"Sorry. I overreacted. Roll over, Monty." She started clipping his belly. "You have an accent. English?"

"I was born and raised in Liverpool."

"Logan says you met years ago in Japan."

He nodded. "When we were both young and green. Well, younger and greener. I was hard as nails and Logan was no pussycat even before Chen Li died."

"Chen Li?"

"His wife. She died of leukemia a few years after I met Logan. Not an easy death and not an easy time for him either. He was crazy about her."

Personal problems. Yes, that would be classified as personal problems. She wished she hadn't asked the question that had led to this revelation. So he'd had a tragedy in his life. Life was full of hard knocks. She would not feel sorry for him, dammit. "I'm sure he was able to handle it."

"Oh, yes, he handled it." Galen finished washing the last plate. "It turned him a little nuts for a while and then the scars formed and he was okay. We batted around the Pacific for about a year before he went back to Tokyo."

"That's when you introduced him to grubs?"

He smiled. "No, that was later. After the first edge had dulled. He would have broken my neck if I'd tried that the first year after Chen Li died." He looked at Monty appraisingly. "He looks like a big yellow bear without all that hair."

"At least he's cooler." She sat back on her heels and began to pick up the shorn hair on the ground. "I wonder where Logan is. He's been gone longer than I thought."

"He might have walked over to the ruins after he left Castleton." He frowned. "Nasty. They must have been like sitting ducks for Rudzak."

She shivered. "Why would he go there?"

"Maybe he didn't. But I'd bet on it. Logan feels very bad about what happened here. Perhaps he's trying to make some sense of it."

"I can't see Logan being that sensitive."

"But then, you don't want to see him like that, do you?" He wiped his hands on a towel. "Never mind. I'm bored with all this meaningful chatter. It offends my shallow soul. I need a bit of mindless recreation before I hit the sack. Do you play poker?"

"Why did you want to come back here?" Castleton swallowed hard as he glanced around the charred ruins. "God, it's hard for me. We're not going to find anything. I told

73

you I'd retrieved every bit of information that wasn't destroyed. I didn't slip up, Logan."

"I believe you. I know how efficient you are." He didn't look at Castleton as he knelt and picked up a scorched wooden box. "What do you suppose was in this?"

"I don't know. Computer disks, maybe."

Logan was silent a moment. "Four dead. Carl Jenkins, Betty Krenski, Dorothy Desmond, Bob Simms. Did you know Betty Krenski was trying to adopt an HIV baby from an orphanage in South Africa?"

"Yes, but I didn't know that you did."

"She asked for my help. She said that someone had to care for those children. I tried to talk her out of it. Assuming responsibility for a baby with HIV is a heartbreaker."

"But you agreed to help her?"

"People have to make their own decisions. We can influence but we can't dictate. I told her if she still wanted to do it at the end of the year, I'd help her."

"I wish she'd gone through me. It was my job to take care of personal problems."

"Did you think I stopped being responsible for the people I sent down here when I hired you?"

"You're a busy man."

"Not that busy. This was a very special project to me. I read every one of their dossiers when you hired them, and I can quote passages from your monthly reports. I never met those people, but I felt as if I had."

"They were all good people. No one knows that better than me." Castleton paused. "I don't mean to be unsympathetic, but I have to go. I can't do anything about the people who were killed, but I can get those wounded into a hospital in the States."

"Yes, I know. You're in a hurry." He stood up. "And coming here must upset you."

"Why are we here?" Castleton repeated.

"I thought it fitting. Galen says I have no sense of ceremony or protocol, but that's not quite true. Not when it comes to this particular business."

"What business? What did you want me to do, Logan?"

"Just die." He whirled and smashed the ball of his hand upward under Castleton's nose, splintering the bones and driving them into his brain.

"Done?" Galen was standing in the middle of the path as Logan strode through the trees toward the campsite.

Logan nodded.

"What about disposal?"

"No one will find him."

He gazed at Logan curiously. "It's been a

long time since you did a job like this. Did it bother you?"

"No."

"Not even a little? You've been a respectable businessman so long, I'd think you'd find it hard to revert to the old ways."

Logan's lips twisted. "I enjoyed it."

"I don't like traitors either. I told you I'd do it for you."

"I know. But it was my job. I chose him. If I'd kept a closer eye on Castleton, maybe I'd have sensed he'd turn Judas." His face darkened as he glanced over his shoulder. "All those lives..."

"It was probably a crime of opportunity. Castleton might have walked the straight and narrow if Rudzak hadn't tempted him."

"How tempting was it?"

"Sanchez said he was paid one million for helping them set up the attack on the facility, and he was to get another two when he lured you into the trap. How did you guess Castleton was in Rudzak's pay?"

"I didn't guess. I was just exploring every possibility. Castleton was conveniently in town when the attack occurred. I started from there. It could have been coincidence, but I couldn't take a chance on coincidence in a situation like this. I had to make sure. If he was dirty, then the lead he gave me to Sanchez would be bogus. Sanchez would be set up to give me the wrong information on how to find Rudzak, and I'd be led down the garden path straight into a trap. That's why I sent you to Sanchez."

"Because you knew how efficient I am."

"Because I couldn't have any more deaths on my hands. I thought the research center was safe here. But it wasn't safe. Rudzak found out about it."

"Stop beating yourself on the head. You didn't know Rudzak would turn up again. You thought he was in that prison in Bangkok."

"You're wrong. I always had a feeling he'd show up again."

"Then you should have had him killed in that prison. I offered to have it done." Galen glanced sideways at him. "Why didn't you?"

Logan didn't answer.

"I never could understand what went on between you and Rudzak. For a while I thought he was your best friend."

"So did I. Then he started to hate me. But he never let me see it until the end." He shrugged. "And he hates me more now. So maybe he was meant to get his shot at me."

"Fate?" Galen shook his head. "We make our own fate."

Logan agreed with that premise. He'd lived too long in the Far East not to have acquired a healthy respect for the patterns life seemed to weave. But he believed only to a degree. "Maybe. I only know I was dead certain I'd be Rudzak's prime target when I heard he'd finally managed to bribe himself out of that prison two years ago."

"Two years is a long time. I was hoping he might have forgotten you."

"Be for real. After what I did to him? I've

77

been waiting for him. I knew he'd have to reestablish contacts before he'd go after me. But, Christ, I was hoping he wouldn't find out about the research facility."

"How long has it been operating?"

"Three years."

"Progress?"

"Early stages, but promising. Very promising. Bassett was brilliant."

"Was?"

"Freudian slip. He may still be alive. But since money isn't Rudzak's prime motivation, it could go either way."

"That was my reading. We're going in regardless?"

Logan nodded. "I won't have Rudzak killing my people or hovering over me like a dark cloud any longer. We're taking him out."

"When we find him. Just how good is Sarah and her dog?"

"Do you think I'd be taking a chance on anyone I didn't think could perform? But I want you to watch out for her, Galen. If anything happens to me, get her and Monty out."

"I'll do everything I can." He was silent a moment. "You do know if Rudzak survives, she may be on his hit list too."

"I'm not a fool. That's one of the reasons I didn't tell Castleton about her and Monty. I'll make sure from now on that she's kept out of sight of any of Rudzak's men and hope for the best."

"And if the best doesn't happen?"

"I'll worry about it then. I need her." He

changed the subject. "Something's been nagging at me. Rudzak may be playing games with—" He shook his head. "I don't know. I just feel uneasy. When he called, I felt he was giving me some kind of puzzle to solve."

"The decoy camp?"

"Maybe." He thought for a moment. "You know, he sent me a scarab just before he hit the facility. Chen Li's scarab."

"You didn't tell me that."

"I wasn't sure it had any meaning. I still don't."

"How did he get ahold of it?"

"He stole the entire collection from her bedroom before he left Tokyo. The police in Bangkok looked for it but didn't find it. I thought maybe he'd sold it and stashed the money. It would have been enough to get him out of a dozen prisons."

"Evidently he didn't sell it or he would have gotten out of that prison a lot earlier. It must have meant something to him."

"It meant something to him all right. He talked to Chen Li for years about ancient Egypt, tried to brainwash her for years. He bought her books and took her to museums. He gave her that scarab when she was only fifteen."

"Why go to all that trouble to—" Galen gave a low whistle. "That scheming asshole."

"And then I came along," Logan went on. "I think if Chen Li hadn't gotten sick, I would have had an untimely accident. And he might have gotten away with it." His lips twisted. "Like you said, I thought he was my best friend."

"Then maybe the scarab was some kind of taunt."

"Maybe. But I feel as if— Who the hell knows? That scarab just makes me uneasy. Has Sarah turned in?"

Galen grimaced. "After she beat me three games at poker. She could make her living in Las Vegas. Sharp."

"I know. She took me to the cleaners once when I first met her. She told me poker is the game of choice when the rescue teams are waiting to go to work at a disaster site."

"Well, let's hope this job doesn't qualify as a disaster." They had reached the campsite and he lowered his voice to avoid waking Sarah, who was lying with Monty beside her across from the fire. "What are the chances?"

"I bought time tonight. I figure we have two days before Rudzak gets suspicious. If we move fast and have surprise on our side... seven out of ten."

Galen dropped down on his bedroll. "We'll have to make sure of both. I have a lot of living to do. There are millions of people out there who haven't yet experienced my intelligence and charm."

"I'll keep that in mind." Logan stretched out on his bedroll and closed his eyes.

Death.

Galen was right. It had been a long time for Logan, but he hadn't felt a moment of hesitation. He had always believed in an eye for an eye. Primitive but fair.

Rudzak understood that philosophy. He

had waited almost fifteen years to get Logan, and he was out there now, salivating.

Logan had gone over and over in his mind the possible targets. Which one would Rudzak pick next?

Screw him. No use worrying about future targets until Bassett was free and he had Sarah, Monty, Galen, and his team to help do that job.

And seven out of ten odds weren't that bad.

Seven out of ten.

Sarah stared into the darkness as she heard Logan lie down across from her. Those were good odds, better than what she had gone up against in a dozen situations in her life. And the chances of survival for her and Monty had to be even greater because their part would be finished the moment Rudzak's camp was located. She would have no part in the attack, and even if Logan and Galen were captured or killed, she and Monty had the training and experience to survive alone in the jungle.

Jesus, that was cold.

No, it wasn't. She had a perfect right to preserve her life and that of Monty with no sense of guilt. She liked Galen, but he had been hired to do a job and evidently he was a mercenary who was paid well to take his chances. As for Logan, he was the one who had drawn all of them into this web. Even if his motive in rescuing his employee was compassionate, his methods were certainly not. No, she was in this alone and would act accordingly.

Monty whimpered and put his head on her arm, sensing her tension. She reached out to stroke, quiet him. No, she wasn't alone. Not as long as she had Monty. "Go to sleep, boy."

Scared?

She was scared. She'd been scared since the moment she'd caught sight of that burned-out research facility. *Premonition?*

Hell, no. Imagination.

But Monty wouldn't believe that, not when he could feel the tension tightening her muscles.

She gently stroked his throat. "A little, but it's okay."

He relaxed. Monty knew about fear. How sometimes you had to keep on going even if you were scared. Once he'd crawled down a tunnel in a crushed parking garage when he'd caught scent of a victim. She'd gone in after him and the shaft had crashed down behind them. There had been no going back, and there had been nothing but darkness and fear ahead. She had felt Monty trembling beside her and could smell his fear and her own. He could have frozen, but he'd crawled on his belly through the long tunnel, guiding her until she could see light ahead.

If they survived that nightmare, they could survive anything.

And seven out of ten odds weren't bad at all.

. . .

"Wake up. It's time to leave."

Sarah's eyes flew open to see Logan's face above her. "Okay." She sat up and threw aside her blanket. "Monty."

Monty stretched and then trotted over to the nearest tree to take care of morning business.

"Here's your backpack." Logan dropped it beside her. "I took a few bottles out and put them in mine. I didn't have room for many."

"I don't need your help. I could have managed."

"I wasn't being gentlemanly." Logan was smiling, but the words were crisp. "I can't afford to have you falling behind."

She put on the backpack. "I won't fall behind. You worry about keeping up with me. This stroll through the jungle is going to be a little more demanding than playing tennis at one of your fancy country clubs." She looked around and suddenly realized they were the only two in the clearing. "Where's Galen?"

"He went on ahead."

"Why?"

"To take care of a few things. We have information that Rudzak may have set up a decoy camp about ten miles to the west. Galen will join us later."

"And what direction are we taking?"

"East." Logan was putting out the fire. "We should reach the search area by noon. After that, it's up to you and Monty."

"Right. Do you have anything belonging to Bassett?"

"Margaret expressed me an old baseball cap he'd left in his locker at the Silicon Valley plant. But he hasn't been home in six months. Will the scent still be strong enough?"

"Probably. But couldn't Castleton have gotten you something down here belonging to him?"

"No." Logan turned away. "That wasn't an option."

"Why wasn't it—"

"Does Monty eat this early?"

She shook her head. "He can do that after we've been on the trail for a while."

"Then let's get going."

No question about breakfast for her. He was as cold and efficient as a surgeon's scalpel and she didn't like the fact that he hadn't told her earlier about the decoy camp. "Do you suppose I could brush my teeth and go to the bathroom?"

The sarcasm didn't faze him. "If you hurry."

She stiffened when she saw his gaze go to the trees at the edge of the clearing. "What are you looking at? Do you think someone's watching us?"

"No, Galen reconnoitered the area before he set up camp, and he didn't think it was necessary to take turns on guard duty last night."

She hadn't been aware there had even been a discussion about setting up guards. She had thought they were safe for at least that one night. "Then why are you behaving as if you think someone is—"

"It doesn't hurt to be careful. Rudzak seldom does the expected." He moved toward the trees. "But this time neither are we."

They stopped to eat at ten and reached the search site at twelve forty-five. By that time Sarah's shirt was plastered to her body with perspiration, but Monty was still moving swiftly. She gave him his third bowl of water and sank down beside him as he drank it.

"We need to hurry." Logan had come back to stand beside her.

"Fifteen minutes. Monty needs rest." She took off her backpack, then took a drink of water herself. "From now on we'll be leading, not following. Give me Bassett's cap."

He reached into his pack, pulled out a faded Giants ball cap, and tossed it to her.

She put it aside and dug into her pack for the canvas utility belt. It was a little large, and she took out her knife and cut additional holes. Then she got out Monty's leash and tossed it on top of the utility belt.

"Why do you need the utility belt?" Logan asked.

"I probably won't need it this time, but I always wear it when I'm on a search. When I put it on, it's a signal to Monty that we're going to go to work." She leaned back against a tree. "I'd advise you to rest. If Monty catches the scent, we'll stop only to give him water."

He sat down across from her and took off his hat. "Okay, I could use some rest."

He didn't look tired. He looked tough as hell. His shirt was as damp with perspiration as hers was, but she could feel the waves of energy and tension he was emitting. Was the tension caused by fear? Maybe. But if he was afraid, he wouldn't give in to it. He was totally relentless as he had led her through the jungle.

She stroked Monty's head. "You set a pretty hard pace."

"I told you we were in a hurry." He smiled sardonically. "I'm sorry if you were disappointed. I know you would have enjoyed leaving me in the dust."

"You're in good shape," she said grudgingly.

"It must be all that tennis at the country club."

"Maybe." At that moment she couldn't imagine him in a country-club setting. He looked more like a scruffy gunrunner than a tycoon. After a short silence she asked, "What's Galen up to?"

"What?"

"You said Galen was taking care of a few things. What's he planning on doing? Or aren't I supposed to know?"

"You want details? I thought you weren't interested in anything but your and Monty's involvement."

"This does involve us. If you manage to get yourselves killed, I want a decent chance of getting out of this jungle. What's Galen doing?"

"Attacking the decoy camp."

Her eyes widened. "By himself?"

"No, Galen's good, but he's not Superman. When he's ready, he'll radio for his team to come in by helicopter."

"How many are in his team?"

"Twelve."

"Against how many of Rudzak's men?"

"Our informant, Sanchez, said at least twenty. That leaves eight at the real camp, where Bassett should be."

"And the plan?"

"Galen's unit hits the decoy camp and makes Rudzak think we've fallen into the trap. Galen pretends to get out by the skin of his teeth and proceeds to the main camp to rendezvous with us. We get Bassett out, hop on the helicopter, and head for home."

Her lips twisted. "Very simple."

"Not simple at all. If Galen's not convincing enough, Rudzak will head back to the base immediately and we'll be in deep shit."

"Why even go after the decoy?"

"Rudzak will be getting suspicious that he hasn't heard from Sanchez or his man in Santo Camaro. If an attack on the decoy doesn't occur by tonight, then he'll think we're onto him and we'll lose the element of surprise." He glanced at Monty. "That's why Monty has to find this base by nightfall."

"I can't promise that. What do we do if we don't find it? What if Rudzak isn't fooled by Galen's attack?"

"Then we try to get out of the jungle before Rudzak tracks us down."

There were too many things that could go wrong. She didn't like it.

"I don't like it either." He was reading her expression. "But it's our best shot." He got to his feet. "Monty's had his fifteen minutes. Let's go."

She slowly stood up and looked at the sun. Seven, maybe eight hours until nightfall.

"Ready?"

"Yes." She didn't look at Logan as she picked up the utility belt and fastened it around her middle.

Monty froze, his gaze on the belt. Then he jumped to his feet.

"Time to go to work." She took Bassett's hat and let him sniff it. "Find."

He whirled and took off running.

"Won't we lose him?" Logan asked.

"No, he'll keep coming back. When he catches the scent, I'll put on his leash and run with him."

"You're afraid he'll get excited and not come back?"

"No." She started in the direction Monty had taken. "I'm afraid some son of a bitch will shoot him, and I want to be there to protect him."

Two hours later Monty had still not caught the scent.

"I think we're going around in circles," Logan said with a frown.

"We might be." Sarah pushed through a

screen of palms. "But Monty knows what he's doing."

"Does he? He's not even sniffing the ground."

She gave him an impatient glance over her shoulder. "He's scenting the air. He doesn't always have to keep his nose to the ground. Air scenting is much more accurate in cases like this. He lifts his nose high and waves it back and forth until he catches the large end of the cone."

"Cone?"

"Bassett's scent will be dispersed downwind in a cone-shaped pattern. The smaller end will be centered around his body, and as the distance from him grows, the cone widens over a large area. Monty will find the large end of the cone and then work back and forth as it narrows until it leads him to Bassett. Are you sure they're encamped and not moving?"

"So my source told Galen. Would that make a difference?"

"Of course it would," she snapped. "Even if Monty finds the scent, he could lose it again and have to start all over again."

"Sorry. Just asking. This is all new to me."

It would have been new to most people, and she wouldn't have snapped at him if she hadn't been so frustrated. It wasn't unusual for a search to take this long, but she had found herself looking behind every tree, afraid to let Monty out of her sight. God, she wished this were over.

"Will you jump on my ass again if I ask you how long this could take?"

"Monty can't go by your time schedule. It will take as long as it takes. He's doing his best, dammit."

"I know," he said quietly. "Is there anything I can do to help?"

She drew a deep breath. "No, there's nothing either of us can do. It's all up to Monty. We're lucky it's so hot. Bassett's body will be producing a stronger scent."

He grimaced. "At the moment I don't feel lucky."

Neither did Sarah. She felt acutely on edge and so hot, she couldn't breathe.

Find him, Monty. Find him and let's go home.

It was over an hour later that she heard Monty bark.

Relief surged through her. "Thank God."

"He's found something?" Logan asked.

"I think so. I taught him not to bark until he caught the scent. If he comes back to get me, we'll know that he's—"

Monty bounded toward her, barking up a storm, tail wagging with excitement.

"He's got it." She took the leash out of her backpack and fastened it to his collar. "Come on."

"Can you stop him from barking? We don't want to alert—"

"He barks only to signal me when he's on a search. If I'm with him, there's no need for him to bark." She broke into a fast trot to keep

90

pace with Monty. "Keep up, Logan. We can't wait for you."

Christ, she was tough, Logan thought.

Sarah was moving at almost a run ahead of him, weaving, pushing through the brush, pausing occasionally to let Monty sniff the air before taking off again. She must be as tired as he was, but she had kept going at this speed for over an hour. During the last ten minutes the pace had picked up and Monty's eagerness had intensified.

Logan's own breath was coming in gasps, and he could see Sarah's shoulders rise and fall as she struggled to force the hot, muggy air into her lungs. She was covering the ground with the same speed and concentration as her dog.

Then she skidded to a halt.

Logan froze in place as she motioned him to stop. Monty was silent but pulled eagerly, frantically, at the leash. Sarah put her hand on his head, and he instantly quieted. Then she turned and strode back to Logan. "There's something up ahead. I think he's found the source."

"How do you know?"

"I just know, dammit." She glared at him. "And I'm not going to take Monty any farther and chance having some guard shoot him."

"No one's asking you to." He took off his backpack and set it on the ground. "I'll go ahead and make sure before I radio Galen."

"And probably get shot yourself." She scowled. "You don't have to check for yourself just because I don't have any proof that the camp's up ahead. I tell you, Monty *knows*."

"And you know what Monty knows." He opened his backpack. "I believe you. I have a great respect for instinct. Just stay here."

"Of course we'll stay here. Why should I—" She stopped as she saw the assault weapon he pulled out of his backpack. "Shit. No wonder you had room for only a couple bottles of water." She moistened her lips. "Do you even know how to use that thing?"

He smiled. "Oh, yes, I know how to use it. I took lessons at the country club."

Thirty minutes passed.

Then fifteen minutes.

Why the hell wasn't he back? Sarah wondered. He'd probably been caught or killed. Just because she hadn't heard anything didn't mean anything. Not all weapons were as loud as that gun Logan had handled with suspicious familiarity. It was clear his time with Galen had been spent in more deadly pursuits than recovering from grief over his wife's death.

Monty whimpered, his gaze on the dense foliage where Logan had disappeared. He wanted to go too. His search had been cut short and he didn't understand why he couldn't bring it to a satisfactory end.

Find?

"No, it will be okay. We don't have to go after him. Logan will do it."

But where was Logan?

Why was she so worried? She and Monty could find their way out of this jungle. She didn't care about Logan. He had caused her nothing but trouble.

But he didn't deserve to die when he was trying to save a life. He might be totally relentless, but he wasn't a murderer like those men in the camp.

No sound but the shrill sound of birds.

Then Monty's tail started to wag and he rose to his feet.

Relief surged through her. He was coming. She couldn't hear him or smell him, but Monty could.

It was another five minutes before Logan appeared through the leaves. "The camp's there." He moved toward his backpack as Monty ran to him, whimpering in an ecstasy of greeting. "About a mile ahead."

"I told you. What took so long?"

He knelt down and gave Monty an affectionate pat, then reached into his backpack for his radio. "I don't flatter myself that you were worried about me."

"No," she said coolly. "Monty was worried. I was just curious. Could you tell if Bassett was there?"

He gave Monty a hug and then pushed him away. "There's a tent with a guard posted out in front. I'm assuming Bassett's inside. The camp's small. Six tents and the numbers Sanchez gave us seem accurate."

"Did you run into anyone patrolling the area?"

"One man. I managed to avoid him."

"Obviously, or you wouldn't be here."

"Not so obviously. Another pinprick at my ego. But if I'd taken him out, it might have triggered an alert."

"So now you call Galen and get him here? Won't the people in the camp hear the helicopter?"

"The pilot will drop Galen and his men off at the clearing we passed about a mile north. We'll rendezvous with them there. Then the pilot will pick us up at Rudzak's camp when it's clear."

Her mouth tightened. "You mean when everyone's killed."

"I mean when we've gotten Bassett out." He looked directly into her eyes. "Whatever that takes." He bent over the radio. "You can lecture me later. We'll have plenty of time. I figure at least an hour before Galen gets here. Now I've got to talk to him and tell him to attack the decoy camp."

"Six dead. One wounded," Carl Duggan told Rudzak. "But we managed to repel the attack and save the helicopter. And I think we got one of their men. Shall we go after the rest?"

Rudzak gazed around the camp. Two tents were in flames and Duggan was wrong. Rudzak

94

could see seven dead. It had been a savage attack and brilliantly executed. "I didn't see Logan. Did you?"

Duggan shook his head. "But Galen was there and he's Logan's hired man."

Rudzak gave him a scathing glance. "I know that."

"Shall we go after them?" Duggan repeated. "It doesn't have to end here. Give me a chance and we'll still capture them."

"Shut up, I'm thinking." Galen and not Logan. The attack had been brutal, but had Galen been repelled too easily? Seven deaths but no push to completion of the mission.

"I have the men waiting," Duggan said. "We don't want to lose them."

Duggan didn't realize they had probably already lost them. They had not heard a helicopter, but no doubt Galen had one if he intended to get his men out alive.

And transport them quickly to another location.

Ah, Logan, you think you've fooled me.

"We won't lose them." Rudzak turned away. "I know where they're going."

It was almost nightfall when Galen and his men were dropped off at the glade where Logan and Sarah waited. They streamed out of the helicopter like a Delta Force. Galen's expression was grim as he waved the helicopter to leave before turning to Logan. "Let's go."

Logan turned to Sarah. "Stay here until

you hear the helicopter come back. Then come to the camp. We won't radio the pilot until it's safe for him to land."

"How long do you estimate that taking?" Sarah asked.

"At least forty-five minutes." He shrugged. "Maybe longer. Just don't come until you hear the helicopter."

"I've no intention of getting close," Sarah said. "My involvement in this is over. We've done our job."

"Come on, Logan." Galen was moving down the path into the forest, closely followed by his men. "I lost a man to Rudzak. Let's get this bullshit over." The words were curt and his attitude was different from when she had first met him. This was Galen the mercenary, and it was an intimidating change.

The entire situation was intimidating, Sarah thought as she watched the men disappear from view. What was she doing in the middle of a jungle with a bunch of mercenaries and Logan, who carried that damn assault weapon as casually as if it were a briefcase?

Monty pressed closer to her, his gaze on the path.

"No, we wait here, Monty." So many others could die to save a man who might already be dead. Galen had said one of his men had already been killed.

Logan could die.

Don't think about it. Just sit here and listen for the helicopter.

Ten minutes.

Twenty.

Thirty.

Thirty-five minutes passed before she heard the helicopter.

Faint.

Far away.

But coming closer every second.

She snapped the leash on Monty. "Come on, boy."

He eagerly bounded down the path in front of her, dragging her forward through the brush. He knew exactly where he was going even if she didn't.

Gunshots.

Explosions.

She caught sight of the camp and it looked like a war zone. Acrid smoke. Bodies. Blood. Fighting. She stopped on the path, staring in astonishment. What was going on here? When the helicopter came back, the battle was supposed to be over. It wasn't over.

"What the hell are you doing here?" Logan was beside her. "Never mind. Just don't come any closer." He said over his shoulder, "Bassett, stay with her."

The tall, lanky man behind him nodded. "I'm not moving a muscle until you come back for me. That's a promise."

Logan turned and ran back toward the camp.

5

"This is no time for introductions, but I'm Tom Bassett," the man standing beside Sarah said. "And you are?"

"Sarah Patrick." Her tone was abstracted, her gaze on Logan.

What the hell are you doing here? Logan had said.

"I've no idea why you're here, but I'm very glad to see you. Hell, I'm glad to see anyone but those stooges of Rudzak's." Bassett shook his head. "I thought my goose was well and truly cooked. When I saw Logan burst into my tent, I wanted to kiss him."

"I believe that would have upset him."

If Logan had not expected her, then they had not radioed for the helicopter?

But the helicopter was coming. She had heard it.

Dear God.

"Stay here." She ran toward the camp. She could still see Logan making his way through the smoke toward where Galen was standing. She and Monty dodged across the campsite to stand next to them.

Logan was not pleased to see her. "I told you to—"

"Shut up. Do you think I came here just because I wanted to see you kill and maim someone? Did you radio for the helicopter?"

"Not yet."

"Well, I heard a helicopter, dammit. And if it wasn't Galen's pilot, who do you think it was?"

He stiffened. "Shit. Rudzak. You're sure?"

"I've ridden in enough helicopters to know that sound in my sleep. Your red herring didn't work."

"How close?"

"Not close then, but they could be almost on top of us by now."

Galen turned away. "I'll radio for pickup." He waved his arm and shouted to his men. "We're pulling out."

"Tell the pilot to go to the clearing," Logan said. "We have to make a run for it back there."

"Take Bassett and get out of here. We'll be right behind you. It's not—"

Rotors. Loud. Close.

Sarah's heart jumped. She couldn't see the helicopter through the palms, but it must have been near and getting nearer every minute.

Logan took her arm. "Run for it. I'll get Bassett."

She didn't have to be told twice. "Monty!"

Branches hit her in the face as she tore through the jungle with Monty beside her.

The helicopter flew over her, almost on top of the camp.

Bullets.

The helicopter was spraying firepower on the camp below.

Logan and Bassett were next to her now.
More shots from the helicopter.

Galen and his men were behind them, then passing them as they raced toward the clearing.

It was scarcely a mile. It seemed a thousand.

Her lungs ached as she tried to force air into them. God, she was afraid. Stop it. Fear was always the enemy. She had been afraid before and survived. She'd survive now.

The clearing was up ahead. Would the helicopter be there?

It was landing as they burst out of the jungle. Galen's men weren't even waiting until it hit the ground to jerk open the door and tumble into the aircraft. Galen was standing by the door waving his men inside before he jumped in himself.

Bassett reached the helicopter and Galen pulled him inside. "Logan," Galen called. "Hurry. Get the hell inside. They must have spotted us. I hear them coming."

"So do I." Logan was looking up at the sky. "Get Sarah and the dog inside."

She glanced over her shoulder and saw Rudzak's helicopter flying low and fast toward them.

"Hurry." Galen reached for Sarah's hand.

"Monty," she called, and the retriever jumped inside the helicopter with her.

Bullets. Spraying the clearing from Rudzak's helicopter.

Logan moved away from the helicopter, lifted his weapon, and released a hail of bullets at the approaching helicopter.

Another spray of bullets.

"Logan!" Galen shouted.

Logan was down, blood streaming from his thigh. "Get out of here, Galen."

"The hell I will." Galen jumped out of the helicopter.

But Monty was ahead of him, already running toward Logan.

"Monty!" Sarah screamed.

Monty began tugging at Logan's shirt, trying to move him.

Sarah dove out of the helicopter.

More bullets.

Monty. Still. Bleeding.

"No!" She sank to her knees beside Monty. He was still breathing. Thank God.

"Get back in the helicopter." Galen was squatting beside her. "I'll take care of Logan."

"She'll never leave Monty. Get the dog first, Galen," Logan said. "Dammit, get the dog first."

"He's my dog. I'll do—" Sarah broke off when Galen picked up Monty.

"Go take care of your dog," Logan told her. "Galen will—"

"Shut up." She picked up Logan in a fireman's lift and struggled to her feet. Jesus, he was heavy. Three steps and she had him in the helicopter. "Lift off."

More shots.

What if they hit the fuel tank?

"Cover fire," Galen snapped.

Sarah was only dimly aware that Galen's men were shooting as she cradled Monty in her arms.

He opened his eyes and licked her arm. The helicopter lifted and headed north, barely skimming the trees.

Oh, God, Rudzak's aircraft was right behind them.

Then, suddenly, it was gone.

"Got him." Galen's gaze was on Rudzak's helicopter, which was slowly spiraling to the ground. "We must have hit something crucial. He's trying to get back to the clearing to land. I hope he gets a palm tree up his ass. Too bad we used the last of our missiles back at the camp." He turned to Logan. "You always did cause me trouble. Somebody pass me the first aid kit and I'll try to stop the blood."

"How's the...dog?" Logan whispered.

"I'm tending to him." Sarah was pressing a compress to Monty's wound. "I think he's going to be okay. The bullet only skimmed his shoulder and he's not bleeding much." She glanced at Galen. "Do you need help taking care of Logan? I've had training."

Logan tried to smile. "Yeah, she went to vet school. She can take care of my fleas at the same time."

She ignored him and spoke to Galen. "I've also had EMT training."

"Galen can handle it," Logan said. "Just make sure—the dog's okay. I know I'll be on your hit list if anything happens to him."

"You're right." She felt angry and scared and, yes, guilty that Monty had been hurt. She had placed him in harm's way. There was no doubt Logan was ultimately responsible, but

102

he had ordered Galen to save Monty first even though his life had been in danger. "I'll care for Monty. Worry about yourself."

His eyes closed. "Too—much trouble. Galen, you—do it."

He passed out.

Logan didn't regain consciousness until they were transferring him to the jet at Santo Camaro.

"About time you came back to us," Galen said. "You've caused me no end of trouble and made a mess of my copter. Of course, the pooch didn't help."

"He's alive?"

"In better shape than you. Sarah's bandaged him and is trying to keep him still."

"Where is she?"

"Inside the plane with Monty and Bassett." Galen paused. "You still have a bullet in your thigh. I didn't think there'd be any additional damage if I let you go back to the States and have it taken out there. Sarah didn't think so either. So we plugged you up and she'll give you a shot of morphine once you take off. Where do you want to go? Monterey?"

He tried to think. His mind was so blurry, he already felt as if he had the morphine. "It depends on whether Rudzak's alive. Go back and check and phone me. It would be nice if the bastard crashed and burned, but we're probably not that lucky."

Galen nodded. "I was going anyway. I

thought you'd want to be certain one way or the other."

"And don't let her give me the morphine. Tell her you just remembered I'm allergic to it or something. I need to know about Rudzak as soon as possible."

"Why not tell her the truth?"

"And let her find out this may be only the beginning? I promised her when we found Bassett, her part would be over, but the situation's changed and I don't know how it's going to affect her. I'm not up to handling her right now. I have to stall."

"And what do I tell the pilot?"

"Just tell him to get us out of South American airspace and I'll give him his orders when I hear from you."

"Okay, but it's a long flight and you're going to hurt like hell."

"I'm hurting like hell now, but Rudzak had to have seen her and Monty. If he's alive, then he may try to take her out first. She's an easier target and it's pretty clear he doesn't want me dead before he can make me suffer."

"Are you going to tell her that?"

"Not if I can help it. It may get in the way and she's pissed enough at me. I just have to be wherever she is to keep Rudzak in check."

"You're not exactly in prime condition to keep anyone in check. You could get protection for her. You don't have to do it yourself."

"I made her a promise." He smiled crookedly. "And, hell, I probably owe her for more than Bassett now."

"You mean for picking you up and throwing you into the helicopter? It's possible. Seconds were counting at that point." Galen grinned. "And it was an interesting role reversal. Do you suppose she has Amazon blood?"

"All I know is that I could have done without that particular guilt trip." He closed his eyes. "Get me in that plane and go back and check on Rudzak. I have to know."

Logan's eyes were closed, but Sarah knew he wasn't asleep. His mouth was compressed and deep lines were engraved on either side of his lips.

She sat down on the bed beside him. "Take this."

Logan's eyes opened and looked at the glass in her hand. "What is it?"

"Tylenol." She popped two tablets on his tongue. "You're not allergic to that too, are you?"

He shook his head as he swallowed the water. "Thanks."

"Tough luck about the morphine allergy. The Tylenol may help a little. I gave some to Monty too."

"Then I know it's a surefire remedy. You might take chances with my health but never with Monty's. How is he?"

"Better than you."

"That must give you some satisfaction. After all, I was responsible for his being hurt."

105

"It doesn't give me any satisfaction. I hate violence. I never wanted you to be shot." She glanced away from him. "And you told Galen to save Monty before you. Not many men would have done that for a dog."

"Don't give me too much credit. I'm not the selfless type. I wanted to tell Galen to get me the hell on that helicopter."

"But you didn't." She was still not looking at him. "And I've always found it's what you do and not what you think that's the bottom line. Fear's always there."

"Is it?"

"If you're not stupid." She rose to her feet. "I have to get back to Monty. You're probably in too much pain to sleep, but you can try."

"I'm expecting a call from Galen. If I do fall asleep, will you see that I wake up to take it?"

"It's that important? You need to sleep."

"Will you wake me?"

She lifted her shoulders. "Sure. Why not? You're the one who's going to suffer for it."

"How's Bassett doing?"

"Okay. He's covered with mosquito bites and he's got a bad case of nerves. He wants to call his wife."

Logan shook his head. "Not now. Tell him not to worry. She wasn't told he was missing."

"But why can't he call her?"

"It could cause problems. He may not be able to go home yet."

"Isn't that his choice? He's had a rough time." She rubbed her temple. "We've all had a rough time. I'd spit in your eye if you tried to keep me from going back to the ranch."

"Would you?"

"You bet your life. Why shouldn't he go home?"

He didn't answer.

She said slowly, "You're worried about Rudzak?"

"He could still be alive, and he thought Bassett was valuable enough to take as a hostage before. I may have to find a secure place for him for a while."

"What if he won't go? His nerves are already shot, and it would be like being put in another prison."

"Maybe it won't be necessary. I hope not."

"It should be Bassett's choice. Not yours."

"It became my choice when Rudzak destroyed that research facility. Everything Rudzak does is aimed directly at me. I'm the only one who can deflect him."

"You talk as if it's some kind of contest."

"It's no contest. It's a war and Rudzak's as tenacious as a bulldog."

"Don't malign any dog by comparing him to that murderer. He tried to kill Monty."

He smiled. "I wonder what it would take to make you care as much for a human being as you do that dog."

"Unswerving loyalty, courage, humor, companionship, intelligence, and the willingness to give his life for me."

He gave a low whistle. "You're tough."

"You asked me. Total commitment is almost

impossible between individuals. That's why I like dogs more than I do most people. It's a hell of a lot safer."

"You've found that?"

"Haven't you?" She felt his gaze on her back as she walked away from him. He was wounded and in pain, and yet he was still trying to pull Bassett's strings. What a surprise. He'd probably have to be in his coffin before he'd give up control.

Maybe she wasn't being fair. He was trying to help Bassett.

Well, she was too tired to be fair, she thought as she sat down beside Monty. Her emotions were in shreds and she was so tired, she was almost numb. She wanted only to go home and rest.

She glanced at Bassett, who was curled up asleep in the chair across the aisle. He deserved to go back to his wife and kid. He should never have gotten caught up in any project with a man as dangerous as Logan. What was she thinking? But she had not really thought of Logan as dangerous until the past few days. On the surface he was a powerful and eminently respectable businessman. Bassett had probably thought himself lucky to hitch his wagon to a star of Logan's magnitude. Well, not Sarah. She had done her job and was through with Logan.

Monty made a sound deep in his throat and she quickly bent to stroke his side. "I know it hurts. It will be over soon. We're going home."

108

. . .

"I think it's a displaced clavicle," Duggan said. "It must hurt like hell. You'd better not walk any farther."

"Don't be an idiot. I have to keep going. Give me a minute and I'll be able to go on." Rudzak leaned back against the tree, closed his eyes, and let the waves of pain wash over him. He had learned in prison that it was better to accept pain than to fight it. Another lesson he owed to Logan. "Did you radio Mendez and ask him to send another helicopter?"

"Yes, he said that he'd have it waiting for us at the cliffs."

The cliffs. Five miles away. It might as well be fifty in the shape he was in. Dammit, why did the helicopter have to crash? All his plans blown in a moment. "You told him I was hurt?"

Duggan avoided his glance. "He said this wasn't company business and that he wouldn't chance involving his men in a confrontation with Galen. He'll be glad to help you if you reach an area that's relatively safe."

He should have known. Company business was the only passion in Mendez's life, and as long as Rudzak kept the profits coming in, the drug baron would continue to pour unlimited funds into his bank account. If Rudzak did anything that harmed business, he'd be cut loose quicker than the blink of an eye. Mendez needn't worry. Rudzak would do nothing to damage their relationship. Money was God in this world, and he needed money to unleash a lightning bolt at Logan.

"I could call him back," Duggan said. "Maybe he didn't realize—"

"He realized exactly what he was doing." Which meant he had to get to those cliffs before Galen and his team returned. "Help me up."

Agony shot through his upper body as Duggan got him to his feet. It would be all right, he told himself. Accept the pain. Make it work for you. Turn it into hate.

He knew all about hate. Fifteen years...

"Do you want to lean on me?" Duggan asked.

"No." He staggered down the trail. Keep going. Ignore the pain. Think about Logan. Plan the next move. "As soon as we get to Bogotá I want you to arrange transport to the U.S."

"We have to get you to a doctor before—"

"That won't take long. If it's a displaced clavicle, it can be put back. I want to be en route by tomorrow. I don't want Logan to feel safe."

"And we're going to Silicon Valley?"

Duggan was zeroing in on his principal interest. No harm; it would keep him focused. But there were so many more facets to revenge than he was capable of seeing. "Yes, but first I have to check and see if—" He stopped to get his breath as another wave of pain shot through him. Fight it. Clear your mind. "I saw a woman and a dog.... She helped Logan get to the helicopter. Find out who she is."

"As soon as I can."

"Right away. I know Logan. He can be very soft when he's grateful to someone. I've exploited that weakness myself." The pain was getting hard to suppress. But he mustn't be discouraged just because one thing had gone wrong.

I'm coming, Logan. Do you feel my hate? You will soon. It will burn you and everyone around you to cinders.

"He's alive," Galen said over the phone. "We found the helicopter, but he'd managed to land it. No sign of him or any of his men."

Logan cursed. "Keep looking."

"I am, but it's my bet he's safe in drug heaven somewhere in the hills."

"Not for long. He'll be on the move as soon as he can."

"But we may have a break for a little while. What's the plan?"

"I'm working on it. But right now we have to wait for him to make a move. Have Margaret contact the FBI and ATF and tell them we've had an anonymous threat and to give my plants and research facilities additional protection."

"Including Dodsworth?"

Logan didn't answer for a moment. "No, not Dodsworth. She's not to tell them about Dodsworth. I've already tripled the security there. Dodsworth will be safe."

"Don't sell Rudzak short."

"You don't have to tell me that."

111

"Easy."

"I don't feel easy." Dammit, Logan had hoped that Rudzak had been taken out. "Try to find him. If you can't locate him, find someone who can point the way. We need to know what he's up to." He had to think through the pain throbbing through him. "Oh, and tell Margaret to make the pilot head for Phoenix and have a surgeon ready in my house there to take out this damn bullet."

"Phoenix?"

"The house has security. I'll double it and set up quarters for Bassett there."

"What about Sarah Patrick?"

"My chances of getting her to stay at the house are slim to none. Arrange surveillance and protection for her cabin, but make sure she's not aware of it."

"Done. And what about you? You're the one Rudzak wants to slaughter and hang out to dry."

"I'm safe for now."

"Oh, yeah? You have a bullet in your leg to prove how safe you are."

"I think Rudzak would have been very upset if that bullet had killed me. He wants to torture me first. He told me so."

"Just hope he doesn't change his mind." Galen hung up.

Rudzak wouldn't change his mind, Logan thought wearily. He had planned his revenge too long.

"Monty wanted to come." Sarah was standing beside him with Monty in her arms and carefully placed the dog on the floor beside Logan's couch. "He's got that sore shoulder, and I couldn't stop him from trying to crawl over to you. He knows you're hurt and he wants to comfort you. Now that you've gotten your call, will you go to sleep? I don't want Monty disturbed any more than he is right now."

"I'll go to sleep." He reached down and stroked the retriever's head. "I wouldn't want Monty disturbed."

She took the phone from him and put it on the end table. "What about Rudzak?"

"Alive."

"And what are you going to do about it?"

"Wait. Watch. Try to find him." He paused. "But Bassett will have to go to the secured house in Phoenix for his own protection."

"Why there?"

"Why not? It's a pleasant enough place. You stayed there yourself for a while with Eve. I don't suppose you'd want to live there until Monty has recovered?"

"No way. I want to go home."

That's what he'd been afraid of. "Do you mind if we go to the house first before I have you taken home? I need to get this bullet out."

"The house instead of a hospital?"

"Hospitals ask questions."

"Doctors are bound by law to report gunshot wounds."

"But they can often be persuaded to delay or forget the report."

"Money?"

"Or influence. Or even a charitable donation. Doctors see so much suffering, sometimes they weigh legalities against a contribution that can help heal thousands."

"And risk their license."

"It's their choice, Sarah." He closed his eyes. "Now go away and let me and Monty sleep. I'm tired of defending myself."

"In a minute." He heard the sound of pouring water and opened his eyes to see Sarah setting down the carafe. She handed him two more Tylenol. "You can take these now. I don't want you restless and disturbing—"

"Monty," he finished for her. He swallowed the pills and closed his eyes again. "I'll try not to thrash around and bother your dog."

"Monty wouldn't care. It's his nature to want to comfort." She tucked the blanket around him with a gentleness that belied the briskness of her tone. "But I care for him. Go to sleep."

He was already half asleep as he heard her move away from him. It wasn't only Monty's nature to want to comfort. In spite of Sarah's resentment toward him, she found it impossible not to try to ease his pain and equally impossible to admit to that softness.

A truly remarkable woman...

"Bring him into the living room. It's already set up as an operating room." A plump, fortyish woman in a pinstriped suit was standing outside the house, waiting, when the ambulance doors opened and Logan was lifted to the ground. "How are you doing, John?"

"Okay."

"You don't look okay. You're pale as a tombstone. This was incredibly stupid of you." She walked beside his stretcher. "And you've caused me a great deal of trouble. Do you know how difficult it is to arrange this kind of thing with any kind of confidentiality?"

"Sorry." He looked back over his shoulder at Sarah. "This is my assistant, Margaret Wilson. Ask her for anything you need."

"I'll be fine. Stop worrying about me."

To her surprise, he reached out his hand to her. She took a step closer to the stretcher and enfolded his hand in hers.

His grasp tightened as he looked up at her. "Stay," he whispered. "Stay, Sarah."

"I'm not going anywhere right away."

"I'll take that as a promise." He glanced at his assistant. "Take care of her, Margaret. She needs to—"

"Shut up," Margaret said. "I'll take care of everything. You just let Dr. Dowden take care of this stupidity you've gotten yourself into before you lose that leg."

He released Sarah's hand. "Yes, ma'am."

Margaret turned back to Sarah as Logan was whisked into the living room. "They're going to operate at once. How bad is he?"

"The bullet didn't shatter the bone, but it tore through some muscle. Infection is always the problem. He'd be better off in a hospital."

Margaret shook her head. "He won't do it. Where's your dog? I heard he was shot too."

"Still in the ambulance. He's okay. Just a little sore. He hasn't wanted to leave Logan since he was hurt, so we rode here with him. Bassett is being driven here by the pilot and the security guard you arranged to meet the plane." She turned, lifted Monty out of the ambulance, and carried him into the house. "We'll stay until the operation is over."

Margaret lifted her brows. "Because Monty's worried?"

"I'm not so hard that I can't feel compassion for someone in pain. Even Logan." She carried Monty through to the kitchen. "Will you get down a bowl? I need to give Monty water."

"Sit down. I'll do it." Margaret went to a cabinet, got a bowl, and filled it with water.

Sarah took the bowl and pushed the water toward Monty. When he started to drink, she straightened and asked, "Is this Dowden a good doctor?"

Margaret nodded. "You don't know me or I'd be insulted that you'd think I'd put John in some quack's hands." She looked down at Monty. "How about him? Does he need a vet?"

Sarah shook her head. "I'm used to taking care of him unless it's something serious. He's fine. He could walk, but that shoulder is sore. I want him to rest it. He'll be back to normal in a day or so."

"So you're lugging him around like a baby." Margaret grinned. "A seventy-pound baby at that."

"No problem. I'm strong. In my job I have to be."

"I know. I did the research on you." She sat down across from Sarah. "You have a perfect right to be pissed at me, but I'm still going to tell you that I admire what you and Monty have done."

"Why should I be angry with you? It's Logan who pulls the strings."

"That's very fair." Margaret's gaze searched her face. "But you're not as angry with John as I thought you'd be. Why not?"

Because he'd kept his word. Because though she disapproved of his methods, she couldn't fault his motives. Because she'd grown to know him in that jungle, his strength and his determination, even a little of his past. It was difficult hating anyone but a total ass once you understood them.

"It's over." She rose to her feet. "It's a waste of energy being angry. Will you keep an eye on Monty? I want to be at the door to meet Bassett. This is pretty difficult for him. He thought he was going home."

"Sure." Margaret reached down and patted Monty. "I love dogs and he's a sweetheart."

Bassett arrived at the front door five minutes later.

He smiled with relief as soon as he saw Sarah walking toward him. "Am I glad to see a friendly face. When I went through

117

those electric gates, I felt as if I was at Alcatraz."

"So did I the first time I came here. And then there were only two security guards, not the four I saw when I drove through the gates."

"You've been here before?"

"Several months ago."

He nodded. "I should have known you and Logan were old friends. The intimacy is pretty obvious."

Intimacy? A ripple of shock went through her. "Why do you say that?"

"As I said, it's fairly obvious watching you together. You saved his life, and you kept an eagle eye on him all during the trip, though I could see you were trying to be offhand about it. Logan's not a man who likes being coddled, is he?"

"I wouldn't know. I don't coddle."

He held up his hands. "Sorry. Did I make a mistake?"

"Yes. Logan and I aren't old friends. I didn't save his life. I just gave him a boost into that helicopter so we could take off. And I did a job for a friend of his and then this one for him. That's the extent of our 'intimacy.' " She turned and moved toward the stairs. "You're probably tired. I'll show you to a room."

"You're upset. I didn't mean—"

"I'm not upset." It was true. She wasn't upset with Bassett. It wasn't his fault he'd read the situation wrong. That she had felt concerned for Logan was entirely natural. She would have felt the same for anyone who was hurt and

118

helpless. By instinct and training she was a person who tried to save.

If it was entirely natural, then why was she justifying her reaction?

Because at that moment she was tired and vulnerable. No other reason. She'd be better after a little rest.

"This is a nice room. It overlooks the garden." She threw open the door at the top of the stairs. "The telephone is on the bedside table. I assume Logan is letting you at least call your wife."

"Sure. Though he asked me not to tell her I'd left Santo Camaro."

"Asked?"

"Well, strongly suggested." He glanced at Sarah. "But don't get me wrong. I came here voluntarily. Logan offered to fix up a lab for me here so I can get on with my work."

He might have thought the choice was voluntary, but what Logan wanted, Logan generally got. "I thought you wanted to go home."

"He pointed out that I didn't want to compromise the safety of my family. He's put a guard on them, but I'd just be a threat to them right now." He entered the room and looked around. "Private bath. Nice. A lot better than the living quarters at Santo Camaro. Castleton did his best, but he concentrated more on lab equipment than on little luxuries. The damn hot-water heater had to be replaced four times in the time I was there."

"Then why did you stay?"

"It was my dream," he said simply. "You

don't give up a dream because you have to take cold showers."

"What kind of dream?"

He made a face. "I didn't mean to pique your curiosity. I'm sorry, you've been very kind, but I can't talk about my work. It's in my contract."

"And was it in your contract to risk being killed?"

"No, but we all knew there might be repercussions. It went with the territory."

"What do you—" Why was she asking questions when he'd already told her he couldn't discuss it? She wasn't interested anyway. It was time she distanced herself from Logan and everyone around him. "Margaret Wilson is in the kitchen downstairs and I'd bet she's had it fully stocked. Do you know her?"

"No, I worked through Castleton, but I've heard of her. Tough, efficient, and bossy as hell." He grinned. "She's something of a legend in Logan's empire. But you can't expect anything else. He's a legend himself."

"Well, that legend is downstairs having a bullet dug out of his leg. When they're through, maybe they should look you over."

"I'm fine. All I need is to talk to my wife and son."

"Then I'll leave you to it."

"Thanks." He was already heading for the phone as she closed the door.

She returned to the kitchen, where Margaret updated her on Logan. "The doctor just stuck his head in. The operation's over and John's

120

doing fine. He's under sedation, but he should be waking up in a few hours."

Relief surged through her. She had known Logan's injury wasn't critical, but operations were always serious. "Good." She sank down in the chair. "No signs of infection?"

"A little. They're giving him megadoses of antibiotics to combat it. The doctor didn't like the fact that the bullet stayed in him all those hours."

"It was safer to bring him back to the States."

"I'm not saying it wasn't the right thing to do. There are always pros and cons." Margaret stood up. "How about some lunch? I've got a lot of canned stuff. Soup? Stew?"

Sarah shook her head. "It's time for Monty and me to go home. Will you arrange for someone to drive me back to my ranch?"

"Now?" Margaret frowned. "What's your hurry?"

"I want to go home."

"You told him you'd stay."

Stay, Sarah.

She had agreed because Logan's moment of vulnerability and need had caught her off guard. But he was neither vulnerable nor in need. He was surrounded by people who would take care of him and protect him. He certainly didn't need her. "I did stay. He's out of danger now."

"John won't like it. He told me to take care of you. How can I take care of you if you're miles away?"

121

"I don't need anyone to take care of me. I can take care of myself." She bent down and stroked Monty's head. "He's hurt and he needs to be in familiar surroundings."

"John won't like it," Margaret repeated.

"Do you get a car for me, or do I do it myself?"

"I'll do it." Margaret sighed. "But you're making my job very difficult."

"I think you'll bear up. You don't seem very intimidated by Logan."

"We've been together a long time. Familiarity generally casts out fear, but I do have a healthy respect for him."

Sarah studied her. "And you like him."

"Hell, yes. He's tough, but he's always been fair with me. And if life gets a little complicated around him, at least it's not boring." She went to the telephone. "I'll call one of the security men on the grounds and tell him to bring a car around front. Sure you don't want to have lunch before you leave?"

"I'm sure." She listened to Margaret put through the call. In a few minutes she'd be on her way back to the life she loved best—silence, simplicity, and serenity. Let Logan spin his complicated webs around someone else. She was going home.

The howl was eerily exquisite floating on the still night air.

Monty lifted his head. *Beautiful.*

"It looks like our wolf is still around." Sarah knelt to pour vitamins into Monty's food. "I hoped it would be gone by the time we got back."

Hungry?

"Maybe. Those Mexican gray wolves have had a pretty rough time since they were released. Eat your dinner."

Monty nosed the bowl away from him. *Hungry.*

"You need to eat. You're not going to heal without food, and you can't save that wolf by starving yourself."

Monty stretched out beside the untouched food bowl. *Hungry.*

The wolf howled again.

"Shut up," Sarah muttered. "Do you want those ranchers to come looking for you? Your best bet is to keep a low profile and—"

Hungry.

"That wolf is a hundred times better equipped than you to find food in the wild."

Sad. Alone.

The wolf shouldn't be this far east. He might well be alone, separated from his pack. "We can't help. They were released to make their way in the world." She sat down at the table and started to eat the stew she'd just heated. "See, I'm not worried. Now eat your dinner." She glanced over her shoulder and saw him staring at the door. "No, we are not going out to try to find—"

A knock.

She stiffened as the door swung open.

"Sorry." Logan was leaning against the jamb, his face pale, a small suitcase at his feet. "Do you mind if I come in? I think I need to sit down."

"What the hell are you doing here?" Sarah jumped to her feet and ran over to the door. She slung his arm around her shoulders and helped him to the easy chair in front of the fire. "Idiot. They just operated on you this afternoon. Are you trying to break open those stitches?"

"You promised me you'd stay. I woke up and you were gone." He settled back in the chair and closed his eyes. "So I came here."

She got a hassock from across the room and lifted his leg to rest on it. "Who brought you?"

"Margaret. I told her to drop me off and leave."

"I bet she loved that."

He smiled faintly. "Oh, you've gotten to know Margaret. She wasn't pleased."

"Neither am I. What are you doing here?"

"I decided I needed a little rest and seclusion. You have lots of that here."

She blinked. "What?"

"You have a couch." His voice was slurred. "I can sleep there."

"You're not making sense."

"I'm not? I'm a little fuzzy right now. Must be the medication the doctor gave me. I'm trying to ask you to either come back to the house or let me stay here."

"I'm not coming back and you cannot stay here. You can get all the seclusion you want in your house in Phoenix."

"It's not only—I promised you I'd deal with Madden for you."

"Yes, you did, and I'm holding you to it, but you didn't have to get out of a sickbed. And you didn't need to come here. Madden's not been here since the day I threw him out."

"Like you want to throw me out."

"Right."

"Safer. I'm—responsible."

"You're mumbling. I can't understand you."

"I don't mumble." Logan opened his eyes as Monty put his head against his hand. "Hello, boy. I'm glad someone is rolling out the welcome mat."

"Don't be flattered. Five minutes ago he wanted to roll out the same mat for a wolf."

"Wolf? I heard him when I was in the car. Beautiful..."

"Not you too?" She turned away and reached for the telephone. "What's Margaret's cell phone number? I'll call and tell her to turn around and come back for you."

He shook his head. "I told her not to pay any attention. You're...stuck...with me."

125

"The hell I am. I'll call an ambulance and have them— Dammit, listen to me."

"Sorry." His eyes had closed again. "Tired..."

He was asleep.

"Logan!"

No answer. He was probably so heavily drugged, it was a wonder he had been able to stir himself to come here. No, not really a wonder. She knew how determined Logan could be.

But why had he been so determined to come here?

Well, it would do no good to fret about reasons, when his presence was an accomplished fact. It would serve him right if she shipped him back to Phoenix in an ambulance.

Monty mournfully looked at her.

"Okay, okay, we'll let him stay until he wakes up. Maybe it will take your mind off that blasted wolf."

Monty settled down beside the chair.

She sighed in exasperation as she brought Logan's bag inside, then she lay down on the couch. She had thought she was done with him. Yet here he was again, only hours later, and she was sleeping on this lumpy couch instead of in her comfortable bed to make sure the idiot didn't thrash around and hurt himself.

"Wake up."

Logan was dimly aware that Sarah was shaking him.

"Dammit, wake up."

He fought his way through the fog of sleep and opened his eyes. The cabin. She wanted him to go…. "I'm staying."

"And I'm leaving. So call Margaret and tell her to come get you."

"What?" He sat up in the chair as he realized she was shrugging on her jacket. "Where the hell are you going?"

"Taiwan. They've had torrential rains for the past two weeks. A mudslide just buried a village. They think the fatalities are going to mount to over five hundred." She crossed to the kitchen counter and poured steaming coffee into a thermos. "God, I *hate* mudslides. The chances of pulling anyone out alive are so slim, they may as well be nonexistent. They're death searches, not life searches."

"Then why are you going?"

"Hundreds of people are buried underneath that damn sludge. Maybe Monty and I can cut that number down by a few."

"How did you find out about this slide?"

"Helen Peabody, our rescue group's coordinator, called ten minutes ago. You were so zonked, you didn't even hear the phone."

"You're dead tired. You have no business going anywhere."

"It's my job. It's a long flight. I'll be able to rest on the plane."

"What plane?"

"Helen is calling around now to see who'll lend us a plane and pilot. She'll get them." She tucked the thermos into her duffel. "Now, get on the phone and call Margaret."

"What about Monty? He's been wounded. You were so concerned about him and yet you're willing to take him on a rescue like this?"

"It's his job too. He's sore but he'll make it. If I see he's hurting too much, I'll pull him."

"I never thought you'd be that tough on Monty. You're crazy about that dog."

"If there's a chance of saving anyone, neither Monty nor I have any right to hold back. We've been hurt before and gotten through it." She reached in the cabinet, got Monty's vitamins, and threw them in the duffel. "We'll be there for only a few days. After that we'll let the other teams take over the search. Monty's had enough death for a while after Barat."

"What about you? Haven't you had enough?"

"Oh, yes." She turned away and wearily arched her back. "I've had enough. But it just keeps coming."

"Did you ever think about saying no?"

"How can I say no when there's someone waiting for help?"

"I guess you can't." He should argue with her, but he was having trouble thinking. He shook his head to clear it. "Taiwan. Where in Taiwan?"

"A place called Kai Chi. Do you want some coffee?"

"No, thanks."

"Are you sure? You look like you could use it."

"Five hundred dead?"

128

"That's the estimate."

"Then I guess you need some help." He reached for his digital phone. "Though you're making things difficult for me. How many people are in your team?"

"Six."

"And six dogs?"

She nodded.

"Call back this Helen Peabody and tell her you've found a plane and pilot." He wrinkled his nose. "My upholstery and carpets may never smell the same after six dogs running around the cabin."

Her eyes widened. "You're lending us your plane?"

"How soon can you have the team at the Phoenix airport?"

"Most of them are in Tucson. Five hours tops."

"That's too long if the conditions in Taiwan are as bad as you say. We'll fly down to Tucson, pick up the team, and go direct to Taiwan from there."

"We?"

"I'm going with you."

"Are you out of your head? To Taiwan? Why?"

"Maybe it's my way of trying to make up for having Monty hurt in Santo Camaro."

"Then just give us the plane and pilot."

He shook his head. "It's my plane. I call the shots." He dialed Margaret. "Margaret, I'm going to Taiwan. Have my plane and documents ready within the hour." He cut her short when she started to protest. "Not now. Just do it." He hung up.

Sarah was shaking her head. "You can't go with us."

"Why not?"

"This is a rescue mission. We have work to do. You'd get in the way."

"No, I wouldn't. I know the language. I have a small plant on the coast, so I have contacts in the country and I have the plane. What else could you ask for?"

"That you stay here and give us the plane and pilot."

"No deal."

"You've just had that leg operated on. You don't know what kind of conditions we're going to face. What if you get an infection?"

"Then you'd have to take care of me as well as Monty."

"That's what I'm afraid of."

"Don't be. It won't happen. I won't be a burden." He struggled out of the chair and had to suppress a wince as pain shot through his thigh. "If I am, then I promise I'll stay out of your way. Now, make the call while I go to the bathroom and throw some water on my face."

She stood there, undecided.

"Go call Helen Peabody." He limped toward the bathroom. "You know I'm the best game in town."

"Look at you. You can't even walk without hurting."

"What do you care? Serves me right, doesn't it?"

"I don't want you to lose your damn leg."

"I'll take care of me, and you and Monty take care of the suffering millions of the world. I'd say that's fair." He glanced at her over his shoulder. "Wouldn't you?"

She slowly nodded. "You're right. Why should I worry about you?" She turned away and picked up the telephone. "Come if you like. But don't blame me if you get more than you bargained for in Taiwan."

"I won't blame you." He closed the door and leaned against it, fighting the waves of agony. He should take some more painkillers, but he couldn't afford to be fuzzy right now. Once they left Tucson, he could let go for a while. In spite of her toughness, Sarah was a caretaker, and she would find a way to keep him from going if she realized he was hurting like hell. And sick. God, he felt sick. When the pain dulled to a throbbing, he pulled out his phone and called Galen. "I'm at Sarah's cabin, but we're leaving for Taiwan right away. Have you found out anything?"

"Not yet. I'm still tracking Sanchez. Taiwan?"

"It seems there's a mudslide in Taiwan. Her rescue team has been called out. I'm going with them."

"Christ. How do you feel?"

"I just had a bullet cut out of me. Not good."

"I don't envy you."

"Just find Rudzak. Even if he's hurt, I'll bet he's somewhere plotting and planning his next move."

He hung up and closed his eyes, gathering his strength. He'd gotten through the call. He could get through the flight. The trick was blocking the pain, operating on automatic, and not allowing himself to think.

He bent over the sink and splashed cold water on his face.

"Nice guy." Susie Phillips sat in the leather seat, her gaze on Logan at the front of the plane, talking to Boyd Medford. "You'd never know he was some kind of tycoon, would you?"

"Look around." Sarah's tone was dry. "I think anyone would be able to hazard a guess by this plane."

"You know what I mean. He's pretty down-to-earth. Have you known him long?"

"Not long."

"Then he must be a good guy to volunteer to do this for us. Particularly after he had that accident."

"Did he tell you he'd had an accident?"

"No, but it was, wasn't it?"

Sarah changed the subject. "How's Dinah been doing?"

"Fine. But she misses the searches. She looks so mournful when I take Donegan here out to my pickup." She reached down and stroked her German shepherd's head. "She doesn't understand that retiring after years of service is a reward, not a punishment." She glanced at Monty. "I know Monty's nowhere near that point, but it will be hard for him too.

Maybe more than any other dog in the group. You should think about it. You'll need time to train another dog."

Sarah didn't want to think about it. She couldn't imagine working with another dog after all these years, and the thought of Monty growing old hurt her. "There's plenty of time to think about that." She rose to her feet. "Logan's looking a little tired. I think I'll go see if he needs anything."

Susie nodded. "Good idea." She took a paperback book out of her tote. "I'll see if I can read myself to sleep. It's going to be a long flight, and I'd love to spend it unconscious."

"So would I." Sarah could feel weariness dragging at every muscle as she walked down the aisle, stepping over dogs and carry-on baggage on the way to Logan. She couldn't wait until she was able to curl up and sleep as the other members of the team were doing. Actually, there was nothing to prevent her. Logan didn't need her. He could take care of himself.

If he was sensible. But if he'd been sensible, he'd have stretched out on one of the couches when the jet had left Tucson an hour before. Instead, he'd continued talking to Boyd, listening politely and growing more wan and exhausted-looking by the minute.

Men.

Boyd looked up and smiled as she stopped before them. "Hey, Sarah. Pretty nice digs, huh? Remember that cargo plane we hopped to Barat?"

"How could I forget?" She gazed directly at Logan. "You look like death warmed over. Go to bed."

"In a few minutes. Boyd was just telling me about the rescue operation in Nicaragua."

"He can tell you when you wake up." She turned to Boyd. "I'm kicking you out of here. He should have that leg elevated. He probably didn't tell you he had an operation yesterday."

"Hell, no." Boyd stood up. "I'm gone. See you later, Logan."

Logan nodded and watched Boyd walk down the aisle and settle down by Susie. "You know him well?"

"Years."

"I thought as much. You can be rude only to very old friends."

"You'd have been better off if you'd been rude to him. He's a great guy, but he talks a lot when he's not on a search."

"I liked him." He smiled. "And I'm fully capable of being as rude as you, Sarah. He interested me. He was giving me an insight into your work."

"And?"

"It was like a glimpse into hell. Intriguing to hear about, but I wouldn't want to live there."

"You don't have to live there. I do."

"Not unless you—"

"Stop talking. I'm dead tired, and the last thing I wanted was to have to run interference between you and my friends because you were too macho to admit you were in pain. Now,

134

will you go and lie down so that I can get some rest?"

"Sure." He struggled to his feet and stood swaying with one hand on the back of the chair. "If you'll give me a minute to get the kinks out. I've stiffened up."

He probably just didn't want to admit that the long walk down the aisle was intimidating in his present state. "Do you want me to help you?"

He grimaced. "You won't let me get away with anything, will you?"

"Pride's pretty dumb if you're hurting."

"No one can ever accuse you of mincing words. Two minutes. If I'm not okay then, I'll let you sweep me up in a fireman's lift and carry me to my couch. Tell me why you hate mudslides so much."

"I told you, they're death searches. In an earthquake you have more of a chance of finding air pockets. When a mountain of mud comes down on you, you suffocate."

"Like a snow avalanche?"

She shook her head. "Snow is easy because it's porous, scent travels through it. Mud is different, the scent is sealed inside. It's almost impossible for a dog to pick up the cone. And the dog thinks he can walk on mud, which leads to trouble. He can get stuck, get carried away, or go under, and sometimes you can't get to him to help him. You have to watch him every minute."

Her words were shooting out like machine-gun bullets. "You can't search alone because you have to use one person as a spotter in case a searcher gets in trouble. And that happens frequently. Just getting a boot full of mud can be a death sentence. A handler has to make sure her rubber boots are well fitting and duct-taped on. Plus, it's still raining in Taiwan, and we can't search until the rain stops because the mud can shift at any time. So you sit and wait while the victims' relatives stare and curse at you. Is that enough problems for you?"

"Shit."

"Exactly. Are you sure you don't want to stay on board the plane instead of going to the village?"

"I'm sure." His gaze wandered over the occupants of the plane. "Nice people, but they must be as crazy as you to be willing to go through that. I'm afraid I was a little out of it when you introduced me. Tell me about them."

Her gaze followed his. "The fiftyish man with the black Lab is Hans Kniper, he's a vet and dog trainer. The small young man asleep by the window is George Leonard. He works at a supermarket in Tucson and trains dogs on the weekends. You met Boyd Medford, our team leader. I guess I know him best. He was with the ATF K9 unit before he bailed and bought a ranch. Theo Randall is the blond man with the black-and-tan German shepherd. He's an accountant with a luxury hotel. Susie's a stay-at-home mom with two kids and four German shepherds."

"None of you have much in common."

"Except a love of dogs and the willingness to train them to help. That's enough of a bond."

"Monty's the only golden retriever. Three German shepherds, two Labs, and Monty. Are some breeds better suited than others for this kind of work?"

"You'd get an argument from every owner on the team. I think the only true qualifications are intelligence, the search instinct, and a good nose. Are you ready to move now?"

"Slowly." He started carefully down the aisle. "Very slowly. Good night, Sarah."

She watched him walk haltingly, stopping for a moment to step around Susie's dog, Donegan. Susie looked up from her book, and he exchanged a few words with her.

Lie down, you idiot. You don't have to charm everyone on the damn plane.

He had gone past Susie and was sitting down on the couch. He took a vial of pills from his pocket and swallowed a couple with a glass of water. Painkillers? If they were, he should have taken them before. At that moment, when he wasn't aware he was being watched, his expression was haggard...and tormented. She could understand the haggardness—but torment? What devils were driving Logan?

Monty got to his feet, walked stiffly to Logan's couch, and plopped down in front of it. He could always sense illness and pain, which was only another signal that Logan had no business on this trip.

And Sarah would have no business on this mission either if she didn't stop worrying about a man who was too stubborn to worry about himself and get some rest. She sat down in the chair Logan had vacated and pushed it back until it was almost fully reclining.

Sleep. Don't think about Logan.

Don't think about that suffocating mud.

Taiwan would come soon enough.

God, she hoped it would stop raining.

The sun was shining brightly and there was not a cloud in the sky. All was right in Dodsworth, Rudzak thought with amusement.

"Why did you want to come here?" Duggan asked. "I told you it was too well protected to hit right now."

"I just wanted to see it." He gazed at the small brick building surrounded by ivy-covered stone walls. "What do the townspeople think is going on here?"

"Agricultural research."

Rudzak chuckled. "Trust Logan to pick a lie that would appeal to America's heartland." He turned away. "I suppose he's reinforced security?"

"Inside. Outside. Patrols, surveillance cameras, sensors, and personnel checks."

"Have you been able to get a blueprint of the building?"

"Not yet. But I won't need it."

138

"*I* need it. I want to know every structural strength and weakness in that building. Make it a priority."

"The security is too tight. You'd do better to hit one of Logan's other facilities."

"I'll consider it. But Dodsworth is such an interesting challenge, and it's clearly Logan's crown jewel. There's usually a way around security if you study the situation enough." He paused. "And that's what we're going to do. Study the situation and see what we come up with." A new element had appeared on the horizon. Sarah Patrick. He had learned quite a lot about her in the last couple of days, including the fact that Logan had extended his protection to her cabin outside Phoenix. What place did she occupy in his life? Was it worthwhile to remove her now? What about Eve Duncan, who had occupied a central place in Logan's recent past?

So many choices. So many paths to explore. But he had time and leisure to find the answers. He was the one setting the pace. Logan could only counter. He could hardly wait to get going again, but it took time to set up interesting scenarios. *It's coming closer, Chen Li. Just be patient.*

"I've seen what I need to see." He strode toward the car. "Let's go. I want to be in Phoenix tonight."

"Hurry. Into the bus." Logan stood in the road, the rain hammering his face, his local contact, Sun Chang, beside him. "The village is only a short distance from here, but Chang says the road there is going to be washed out any minute. If it's not gone already. The soldiers won't let anyone in or out of the area after the road goes."

"Great." Sarah scrambled onto the bus. "That's all we need. What about air support?"

"No place to land. The terrain is too rough. The best they can do will be supply drops. The village was terraced on the side of a mountain."

"Have they been able to get medical equipment into the village?"

"Yes. And they've set up tents."

"Any other search and rescue teams arrived?" Boyd asked.

"One from Tokyo. They've been here since last night."

"Survivors?"

Logan's lips tightened. "They've dug out six...so far."

Sarah leaned her head against the window, staring blindly out at the driving rain. Six out of five hundred. Dear God.

Logan dropped down in the seat beside her. "I don't suppose there's any chance of you staying here instead of going to the village?"

"No, but you could do it. You won't be any help after we start work. You can barely walk."

"You'd be surprised how helpful a man like me can be. I haven't failed you yet, have I?"

"No." From the moment he had gotten off the plane, Logan had been a dynamo of energy, checking with the handlers to make sure they had everything they needed, talking to Chang, who had met the plane and arranged for the bus. "But there's not much you'll be able to do from now on unless you're a doctor or trained in rescue. It will be—" The bus bounced and skidded across the road, throwing mud on the windows. "And you won't be able to get out if that leg needs more medical attention than the doctors here can supply."

"It's amazing what I can accomplish with a cell phone."

"Don't be flippant. It's not funny."

"Funny is the last thing I'm trying to be." He straightened his bad leg. "I'm trying to reassure you that I'll not be a—Shit."

They had rounded a curve of road and a mountain of mud spread out before them. The village was gone. No sign of houses or streets...or life. Through the driving rain Sarah could see a few search and rescue handlers and their dogs plodding through the mud on the lower slope and a bevy of men digging furiously while balanced on boards placed across the mud to the safe stone banks on either side. Tents ringed the area, and she located the hospital tent with a large red cross.

"Christ," Logan murmured. "Where the hell can we start?"

"Where we always start." She reached down, checked Monty's bandage, then fastened his orange halter with the red cross on both sides. "With the dogs."

Logan's face had turned pale. "My God."

"I told you mudslides were the worst."

"Yes, you did." He took a deep breath and dragged his gaze from the mountain to Monty. "He didn't wear that halter when we were in Santo Camaro."

"It wouldn't have done any good there. On disaster sites it identifies him as a lifesaver, not one of the wild dogs that often scavenge among the ruins. I've seen starving families kill those dogs for their next meal." She put up the hood on her poncho and tied it under her chin as the bus slithered to a stop in front of the hospital tent. "That's not going to happen to Monty."

Logan watched Sarah and the rest of the team disappear into the tent to be briefed by the military. It was getting dark, and the slide looked like a monstrous obscene mass in the half-light.

No screams...

No sobbing...

No children singing...

Silence.

Silent as a tomb.

"You're getting wet, Mr. Logan." Chang was

standing beside him. "There's hot food in the mess tent."

"Not now." He gazed up at the mountain. "Where did the slide start?"

"They're not sure. It happened in the middle of the night." He pointed to a spot near the top of the mountain. "Close to that area."

"I want to go there."

"The military isn't letting anyone up there. The mud is still shifting and the rain—"

"Then take me around it." He jerkily moved toward the mountain. "I want to go there."

The rocks were slippery underfoot as they neared the top of the mountain.

Death.

A monument to death.

No coincidence. It couldn't be a coincidence.

"What are you looking for?" Chang asked.

"I don't know."

It would be protected. He would want Logan to find it.

The beam of his flashlight flared on the rocks around him.

Nothing.

"We should go down," Chang said. "The military wouldn't like it if they knew—"

"You go down." Logan scrambled over the rocks, the light from his flashlight weaving back and forth. The scarab had been small....

So was the blue and white box shining in the beam of the light.

Chen Li's box. He had seen her handle it a hundred times, her fingers tracing the lapis lazuli flowers on the lid.

He sank to his knees beside it.

He wanted to shout. He wanted to pound his fists on the stone.

All he could do was stare at the exquisite jeweled box glittering in the beam of his flashlight.

Five hundred people.

Buried alive.

Rudzak called him six hours later. "Is it still raining in Kai Chi?"

"Yes."

"I saw the news bulletin that you were on a mercy mission. The rain didn't stop you from finding Chen Li's box, did it?"

"No."

"Because you knew it would be there. You're a smart man, Logan. You finally realized what I was doing with Chen Li's treasures, didn't you?"

"Funeral gifts."

"You sound a little numb. Did I wake you?"

"No."

"I didn't think so. You were probably lying awake, staring into the darkness. Isn't that what guilty men do?"

"You should know. You were the one who did this."

"I feel no blame. It's not in my makeup. But now you've been thinking and I'll wager you've figured out why I hit Santo Camaro and Kai Chi."

"Her grave."

"I was very angry when I saw her grave. Chen Li was a queen and you buried her like a pauper. The passing of a queen should be marked by the blare of trumpets and the clash of cymbals."

"So you gave her Santo Camaro and Kai Chi."

"I would have gone after you anyway, but as I stood by her grave, it came to me how it must be done. It was so beautifully clear to me. Santo Camaro was fine for a beginning, but Kai Chi is special. Chen Li was born there, and we spent every summer playing on those slopes."

"After she died and I'd earned a little money, I endowed an orphanage here in her name. Did you know about the orphanage?"

"Of course. Did you think it would make a difference?"

"I suppose not."

"And I remembered that you and Chen Li spent your honeymoon there," Rudzak said. "All the more reason for it to die with Chen Li."

"Is it over? I'd think five hundred people would be enough even for you."

"Of course it's not over. She was a queen and a queen must have her due."

"She would hate you for this."

"She could never hate me. You tried to make her hate me, but even when you met her, she was already mine."

"I never tried to make her hate you. I actually liked you until I found out what a son of a bitch you were."

"You kept her away from me."

"She was dying. I didn't want her hurt. And she didn't argue. By that time she knew what you wanted from her. She didn't want to see you."

"You're lying. It was you who—" He drew a deep breath, and when he spoke, the anger was gone. "I won't let you upset me. I'm winning, Logan. I fooled you, didn't I? You never expected Kai Chi. You thought I was in Colombia when I called you. I set the timer right after I talked to you on the phone."

"You're right, I never expected even you would be this sick. You won't fool me again."

"Don't be so certain. I found it interesting that you brought Sarah Patrick with you to Kai Chi."

"*She* brought *me*. This is her job."

"Then it's doubly interesting. You two seem to be walking the same path, don't you? By the way, do you know that I still have eight more of Chen Li's artifacts?" He hung up.

Logan wanted to lie down again and shut the world out, but he had to call Galen. Galen had to know so he could try to protect—

Protect what? Who? Where was Rudzak going to strike next?

"I've been wondering when you were going to call me." Galen's voice was uncharacteristically sober when he answered the phone.

146

"You didn't tell me you were going to Kai Chi."

"I didn't want it to be true. I wanted it to be an act of God, not Rudzak. But I knew that wasn't likely."

"It was Rudzak?"

"Yes, I went looking and found another of Chen Li's artifacts and some blasting caps on the mountain where the slide started. Christ, I was hoping I wouldn't find it. But when I saw that mountain of mud, I knew. It couldn't be a coincidence. Everything came together. Funeral gifts."

"Funeral gifts?"

"Pharaohs were entombed with the treasures they held precious in life. Chen Li loved her collection. If it couldn't be buried with her, why not use it to honor her passing?"

"Are you guessing?"

"I was until Rudzak just called me and confirmed it. He's got some twisted idea that all these deaths are a tribute to Chen Li."

"So he killed four at Santo Camaro and over five hundred there?"

"In several ancient civilizations it wasn't uncommon for the servants and wives to die with the ruler. Rudzak wouldn't see the difference. Even if he did, it wouldn't matter to him."

"Shit."

"I didn't expect Kai Chi. I never thought about it happening here. I don't want to make another mistake like that."

"Don't be an ass. How could you know?"

"From now on I have to know. He reminded

me that he still has eight more artifacts to spread around."

"Your plants?"

"Maybe." He paused. "And he mentioned Sarah."

"Are you going to tell her about the mudslide?"

"And have her hate me more than she does right now?"

"You didn't cause that slide."

"Keep telling me that. I need to hear it. Get back to me if you spot anything that's even a little suspicious." He hung up.

He lay back down on the cot. He should try to rest though he knew he wouldn't be able to.

You were probably lying awake, staring into the darkness. Isn't that what guilty men do?

It's what he had been doing. Lying there and thinking about that sarcophagus of mud only yards away. Was he feeling guilt? Hell, yes. If he'd had Rudzak killed in that prison, he'd never have been free to cause this carnage. So, yes, the blame was partly his own, and he felt as if that entire mountain were lying on top of him.

As it was lying on top of that orphanage.

He had visited the orphanage many times over the years, and the nuns always had the children sing for him.

He closed his eyes.

He could almost hear them singing....

• • •

Mud.

Sheets of rain.

Death.

How long had it been?

Two days? Three?

It didn't matter.

She had to go on.

Monty had caught the cone. Maybe this one would be alive.

Not likely. She and Monty had found only five survivors. The rest had been dead.

That didn't mean this one wouldn't be alive. You had to keep hope alive. Otherwise the ones who waited might never be found.

She staggered on the makeshift bridge across the mud after the dog.

The man wasn't alive. The pouring rain had freed him from the coffin of mud but not in time. His mouth was wide open in a silent scream.

Monty was whimpering. Too much. Take him down. Get him away from the death.

"Come, boy." She put a stake in the mud beside the body and marked it with orange flagging tape, then started down. She could see Logan below, looking up at her, a shovel in his hands. He was covered in mud like all the rest of the rescue workers trying to dig out the ruins of the village. He shouldn't be there. She had caught only brief glimpses of him in the past few days as he moved around the camp, helping in the medical tent, assisting the handlers, besides spending hours digging. He seemed driven. But she had been vaguely aware of his growing exhaustion, the gauntness of his face, and his worsening limp.

He wasn't looking at her anymore. He was bent over, digging at the mud. But he glanced up as she and Monty passed by him. "Boyd says we're pulling out tonight," he told her. "The team hasn't found a survivor in twelve hours."

"Is the road open?"

"The army's built a bridge over the washout. We got a shipment of food and blankets while you were up there on the search. There will be a truckload of volunteers here within a few hours. Not that it will do any good." His shovel dug viciously into the mud. "None of it is any good. No matter how hard I try, it's useless. I hate it that it's so goddamn hopeless. Why can't we find anyone? Christ, I'll be glad to get out of here."

So would she. It had been an even more heartbreaking search than usual. The rain stopped and started in a seemingly neverending cycle, keeping them from taking the dogs out, and there had been two other slides since they arrived. "I have to go up and try one more time. There might be someone alive out there."

"I'm not arguing." He didn't look at her. "At least get some rest first. I know I can't convince you to be easy on yourself, but Monty looks like he could use it. How's his wound?"

"Almost entirely healed. Do you think I'd let him work if he wasn't okay?" Not waiting for an answer, she walked away from him toward the tent the rescue team shared. Logan had no room to talk about being easy on herself when he was staggering around with that bad leg.

Only Hans Kniper was asleep on his cot with his Lab beside him when she went into the tent. She didn't bother being quiet as she watered and fed Monty. No danger of waking Hans. They were all operating on practically no sleep and fell unconscious when they got the chance to rest.

She washed enough mud off Monty to make him a little more comfortable and then scrubbed her own face. No use doing anything else when they'd be back in the mud within a few hours. She lay down and cuddled next to Monty. It was raining again. She could hear it pounding on the canvas of the tent. God, she wished it would stop.

"Sarah."

Logan. She came instantly awake.

Logan was kneeling beside her. He nodded at the Asian woman standing in the entrance of the tent. "This is Ming Na. She wanted me to ask one of you to find her baby."

Sarah felt sick as she looked at the young woman's desperate expression. "Did you tell her how hard we've been trying?"

"She says we've been looking in the wrong place for her child. He wasn't in the village. They were walking down the mountain after

151

visiting Ming Na's grandparents. A flash flood took him away from her and swept him down the mountain to the creek that runs beside the village."

"How old is her baby?"

"Two."

"The chances of his surviving a flash flood are practically nil."

"She said he did survive. She saw him thrown up on the bank and crawling away. She tried to run after him, but the mudslide came and she couldn't get over to get him. She heard him crying."

"It's been four days," Sarah whispered. "If he survived the flood, who's to say he would survive the exposure? You're grabbing at straws."

"Hell, yes, I want that baby to be alive." His lips twisted. "I want a miracle. After these last few days I need a miracle."

She could see that in his face. She needed a miracle too. You never knew when you'd find one, so you kept trying. "I'll go take a look." She got to her knees and put Monty's halter on. "Ask her if she'll take me to the place where she heard the baby crying."

Logan turned to the woman and spoke to her in rapid Taiwanese. She nodded and answered. He turned back to Sarah. "She'll take us."

"Us?"

"I'm going," he said firmly. "I promised her I'd bring back her baby."

She shook her head.

"I want to do something besides pull corpses

from beneath that goddamn mud. I want to find that baby...alive."

She opened her mouth to protest and then closed it. She understood his desperation and weariness; how many times had she felt the same way? How many times had she tried to fool Monty into thinking there was life in a sea of death? "Come if you like. But if you can't keep up, I'm not going to wait for you."

"I'll keep up."

"Over there." Logan pointed over the lake of mud to the rocks on the other side.

"The child was thrown on the bank there?" Sarah asked.

Logan nodded, then moved toward the boards that bridged the mud. "Let's get the kid."

"Let Monty and me go first, give him a head start." She and Monty carefully picked their way across the narrow bridge to the safety of the rocky ground on the other side. She took off the leash and let Monty run down the mountain.

She tried not to look over her shoulder at Logan but couldn't resist a glance before she started after Monty. He was okay, she saw with relief. Though God knows how he was keeping his balance on the wet boards with that bum leg. "Don't try to hurry. Monty may come back to me a dozen times before he gets the scent." She set off after the dog. "If he gets the scent."

Monty was running around in circles as he tried to pick up the cone. The rain had increased in the last few minutes and she could barely see him.

"Monty's not picking up anything," she told Logan when he was beside her. She watched the retriever barrel down the bank.

Logan limped ahead of her to follow Monty. "Let's go."

She saw his expression and felt a ripple of shock. He was tense, totally absorbed, completely driven, and desperate.

I want to find this baby alive.

Oh, God, I hope you do, Logan.

Monty wasn't picking up the scent. He was running around in circles.

"What the hell is wrong with him?" Logan's tone was harsh. "Can't you do something?"

"He's doing the best he can."

Logan drew a deep breath. "Sorry. I know he is."

Fifteen minutes later Monty barked. He came running back in a delirium of joy and then took off running down the mountain.

"He's found him." Quickly following, Logan slid and slipped down the bank. "He's found him!"

Sarah muttered a prayer as she stumbled after Logan.

The rain was so heavy, she could no longer see him or Monty, but they had to be straight ahead. "Logan!"

No answer.

"Logan, where—" Then she saw him.

And she saw Monty standing over a mound of mud beside the creek, whimpering.

"Sweet Jesus, no," she whispered.

"It may not be the kid." Logan fell to his knees and clawed desperately at the mud. "It may not be—" He stopped, staring down at the delicate arm of a child he had uncovered. "Shit." He dug frantically until he'd uncovered the still, small body. "Shit. Shit. Shit." He sat there, his shoulders slumped as he gazed down at the baby. "It's not fair. He's only a little kid."

"One of the later mudslides must have gotten him." Sarah knelt beside Logan. Poor baby. Poor Ming Na.

She couldn't move for a few minutes and then she slowly struggled to her feet and got out her flagging tape. "Come on, Logan. We've got to get back to Ming Na."

"What are you doing with that tape?"

"You know what I'm doing. You've seen it before. Marking the spot."

"Not him." Logan reached out, picked up the little boy, and rose to his feet. "I promised Ming Na I'd bring back her baby. I'm not going to leave him here in the mud."

"You can't carry him up that mountain. You barely made—" She stopped as she saw his face. The cords were standing out in his neck, and tears were running down his cheeks. "Can I help?"

"No. I'll make it." He started up the mountain. "I promised her."

She stood there with Monty, watching him struggle up the slippery slope. Why was it so heartbreaking to see a strong man like Logan

155

with that baby in his arms? She wanted to rush forward and help him, comfort him. She knew what agony he would face when he handed the baby to Ming Na. She had faced that agony any number of times in a hundred different places over the years.

But he wouldn't let her help.

"Come on, Monty." She slowly started up the mountain after Logan.

The team washed their dogs, showered, and changed at the airport before they boarded Logan's plane. They took off at a little after eight that evening.

Logan was quiet. Too quiet. He'd spoken only a few words since he'd placed the baby in Ming Na's arms and walked away. Well, she hadn't been very talkative herself. There was a pall over the entire team. It had been a nightmare of a search operation. She started to settle down for the night.

Oh, what the devil. She strode over to the chair where he was sitting. "Are you okay?"

He smiled faintly. "You held out longer than I thought you would."

"You shouldn't have come. I warned you that you didn't belong on the search."

"I had to come."

"Just as you had to go after that baby."

He nodded.

"It happens. Searches don't always turn out as they should. You have to think about the good ones."

"Since this is my first, I don't have a happy experience for comparison. And I don't think I want to try another one." He looked out the window. "How the hell do you take it?"

"Hope. And the knowledge that almost always there's someone waiting for us to come. Maybe it's only one or two, but those lives are precious." She rubbed the back of her neck. "But this was a rough one."

"Yes, it was." He looked back at her. "So stop trying to make me feel better and go lie down and sleep. I'm okay. It's not as if I haven't dealt with death before. It's just that babies are...different."

"Yes, they are."

"I wanted that kid to live."

"I know."

"But he didn't and I have to put it aside. I'll bounce back. I always do." He closed his eyes. "So go take care of your dog and let me sleep."

She stood looking at him uncertainly.

"Sarah." He didn't open his eyes. "Scat."

They heard the wolf howl as they were driving to the ranch. Monty sat upright in the backseat, looking eagerly at the mountains.

"I'd forgotten about the wolf." Sarah's gaze followed Monty's. "At least he's still alive."

Beautiful...

"But dangerous, Monty. And you don't need a challenge after what you've gone through lately."

The wolf howled again.

"Call of the wild," Logan murmured. "Incredible."

"And the National Wildlife Federation wants him to stay wild. So do I. I wish the damn wolf would quit coming down and raiding the ranches." She parked in front of the cabin and jumped out of the jeep. "Come on. I'll give you a cup of coffee and then you can call Margaret or whoever is available to come get you. I don't know why you didn't let me drop you off at your Phoenix house."

"I had to deliver you to your door. Galen would have said it was the polite thing to do. I'll take that cup of coffee." He got out and limped into the house. "I can use it."

She flicked on the lights and went to the cabinet. "You don't look so good. You need more than a cup of coffee. I didn't see you taking any of your painkillers on the plane."

"I ran out yesterday. I guess the doctor thought I wouldn't need any more."

"He didn't know you were going to abuse yourself like you did these past five days." She started the coffee. "I don't think he would have recommended all that digging, much less sliding down that mountain."

"It had to be done." He settled himself in the easy chair and propped up his leg on the hassock. "You should understand. I've never known a more passionate advocate of that philosophy."

The wolf howled again.

She stared out the window into the darkness. "I wish he'd stop. He's unsettling Monty."

"We wouldn't want that to happen. I seem to have a calming effect on him. Why don't I stick around for a while?"

She had been half expecting that suggestion from him. She should have followed her instincts and dropped him off in Phoenix. If she hadn't been so tired, she would never have let him get his foot in the door. "Nothing's changed since the night you first came." She brought him his coffee. "I don't want anyone staying here."

"Things have changed. We've gone through a lot together. I don't think you regard me as the enemy any longer."

"That doesn't mean I want you in my house. Why the hell did you come anyway? When you first showed up I thought you were just out of your head. We both know any action you take against Madden doesn't have to be done from here. Something's weird."

"Can't we argue about this in the morning? I'm pretty tired."

"Then finish your coffee and call Margaret."

"I'm too tired." He set his cup on the table beside him and smiled faintly. "You wouldn't kick a wounded man out of your house."

"Maybe I would." She let her breath out in a resigned sigh. He was playing on her feelings, but he did look terribly pale, and she knew what he had gone through in Taiwan. "Okay. Tomorrow. But that chair isn't as comfortable as those cushy recliners on your plane. By morning you may be ready to leave."

He closed his eyes. "You can never tell...."
He was asleep.

She sank down on the couch and gazed at him in frustration. Déjà vu. Why couldn't she get rid of him? She didn't want him there. That he had become too much a part of her life in these last days made her uneasy. She had seen him tired and discouraged and hurting. She had seen his tears. He disturbed her, and she had enough disturbance in her life. This was her home, her haven, and she wanted no strangers—

But that was the crux of the problem. He was no longer a stranger. She didn't know exactly what Logan's place was in her life now, but he could never be a stranger again.

The wolf howled.

Monty lifted his head and whimpered deep in his throat.

She couldn't blame him. The wolf's cry was terribly melancholy and heartbreakingly wistful.

And closer.

Stay in the mountains, she prayed. Those ranchers will shoot you. There's danger here. They think you're a threat and don't care if you're wild and free and beautiful.

Monty put his head on his paws. *Beautiful...*

8

"Get up, Sarah."

She opened her eyes to see Logan standing over her. She had been sleeping hard and for a moment she thought she was back in Taiwan.

"Come on. He's gone. I can't go after him by myself." He half walked, half hopped toward the door. "Hell, I couldn't catch up with a turtle."

She sat up and rubbed her eyes. "What is it?"

"Monty. He took off out that dog door like a bat out of hell. He heard something."

She swung her feet to the floor. "What?"

"I don't know. I didn't hear anything. I'd just opened my eyes and saw Monty get up. He listened for a minute and then took off." He opened the door. "Does he go out much at night?"

"No, but it's not completely unusual."

"I tell you he heard something. We'd better go after him."

Logan was clearly worried, and his concern was infectious. Monty had probably just gone outside to relieve himself, but she had to check. She grabbed a flashlight and followed Logan. "Monty!"

She waited.

"Monty!"

For the first time, fear iced through her. Monty always answered her.

Unless he couldn't.

She heard something in the distance. Not a bark. A moan?

"I hear something." She set out at a run. "Go back to the house."

"The hell I will. Where are the keys to your jeep?"

"I always leave them in the ignition."

"Well, that's safe."

She paid no attention as she ran west, where the sound had come from.

Darkness.

Silence.

"Monty!"

No sound.

"Answer me!"

A low moan in the distance.

Monty. She knew it was Monty. She flew over the hard-baked sand, the beam of her flashlight spearing a wide circle from side to side in front of her.

Then she saw him.

Blood.

Monty was lying in a pool of blood.

"Oh, God." She flew toward him, tears running down her face. "Monty."

He looked up at her, his eyes full of pain.

She was almost to him when she saw what his big body had blocked from view.

Gray fur, silver eyes staring fiercely in the light, and lips drawn back from gleaming white teeth.

And a front paw caught in an iron-jawed trap. The blood was trickling from the wolf, not from Monty.

162

Monty nestled closer to the wolf. *Pain.*

"Get away from him, Monty. He'll hurt you."

Monty didn't move.

She knelt down beside them. "I'm going to release the trap. Just get out of the way."

He didn't move.

"Okay, be stupid." He wasn't the only one who was stupid. Trying to free the wolf from this trap without putting him to sleep first was asking for trouble. She took off her shirt and wrapped it around the arm nearest the wolf. "I'm going to get you out of this," she said softly. "Give me a break, will you?"

The wolf snapped. Sarah snatched her arm out of harm's way just in time.

"Okay, no break." She reached for the iron teeth of the trap. Quick. She had to be quick.

The wolf snapped again. This time he drew blood.

She sat back on her heels. "Look, do you want to bleed to death? Let me help."

The wolf lunged toward her and then collapsed with a cry of pain.

Monty crawled closer to the wolf.

"No!"

Monty ignored her and laid his head across the wolf's throat.

She held her breath. "What are you doing, boy?" Any minute she expected the wolf to rise up and slash at Monty.

But the wolf lay still.

Unconscious?

No, she could see the gleam of his slitted eyes.

What was she doing, sitting there? It didn't matter what weird thing was happening between Monty and the wolf. Seize the moment. She started working at the trap, every moment expecting the wolf to make a move.

Lights suddenly speared the area.

The jeep.

"Stop, Logan." She froze, her gaze on the wolf.

No motion. As if Monty's touch on his throat were paralyzing him.

"Can I help?" Logan called from the jeep.

"Get the first aid kit under the front seat and then come and help me with this trap. I'm not strong enough to do it alone."

A moment later Logan was kneeling beside her, his gaze on Monty and the wolf. "What's happening here?"

"I've no idea. I think Monty's hypnotized him or something." She opened the medical kit and withdrew a hypodermic and sedative. "Get ready to spring the trap after I give him this shot."

"Why not afterward?"

"He'll run away. I have to take care of that leg before he bolts." She kept her eyes fixed warily on the wolf as she gave him the injection. No movement. Maybe the pain of his leg dwarfed the little pinprick.

Monty was the one who gave a low moan as if in sympathy with the wolf's agony.

"Just keep him quiet a minute more and we'll have him out, Monty," she murmured. "I

164

don't know what you're doing, but keep doing it." She said to Logan, "Be ready to jerk open that trap when I tell you." She put her hands beside Logan's on the iron. "On the count of three. One, two..." She glanced at the wolf. He had gone limp. "Three."

She and Logan pulled with all their strength. The iron jaws slowly parted. "Can you hold it open while I get his foot out?"

"Do it," he grunted.

Carefully she freed the wolf's leg. "Let it go."

The trap snapped shut with a lethal click. How she hated those traps. She unwound the shirt from around her arm, formed a pressure bandage, and bound the wolf's leg. "Get in the jeep, Monty."

Monty hesitated, then got to his feet and ran toward the jeep.

"What now?" Logan asked.

"We get the wolf back to the cabin, where I can tend him."

"A wild animal?"

"A wounded animal." She picked up the wolf and carried him toward the jeep. "Come on. I need your help. You'll have to drive while I keep an eye on him."

"Okay." He struggled slowly to his feet as she settled the wolf in the backseat. "There's blood on your arm."

"He barely broke the skin." She jumped in the passenger seat. "Hurry. I'm not sure how long he'll be under, and I want to work on him without giving him another shot."

"Right."

Logan pulled the jeep in front of the cabin in less than five minutes and Sarah jumped out. "Go on ahead and open the door beside the fireplace. It leads to a small screened-in back porch."

He limped into the cabin. "Anything else?"

She followed him. "Grab that throw on the back of the couch and put it on the floor of the porch."

He did, then asked, "Next?"

She set the wolf carefully on the throw. "Bring me the bag with the medical supplies in that first kitchen cabinet."

She knelt down and gently stroked the wolf's muzzle. "What a beautiful boy you are. Don't worry, we're going to take good care of you."

Monty settled himself beside the wolf.

"You'll have to get out of the way," Sarah told him. "I'm going to stitch up that cut and set the leg. It's fractured."

Monty laid his head on his paws, his gaze on the wolf.

"Here's the bag." Logan fell to his knees beside the wolf. "Tell me what to do to help."

She looked across the wolf's body at him. So far he had taken orders without question, and heaven knows she needed help. "First we have to clean the wound."

"Are you going to leave Monty in there with the wolf?" Logan asked as he followed Sarah from the porch an hour later.

"I don't think I could budge him." Sarah set the medical bag on the counter and washed the blood from her hands at the sink. "Not until he's sure the wolf's okay. Coffee?"

"Yes." He carefully lowered himself into the easy chair and raised his leg onto the hassock. "I could use it. How long will he sleep?"

"I hope another hour or so. And it's she, not he. I assumed it was a male too, until I started working on her. I'm surprised you didn't notice."

"I was preoccupied." His gaze shifted to the fire. "Aren't you a little cold?"

"No."

"Well, neither am I. Will you go put on a shirt?"

She glanced at him in surprise. "I'm wearing a bra. That's no different from wearing a bikini top."

"Trust me, there's a difference."

She inhaled sharply as she met his gaze. She quickly averted her eyes. "Oh, for God's sake. I suppose I should have expected it even in a situation like this. It's a guy thing. I read an article once that said men think of sex once every eight minutes."

"Then I must be a cold fish. I'm sure it doesn't pop into my head more than every ten minutes."

His tone was flippant, and the disturbing moment was gone, she realized with relief.

She went into the bedroom and came back pulling a white T-shirt over her head. "Satisfied?"

"No." He changed the subject. "What are you going to do with the wolf?"

"Get her well and then turn her back over to the Wildlife Federation to relocate." She made a face. "If I can keep my rancher neighbors from busting in here and trying to kill her again."

"Maybe I can help there."

"What are you going to do? Pay them off?" She shook her head. "These ranchers are independent as the devil and they're not about to be bought. They've lost livestock and they're mad as hell."

"I'll think of something." He drew a quick breath. "I wonder—if I could—trouble you to get out your medical bag again. I may need a little first aid myself. I believe kneeling beside that wolf may have been the last straw."

Her gaze flew to the leg propped on the hassock. A wide dark stain was spreading on the inner side of his thigh. "Dammit, you tore open the stitches." She grabbed the bag off the counter and moved over to the chair. "Why didn't you tell me?"

"You were busy. We were both busy. You seem to live in a constant state of emergency. I'm almost afraid to close my eyes around— What are you doing?"

"Taking off your jeans."

"You seem to have no compunction about nudity in yourself or others."

"There's nothing shameful about nudity." She wriggled the trousers off his hips and down his legs. "I can repair those stitches— unless you want me to call an ambulance."

"No, you do it." He closed his eyes and smiled faintly. "Just please don't enjoy sticking that needle in me too much."

"I never enjoy inflicting pain." She bent over his thigh. "You didn't break all the stitches. This shouldn't take long."

"That's good. I've never been good at—" He inhaled sharply as the needle went into his flesh. "I should have asked for a shot like our wolf friend."

"I would have given you one, but I have only morphine, and you're allergic to it."

"Oh, shit. I knew that would come back to haunt me."

"Just a couple more."

Actually, it was three more before she was able to rebandage the wound. "That wasn't so bad, was it?" she asked as she pulled up his jeans and fastened them.

"It wasn't good." He opened his eyes. "But since most of it was my fault, I guess I can't complain. Could I have that coffee now? I need it."

"Sure." She moved toward the counter. "I could use a cup myself."

"I can see how you would. It's been a difficult night for you."

She poured the coffee, gave him a cup, and then sat down on the hassock with her own. "And for you. And it wasn't your fault that you broke open those stitches. You were trying to help Monty and then the wolf. If anyone's at fault, it's me."

He shook his head. "No, my responsibility."

169

"You said that before. You're big on responsibility."

"It's one of the few codes I never break. Whatever I do, I shoulder the responsibility for my actions."

She took a sip of coffee and was silent a moment. "Why did you come here, Logan?"

"Why do you think I came?"

"I don't know. I thought it might be the medication that caused you to stumble here from a sickbed. But I can't see you being that woozy even under drugs. So it was something else."

"Go on."

"Tell me."

"I'm enjoying watching you work it out. Did I ever tell you how much I admire that fine brain of yours?"

"Don't flatter me, Logan."

"I wouldn't presume. We may have had our differences, but I've never underestimated you."

"Just used me."

"That's done. I'll never use you again, Sarah."

She studied his expression.

"Believe me."

She did believe him. "If that's true, then it narrows down the reasons you'd show up here. You made me a promise about Madden, but you wouldn't have thought it necessary to drag yourself here to keep it."

"I would if you'd told me you wanted it done immediately."

"But I didn't tell you that." She tilted her head, thinking. "And you were more scared than I was when Monty ran out of here tonight. You were afraid something would happen to him."

He was silent, waiting.

"Responsibility." She met his gaze. "You were afraid someone would hurt Monty."

"Or you. You nearly gave me a heart attack when you took off running. I knew I'd never catch you with this bum leg."

Her eyes widened. "Rudzak? Why?"

"He had to have seen you when you jumped out of the helicopter after Monty."

"And that's enough to target me?"

"More than enough. You helped me, and no one believes more in revenge than Rudzak. He'll regard his defeat as a humiliation, and you both participated in and witnessed that humiliation."

Her hands clenched into fists. "I thought I was out of it."

"Will you come back to Phoenix with me?"

"No, I think you're off base about any threat to me, but if there is, I'll take care of myself."

"I thought that would be your response. I told Galen to get some security out here, but it would be much easier if you go back to Phoenix."

"I want my life back. I don't want to make it easy for you."

"Then if you're going to stay here, let me stay too. I'll be chief cook and bottle washer. You have your hands full with the wolf and Monty."

"I told you I don't want you here."

"Just imagine me humble and at your beck and call. Doesn't the picture appeal to you?"

"Like a dream come true. But you'd probably break open the stitches again and I'd be waiting on you too."

"I trust your stitches." He grimaced. "They hurt too much not to be tight as a drum."

"And you'd be more danger to me here than behind those gates in Phoenix. Rudzak would probably crawl up to my cabin and blow it up just to get you."

"No, my presence will actually make you safer. Rudzak doesn't want me dead yet. He wants me to suffer first."

"What the hell did you do to him?"

"I took away fifteen years of his life. I should have killed him, but things didn't work out." The words were cold and the tone without feeling. Then he smiled. "But that's the past. We have to worry about the future. Just let me stay until you get the wolf in shape. Maybe by that time we'll have located Rudzak. And I have some strings I can pull to get the IRS to persuade the ranchers not to go after the wolf again."

"I wouldn't sic the IRS on my worst enemy."

"Just a mild attack? To save the wolf?"

"Maybe." She stood up. "I've got to check on her."

"Don't you think we should give her a name? Something exotic, perhaps. Ivana or Dest—"

"I hate cutesy names." She headed for the porch door. "Her name is Maggie."

172

"Margaret will be flattered...I think."

"It's not about her. I just like the name."

"Sarah."

She glanced over her shoulder.

"I'm making sense," he said soberly. "I know Santo Camaro seems far away and unreal. But it's not. Believe me, Sarah."

He was right. The threat from Rudzak did seem completely unreal to her. "You could be wrong."

"I'm not wrong. Let me stay. Let me help you. I promise I won't be a disturbance." He made a face. "And just think how you'll love ordering me around."

"It might almost be worth it."

"Then think about it."

She was silent a moment. "I will."

He watched her disappear to the porch. Had he been persuasive enough? He had laid the facts out before her with complete honesty; anything else would have been the height of idiocy. She would never accept deception in herself or anyone else. She had a directness he had seen in very few women and a passionate caring for the helpless he had never experienced. She had worked over that wolf as if it were her child, stroking it, talking to it, soothing even though the animal couldn't hear her. There had been something beautiful about Sarah Patrick in those moments. Fine-boned hands that were gentle as well as deft, tousled hair that she'd had him push back once so she could better see what she was doing. Strong shoulders, breasts lifting and falling with the intensity of her emotion...

Oh, shit. He didn't need this physical response right now. He certainly didn't need it in connection with Sarah Patrick.

Then forget it, block it out.

Easier said than done. Every time he looked at her, he'd remember how he'd felt at that moment.

Nothing was easy. Do it. Forget how she'd looked in that simple white bra.

Remember only what he had to do to keep her alive.

Monty was stretched out next to the sleeping wolf, almost nose to nose. He didn't lift his head when Sarah walked into the room. Good. She was glad she had a moment to herself. Too much had happened that night and she was upset and off balance. Logan had thrown her another curve and now she had to deal with it.

This cabin was her haven; she didn't want anyone here. Particularly a presence as strong as Logan. He had said he wouldn't disturb her, but there was no way a personality that forceful wouldn't prove a disturbance.

Yet he hadn't exerted that strength when he helped her with the wolf. He took a backseat, ready to help but not interfere, same as in Taiwan.

But living comfortably with him wasn't the real issue. Was it safer for her and Monty to

174

have him there? Did she trust his judgment and motives? He was a complicated man, but she had grown to know something about him and she had believed him when he had said he would never use her again.

She stared across the room at Monty and the wolf. "We have a problem, boy."

Monty lifted his head and looked at her inquiringly. *Okay?*

"Me or the wolf? We're both going to be fine. You shouldn't have gone out looking for her, you know. You're not in top shape yourself, and there's no telling what could have happened. She's no gentle soul."

Monty put his head back down. *Beautiful.*

"Yes, she is, and she's clearly a maiden in distress, but she could take you apart in minutes. You don't have the killer instinct."

Hurt.

"Right now, but in a few weeks she'll be well again. And I don't want you pulling that trick of putting your head on her throat again. It's a good way to get mauled and you—"

The wolf opened her eyes and stared directly into Monty's.

Beautiful.

"Oh, shit." Sarah's heart sank as she watched them together. "No, boy. She's definitely from the wrong side of the tracks. Hell, the wrong side of the universe. Believe me, you have nothing in common."

Beautiful.

"If you had a domestic squabble, she'd take you apart."

Beautiful.

"And what kind of kids would you have?"

Beautiful.

They might be at that. Golden retriever and this gorgeous wolf... "It would definitely be a one-night stand. The Wildlife Federation has other plans for Maggie."

Monty delicately licked the fur beneath the wolf's eyes.

Maggie drew back her lips in a snarl.

Sarah tensed, ready to jump forward to protect him. "Stop."

Monty didn't stop.

And Maggie's snarl slowly disappeared. She closed her eyes, accepting.

"I'll be damned." Sarah shook her head. "Maybe it's mutual after all." She moved forward and knelt by the wolf. "I have to give her another shot, boy. Try to distract her."

Maggie opened her eyes and snarled at Sarah when the needle entered, but she didn't attack. A few moments later she was asleep again.

Once more Monty stretched out beside her.

"You're not listening," Sarah said. "It's strictly Montague and Capulet stuff. Her folks would never accept you."

Monty sighed, his gaze never leaving the wolf. *Beautiful.*

Logan was asleep in the chair when she left the porch.

She marched across the room and shook him awake. "You can stay. But you'd better get well

176

fast. I'm going to work your tail off and enjoy every minute of it."

He yawned. "I'm glad you informed me in such a gentle manner."

"I don't feel gentle. I have problems." She headed for her bedroom. "I have to get Maggie on her feet and out of here quickly and I may need your help with some repercussions."

"What repercussions?"

"Monty's ga-ga over her."

Logan chuckled. "So?"

"It's not funny. I have to get them apart before they decide to mate. Wolves mate for life, and Monty... I won't have him hurt."

"Isn't it unusual for a rescue dog not to be fixed?"

"ATF wanted to do it, and I told them to leave it to me. I meant to . . . but then I didn't." She glared at him. "Okay?"

"Maybe for Monty it will be only a fling."

"That's crazy. Monty's the most loving dog I've ever known."

"I can see the problem."

She scanned his expression. He wasn't laughing or mocking any longer. He did understand. "Most people would think I'm being weird, but it's...important to me."

"Then it's important to me. And I can understand why you wouldn't want your best friend to make a bad match." He closed his eyes. "But could I go back to sleep now? If you're going to work my tail off, I'm going to need all the rest I can get."

He waited until the bedroom door shut behind her before he reached into his pocket for his phone and called Galen. "I'm at Sarah's cabin and I'll be here for a while. Have you heard anything?"

"Not yet. I'm still tracking down Sanchez. How were those last days in Kai Chi?"

"Hell."

"Is Sarah okay?"

"As good as can be expected. She's having a few domestic problems. Monty's in love with a wolf."

Galen burst out laughing. "That ball of fluff?"

"Believe me, it's not funny to Sarah. Call Margaret and have her find out everything she can about the Mexican gray wolves that were released in this area."

"Why don't you call her yourself?"

"She was pissed at me for coming here, and Taiwan won't have made her temper any better. I've had a rough night and I don't want to deal with her right now."

"Say no more. I wouldn't want to contact her either."

"Have you secured the cabin?"

"Six of my best men."

"I haven't seen anyone."

"They can see you. They're camped up in the mountains and they can see trouble coming for miles. I'll give you Franklin's number."

"Tomorrow. I don't have a pen and I don't want to move. I'm hurting like the devil. Bye."

He had to get a few hours' sleep. It was almost dawn, and he hadn't the slightest doubt Sarah would soon be up and tending the wolf. As usual, she'd be fighting any softness toward him and would have no compunction about putting into action her threat to "work his tail off."

"Just what do you think you're doing?" Sarah stood in the bedroom doorway with her arms folded across her chest.

"Feeding Monty." Logan patted the dog on the head. "He was hungry, and I didn't want to wake you."

"No one feeds Monty but me. I've trained him not to accept food from anyone else." But Monty was eating, she realized with a mixture of amazement and annoyance. "Damn."

"He was hungry," Logan repeated as he filled up Monty's water bowl. "I thought I'd give it a try."

"I can't have you interfering with Monty's training."

"I can see why you wouldn't want to have strangers feed him, but I'm no threat."

179

"Practically no one is a stranger to Monty. He loves everyone. That's why I can't have him fed by anyone but me."

"Maybe he has better judgment than you think." He put down the water bowl. "Here you go, boy."

"I can't take the chance. So please leave my dog alone."

"Okay. Just trying to help. Anything else I can do?"

"You can go sit down and rest that leg. You haven't been off it in the last three days."

"Whatever you say." He limped back to his chair. "But it's getting better. Did you notice I was able to do a lot more yesterday?"

"Yes." Since the night they'd brought home the wolf, Logan had kept himself busy doing everything from sweeping the cabin to helping nurse Maggie. When they weren't working side by side, he was cooking or cleaning or on the phone, trying to wield influence to keep the ranchers away from the wolf. She scowled. "Too much."

"Do I perceive a softening?" He stretched his leg out on the hassock. "You're the one who wanted to work me to the bone. You asked, I obeyed."

"I know."

He grinned. "But you don't like the fact that I didn't mind it."

"Nonsense. I just didn't—" She smiled reluctantly. "You've not been any fun at all. What good is a slave if he's so obliging? It takes all the joy out of the situation."

"Sorry."

She studied him. "And you've been doing a heck of a lot more than I ask. I don't like that."

"I'm just a self-starter."

"You're also a prime manipulator. You knew it would bother me to see a wounded man overextend himself."

He gazed at her innocently. "Did I?"

"Knock it off."

"I'm surprised it took you this long to call me on it."

"I'm not that soft." She made a face. "And I thought you'd stop. I knew you were hurting."

"Just doing my job, ma'am."

"And getting a little of your own back."

"I admit I have a problem with total subjugation."

"Any subjugation."

"I do prefer partnerships. I think we've proved we work pretty well together, don't you?"

She didn't speak for a moment. "Yes."

"Then why not call a truce? You don't have to force me to do anything. I'd go nuts if I didn't have something to do. Even nursing your wolf is better than twiddling my thumbs. We're living together, let's do it as painlessly as possible."

"I'm not in any pain. I could go—" She broke off as the phone rang. "And we're not living together," she said as she crossed the room and picked up the phone. "Hello."

"You didn't call me," Todd Madden said. "How did the Logan job go?"

181

"What do you care, Madden? It's over. That's all that's important."

"Good. Then you can come up to Washington for the weekend. I've set up a press conference about the Barat earthquake, and what about this Taiwan mudslide? That will be excellent copy."

"Go to hell."

"Don't be ugly, Sarah." Madden's voice was silky smooth. "You know it doesn't do you any good to be nasty to me. Shall I make your reservations or will you?"

"I'm not coming to Washington. I'm busy."

"You know how I hate to pressure you, but I can't tolerate—"

"Screw you." She hung up the phone.

"You should have let me talk to him," Logan said.

"I got too much satisfaction out of telling him to go chase himself."

"That wasn't exactly the term you used," he said lightly.

The phone rang again.

She didn't answer it. "It's him again. He can't believe I'm not jumping through his hoop."

"Are you going to answer it?"

"No. I'm burning my bridges. If you don't keep your promise, I'm going to go down in flames."

"But you trust me to keep it. Or you wouldn't have burned that bridge."

She was silent a moment. "Yes, I trust you."

"How much time do I have?"

182

"A few days, maybe a week. Madden will have trouble believing that I won't change my mind. Then he'll get angry and want to punish me."

"And then what happens? What will he do to you?"

"He'll take Monty away from me."

"What?"

"Monty doesn't belong to me. ATF owns him. I do what Madden wants or he uses his influence to have them take Monty away and give him to someone else."

Logan swore softly. "Can't you buy him from ATF?"

"Don't you think I've tried? They won't sell him. Madden wants that hold on me."

"Are you sure he can get them to take Monty away?"

"He's done it before. Two years ago I'd had enough and told him to go jump in the lake. ATF snatched Monty out of my jeep while I was in the supermarket getting groceries. They left a very businesslike note. They were sending him to a handler in Europe and I'd be notified of the new dog I'd be assigned."

"Europe?"

"The K9 Corps trains dogs for other law enforcement bodies overseas." She continued bitterly. "Madden was very clever, wasn't he? He didn't even tell me what country. I was frantic. I begged everyone from mail clerks to senior officers in ATF to tell me where they'd shipped Monty. It took me over a month to find out they'd sent him to a police department in Milan. I thought it might be too late."

"Too late?"

"It's not only that he won't eat or drink for anyone else. Monty loves me. We're...close. He would mourn. A dog as loving as Monty can die of sadness." She blinked her stinging eyes. "He did mourn. He was sick, so sick, when I found him in Milan."

"And what did you do?"

"What do you think I did? I called Madden and told him I'd do anything he wanted if he'd give me back my dog." She looked straight into his eyes. "I won't let that happen to him again. If you can't find a way to get Madden off my back, Monty and I will just go away and disappear."

"I'll find a way." Logan's lips tightened grimly. "Count on it."

"I am. Heaven help you if you let me down."

"I won't let you down." He took out his phone. "Now go tend your wolf while I take care of Madden." He looked up after he'd dialed a number. "Since we're joined in putting Madden down, couldn't you ignore all my sins and give me my truce?"

"Maybe." She smiled. "If you promise not to feed my dog again."

"Only if he's starving." He spoke into the phone. "Margaret, what's the word on Madden?"

Sarah was still smiling as she and Monty moved toward the back porch. There was something very comforting about Logan's immediate and focused response to her problem.

Monty looked back at Logan. *Nice.*

"Cupboard love. You shouldn't have eaten until I fed you. You know better."

Trust.

"You still shouldn't have broken the rules." But she, too, was breaking the rules and trusting Logan. How had he managed to get past her defenses?

Nice.

Charisma? No, heaven knows he hadn't tried to charm her during these last days. He had just been straightforward and hardworking.

Why was she worrying anyway? All she had committed herself to was a truce for the next week or so.

Beautiful. Monty was trotting toward Maggie, who looked at him balefully. He plopped down beside her. *Love.*

She curled her lips in a snarl.

Sarah shook her head. "She's not feeling very romantic, boy. That wound's giving her a fit." She moved toward Maggie. "Come on, let's see if I can make it feel better. No snapping. Let's see if we can have a truce too."

The dog was romping and playing, his golden tail wagging happily as it ran circles around the Patrick woman.

Duggan sighted down the rifle squarely on the dog's head. His finger slowly caressed the trigger.

"What are you doing?"

185

He looked up to see Rudzak coming toward him over the ridge.

"The Patrick woman and the dog are outside the cabin. I'm going to give her a little surprise. I didn't do a good job of getting the dog at Santo Camaro. I'm going to blow his fucking head off now."

Rudzak looked down at the cabin. "That's not why we're here. We just managed to avoid Galen's men patrolling this area. They're all over the place. You'd think they were protecting Fort Knox. We may have only a short time before they come back. Have you seen Logan?"

"He's standing in the doorway."

"Ah, yes," Rudzak murmured. "His attitude is very protective, isn't it?"

"You told me we weren't going to touch him or the woman yet. But there's no reason I shouldn't kill the dog, is there?"

"Do you think you can do it? We weren't able to get very close. It's way out of range for most shooters."

"I can do it."

The golden retriever was lifting his head in the air and joyously barking.

"I've always hated barking dogs." Duggan sighted down the barrel again. "What do you bet I can put him down with one bullet?"

"No bet." Rudzak smiled. "I know you're an excellent marksman."

Yes, Rudzak always appreciated him, Duggan thought. Ever since he'd joined Rudzak a year earlier, he'd been given due respect. "Then watch me blow that pooch away."

"I'm looking forward to it." Rudzak crossed his arms across his chest. "Actually, this may be a stroke of genius on your part. I imagine Logan is feeling very safe in that little cabin with Galen's men protecting them on that far ridge. What better way to shake him up than this little statement? By all means, shoot the dog."

Duggan could almost see the after scene play out before him. The dog falling, covered with blood. Sarah Patrick staring at her dog, screaming, and then she and Logan running toward him.

"Wait a minute."

He followed Rudzak's gaze to the woman. She had whirled around and was looking up at the mountains.

"Interesting," Rudzak said. "Do you suppose she senses something? She's calling the dog."

"Goddammit." The dog and the woman were moving quickly toward the cabin, Duggan realized with frustration. He had to act fast. "Don't worry. I can still kill that dog."

"No."

He glanced up at Rudzak with a frown.

"I've found out what I wanted to know, and Galen's men aren't fools. They'd be able to locate the direction of the shot and be down on us in a heartbeat. It would be worth the risk if it was important, but it's not." He shrugged. "Besides, killing a dog would hardly be a worthy follow-up to Kai Chi."

"But it wouldn't hurt anything to—"

187

"No, Duggan," Rudzak said gently as he turned away. "Trust me. We'll just have to think of something more fitting."

"What's wrong?" Logan asked as Sarah shooed Monty in the front door. "What did you see?"

"Nothing."

His gaze narrowed on her face.

"Nothing," she repeated. "I just felt... something wasn't right. I know it sounds crazy. But I've learned to go with my instincts."

"It doesn't sound crazy at all. I imagine you've developed very good instincts over the years." He took out his phone. "I'll call security and ask Franklin to check out the area for any sign of Rudzak."

"If there's any threat, it's more likely that ranchers have found out I'm taking care of Maggie. They might have decided to teach me a lesson." She made a dismissive gesture. "As I said, it's probably nothing but maybe I'll take Monty out after dark from now on."

"Good idea." He spoke into the phone. "Franklin, what's happening up there?"

"Come on, Monty." Sarah headed for the kitchen. "I'll get you some fresh water."

Logan hung up as she finished filling Monty's dish. "No one's been sighted but they're checking."

"I told you, I didn't *see* anything." She moved toward the back porch and Maggie. "But if it was one of those ranchers, it won't hurt for them to know they're not alone out there."

•••

"Are you letting me win?" Sarah leaned back in her chair and gazed at Logan suspiciously. "I'm good, but you can't be this bad."

"Believe me, I am. Poker's not my game. I've never been into instant gratification. I'm better at chess."

She studied him and then nodded slowly. "I can see it. Strategy and war games. I've never gotten into chess. I vote for instant gratification every time."

"Who taught you to play poker? Someone on the search team?"

"No, my grandfather. When I was a kid, we'd sit here before the fire and play for hours."

"What about your mother?"

"She lived in Chicago. She didn't like it here."

"But you did."

"I loved it." She grimaced. "And I loved getting out of the city. It was dirty and crowded and—" She stood up. "I'm thirsty. Want some lemonade?"

"Please."

"It's not as cool as it usually is this evening." She went to the refrigerator. "Maybe we should put out the fire."

He crossed to the fireplace. "Your mother liked the city?"

"She liked lights and movies and bars and people. Lots of people. She got bored a lot." She gave him the frosty glass. "She was married four times."

189

"Tough for you."

"I survived." She sat down and stretched out her legs. "In fact, I was lucky. I got to go to my grandfather for a while every time she got married. I liked that. The third time she let me stay for two years."

"Why didn't she just turn over custody?"

"She'd get lonely. She had to have someone around."

"Nice."

She looked at him over the rim of the glass. "Look, I'm not complaining. That's just the way things were. I wasn't abused. Some people are just needy."

"But not you."

"Who'd take care of the needy people if we were all the same? It all balances out."

"Did your grandfather need you?"

She didn't answer right away. "I think he did. It was hard to tell. I know he loved me. He told me so at the end."

"Not before?"

"He didn't talk much. He worked his fingers to the bone to get the money to buy these few acres. When he moved into this cabin, he swore he would never leave until the day he died."

"How did he make a living?"

"Training horses and dogs. He was wonderful with animals."

He sipped his lemonade. "So are you."

"Animals are easy. They don't demand anything. All you have to do is love them."

"Some people are like that too."

190

"Are they? I haven't found that to be true."

"Why? Because you had a selfish mother who obviously didn't know how to take care of her own kid? You've been around enough to know there are plenty of great people in the world."

"I don't resent— It's none of your business, Logan."

"I know. It was just an observation."

"Screw your observations. You don't see me asking you the story of your life and then judging you."

"Go ahead. Turnabout is fair play."

"I don't want to know anything about—" She stared at him challengingly. "What were you doing with a research facility in Santo Camaro?"

"That's not the story of my life."

"So you won't tell me."

"I didn't say that." He looked down at his drink. "It's a medical research facility. We're making some interesting breakthroughs."

"Medical?"

"It's a field of research I've been funding for some time."

"Breakthroughs in what?"

"Artificial blood."

Her eyes widened. "What?"

"A substitute for blood. You haven't heard about it? There's been some news coverage about the research."

"I've heard a little." Her eyes narrowed. "It's because of Chen Li, isn't it? Because of her leukemia."

"It started off with Chen Li. It nearly killed

191

me when I couldn't help her. But I'm not so selfish that I can't see the application to other diseases."

"But why bury the facility in the jungle? What's the big secret?"

"Industrial espionage. We're so damn close. The company that gets there first will control both development and the market."

"Money?"

"Control," he repeated. "I haven't devoted all these years to finding answers to give up control now."

"And that's what Bassett's working on?"

"Yes, he's trying to reconstruct the last month of research by the Santo Camaro team. They sent reports every month, but we didn't get the last report, and a hell of a lot was done right before the attack at Santo Camaro."

"Does Rudzak have anything to do with industrial espionage?"

"Rudzak doesn't give a damn about anything but getting me where it hurts the most."

"How was he able to find out what you were doing and about the facility? Did he know about your wife and how she died?"

"Oh, yes, he knew about Chen Li." He set his glass down on the table beside him. "See how I trust you? I've told you all my secrets."

Not all his secrets. "You must have loved Chen Li very much."

"Yes, she knocked me for a loop the first time I saw her. She was half Old World and half new technology. She was a computer whiz, but there was something serene and gracious about

192

her. We were married a month after I met her." He paused. "She died three years later."

"And you're still hurting." She added brusquely, "That's why it's safer to love dogs."

"That was a long time ago and I was a different man. And I don't think you're totally devoted to the canine species or you wouldn't do the work you do."

"Think what you like. I knew from the first search I ever went on that this was what I was meant to do. A little girl got separated from her folks in the mountains near Tucson." She looked down into her glass. "She was only five and it was freezing cold. I wasn't sure we'd find her alive, but we didn't give up. Three days later Monty zeroed in on her, and she was alive. When I picked her up and wrapped her in a blanket, she whispered that she knew someone would come. She had been waiting. And I knew that she'd been waiting for *me*. I was the one who had saved her. There's nothing like that feeling on the face of the earth."

"Sometimes you can't save them."

"No, but then I can bring them home."

"You sound like Eve."

She shook her head. "I keep telling you, I'm nothing like Eve. Stop trying to dig into my psyche. Look, I'm just what's on the surface. I don't have a tragic past like Eve and I don't harbor resentments. I accept people as they are and go along with it. Understand?"

"I understand. But I don't believe you. If

193

I've learned anything about you in the past weeks, it's that you're more complicated than you'd ever admit."

She snorted with disgust. "Bull."

"You're intelligent, hardworking, and crack a mean whip. And beneath all those prickly thorns, you're probably the most loving and giving woman I've ever met."

She glanced away from him. "Don't be sappy."

"You don't like that. Why not?"

"Because I just do what needs doing. Everybody has a purpose, a job to do. This is my job."

"You don't admit that your job is more selfless than most?"

"No more than a firefighter's or a policeman's or any number of other—"

"And you're embarrassed that I'd suggest you care for people as much as you do your four-legged friends?"

"I'm not embarrassed." She stood up. "I've got to check on Maggie."

"Are you running away?"

"No." She gave him a steady glance over her shoulder. "You couldn't make me run away, Logan. I'll check on Maggie and then I'll come back and give you another trouncing in poker."

"And I'll accept it. Do you know why?"

"You're a masochist?"

"No." He picked up his glass and lifted it in a toast. "I'm a friend."

She stared at him.

"Resign yourself. It was bound to happen

after the time we've spent together and now, we've exchanged confidences. That seals it. I'm very impressionable. Don't worry. I'm not going to demand anything of you. Just pretend I'm a dog or a wolf."

She didn't know what to say.

"It's okay, Sarah," he said gently. "Really."

It wasn't okay. She felt awkward and uneasy and oddly...warm. "Are you trying to kid me?"

He started to stack the cards. "No way."

Two days later Logan got a call from one of the security men camped out in the foothills.

"Okay. No, just keep watch. I think I know who it is." He turned to Sarah. "We have a visitor. He should be here within a few minutes."

She stiffened. "Rudzak?"

He headed for the door. "I think it may be your friend Madden."

"What?" She followed him. "Why the devil should he come here?"

"If Margaret did her job, he should be hopping mad." He shaded his eyes to watch the approaching Buick. "Though I expected him to call you, not come here."

"Why should he be mad?"

He grinned. "It was taking too long to find the dirt on the prick so I hit him where it hurts. The wallet. He has an election coming up, and I called two of his biggest campaign contributors a few nights ago and persuaded them to drop their support. Then I had Margaret call Madden and tell him that would only be the beginning if he didn't persuade ATF to sell you Monty."

Her mouth fell open. "I'll be damned." Her gaze went to the Buick. "No wonder he's here."

"Like I said, I thought he'd call."

"No, that's not Madden. If he's frustrated, he's going to want to strike out and see my pain."

"Go inside. I'll talk to him."

She shook her head. "Stop trying to protect me. He'll be ugly, but it's nothing I can't handle." She braced herself as the car screeched to a halt before the front door. She hoped she was telling the truth. Madden was an expert at inflicting pain, as she'd learned all those years ago. But she wasn't that young, inexperienced girl any longer. She stepped forward as Madden got out of the driver's seat. "I told you never to come here again, Madden."

"You bitch." His face was flushed with anger. All the smoothness he usually showed Sarah was gone. "What the hell do you think you're doing?"

"A little more respect, please," Logan said softly. "And I think you're aware of what we're doing."

Madden's gaze shifted to Logan. "And what are you doing here? I did you a favor, dammit. You were supposed to help me."

"Circumstances changed. As a politician, you know how empty promises can be. Have you called ATF?"

196

"I won't be pressured by you."

"If you want to keep your seat in the senate, you will. We've only just begun to play. I'll stop your contributions cold and if you've even jaywalked, I'll find out about it and put it on every front page in the country."

"You son of a bitch."

"I want this, Madden. Give it to me and I may let you survive to run again."

"May?"

"I don't know if I can stand the thought of you sitting fat and healthy in the capitol, but it will definitely make my mind up if you turn me down."

"I will turn you down, you asshole."

"No, you won't. You're an ambitious man and I'm probably the biggest obstacle you've ever run across. Think about it. Why risk everything just for a little goodwill and publicity? Go get them somewhere else. You've used her and Monty enough."

"Have I?" Sarah could see him struggling to contain his rage as he whirled on her. "Have I used you enough, Sarah?" His voice was thick with malice. "Speak up. It's not like you to stay in anyone's shadow."

"Go away, Madden."

"Now you're giving *me* orders?" His gaze went from her to Logan and back again. "You think just because you're sleeping with the big man, you can pull the strings."

"I'm not sleeping with Logan."

"He's just staying in this crummy shack because he likes it? I'm not an idiot. I can see how he looks at you. Money and sex make the world go round. You couldn't give him money, but sex is no problem for you, is it?"

"Shut up, Madden," Logan said.

"So protective." He shot him a mocking glance. "I can't blame you for letting her talk you into—"

"Shut up."

"She fucks like a wild animal, doesn't she? She's the only woman I ever screwed who never said no. It didn't matter what I asked her to do, she—"

Sarah's fist connected with his nose. Blood spurted and he staggered back against the car.

"Go away, Madden," Sarah said. "Now."

"Whore." He reached for his handkerchief and covered his nose. "You *are* an animal."

"Maybe. I know I'm tempted to go for your throat."

"Hit the road." Logan's expression was grim. "And get on your phone the minute you hit the highway. I want a call from ATF within thirty minutes offering to sell Monty to Sarah."

Madden began cursing.

"I'm not going to repeat myself." Logan took a step closer. "Listen to me. I was annoyed with you before, now I want to break your neck. Do what I tell you."

"I'm not afraid of you." But Madden backed away. He gave Sarah one last malevolent look as he got in the car. "You think you're so clever. Oh, you've got him now, but he'll get tired of you and I'll still be around."

198

"I don't doubt it," she said. "Cockroaches are great survivors."

"Unless they get stepped on," Logan said.

Madden opened his mouth and then closed it without speaking. A moment later he was in the car, streaking down the road.

"God, that felt good," Sarah said. It felt better than good, as if a gigantic weight had been taken off her shoulders. "Do you think he'll make the call?"

"I almost hope he doesn't." Logan turned on his heel and went into the house.

She stared at him in surprise before following him. "Why?"

"Because I want to crucify the son of a bitch." His tone was savage. "But you're feeling just fine because you punched that bastard in the nose, aren't you?"

"Yes. Why are you so angry? Madden attacked me and I took care of it."

"Did it occur to you that I would have done it for you?"

"No."

"I didn't think so."

"Why should you? It was my job."

"The hell it is."

"Stop pacing around the room and sit down. You've been on your feet too much today."

"I'll sit down when I feel like it."

She held up her hands. "Whatever you say. I don't care if your leg aches all night. It would serve you right." No, it wouldn't; he had just done her a great favor. She tried to hold on to her patience. "Look, I'm sorry I involved you in that ugliness with Madden. I owe you and I—"

"You don't owe me shit. We made a deal and I paid it. Do you think that's what this is all about?"

"All I know is that you're not behaving reasonably. It's not my fault that Madden is the bastard he is."

"It's your fault that you didn't let me help you. You're not alone in this world, you know. Would it have hurt you to let me protect you? Just once?"

She blinked. "I didn't need protection."

"No, you don't need anyone, do you? You're not wounded. You haven't got a scar to your name. Bull*shit*."

She stiffened. "Shut up, Logan. I'm sorry if your ego was hurt, but don't take it out on me."

"You should have let me help you."

"You did help me."

"Is that why your knuckles are bleeding?"

She looked down at her hand in surprise. "It's nothing. Just a graze."

He stopped before her. "And you're so tough that it didn't faze you."

"No, dammit, I was too busy trying to understand why you were overreacting to a little— Let me go, Logan."

His hands tightened on her shoulders. "Why? Will you sock me too?"

"Maybe. If you deserve it." She looked up at him. "What the hell is wrong with you?"

"Nothing's wrong with me. No, that's a lie." He shook her. "You're driving me crazy.

You're not alone in the world, dammit. You don't have to do everything for yourself."

"Let me go."

His hands opened and closed on her shoulders. "What's the matter? Are you afraid I'll jump you like your friend, Madden?"

"I know you better than that."

"Do you?"

Her chest tightened. He was gazing at her with an intentness that made her feel... She hurriedly looked away from him. "You're not Madden. And you said you were my friend. Was that a lie?"

He went still. "No." His hands dropped away from her shoulders. "It wasn't a lie." He walked back to the open doorway and stared at Madden's car, which was faintly visible in the distance. "And I'm not Madden. Why didn't you tell me you were lovers?"

"You didn't need to know to help me. It wasn't important."

"No? It feels damn important."

"It shouldn't. That was a long time ago and doesn't affect the present situation. The only use he has for me these days is to help his career."

"And what about you?"

"Get real."

"What about you?" he repeated.

"For God's sake, I was only a kid. I met him right after I joined ATF. I was lonely and I thought he— He was very smooth. He fooled me for over six months. Then I broke it off. He didn't like it."

"Evidently." He didn't look at her. "He clearly found you very entertaining."

She felt heat rise to her face. "So?"

"Just commenting. I take it he's been fucking you in other ways since you stopped letting him come to your bed."

"That was crude."

"But true."

She didn't speak for a moment. "Yes. He always wanted to be the one holding the whip."

"I trust you're not speaking literally. I think even you would have said no to—" He broke off and shook his head. "Sorry. That wasn't necessary."

"No, and that was crude too. And none of your damn business."

"You're right. As I said, I'm sorry." He turned around to face her. "I suppose I felt a little hurt that you'd close me out. Friends don't do that."

The tension between them was gone, she realized with relief. Or had it just eased? She'd take it either way. "I never said I was your friend."

"But you are, aren't you?"

Days of closeness and working together. Nights of tending Maggie. Jokes, humor, familiarity. "I suppose I am," she said slowly.

"You're damn right you are. I've worked too hard to make sure you—"

The phone rang.

"I'll get it." Logan crossed the room in four steps and picked up the phone. "She's not available. This is John Logan. Talk to me."

He listened for a few moments. "I'll have someone stop by your office with a certified check within the hour. Give him a notarized bill of sale in exchange. Thanks." He hung up the phone and turned back to her. "Sanders with ATF. He said he's the head of the K9 unit. You know him?"

"He's my boss." Excitement was surging through her. "Madden called him? He's going to sell me Monty?"

He nodded. "Tomorrow you'll have the papers on him."

Oh, God, it was too good to be true. After all this time and heartache, it was going to happen. "Really?"

He smiled. "Really."

Her knees felt weak. She sank down in the easy chair. "I was afraid he wouldn't do it. I couldn't believe..."

"Believe."

Monty was hers. No more threats. He was safe.

Logan's gaze was on her face. "You're... radiant."

She felt radiant. She felt as glowing as the sun. "He's safe."

"Yes."

She closed her eyes. "I've been so worried about him. Dogs are helpless. They can't protect themselves from cruelty."

"But you protected him."

She opened her eyes as she felt his handkerchief touch her cheek. "What are you doing?"

"You're crying." He wiped her tears and then handed her the handkerchief. "Why do women always cry when they're happy? It doesn't make sense." He went over to the sink. "And it's disconcerting as hell."

"Why?"

"Tears are a sign of sorrow, and it's primitive instinct for a man to try to heal sorrow in a woman." He was returning to her carrying a damp dish towel. "It messes up our minds when there's no sorrow to heal. Give me your hand."

"What?"

"You're bleeding." He took her right hand and gently dabbed her bruised knuckles with the towel. "And that's a wound I can heal."

"It's barely a—"

"Hush. You've got a wicked right hook. Where did you learn it?"

"Ray Dawson."

"Who's Ray Dawson?"

"He's a fireman, one of my EMT instructors. He said that in natural disasters or tragedies people sometimes go crazy. Looters, relatives of people you can't manage to save. You have to be able to protect yourself."

"I can see that." He lifted her hand to his lips and kissed the bruised knuckles. "To make it better. Not scientific, but it satisfies my primitive instinct." He rose to his feet. "I have to call Margaret and make sure that she gets a man out to ATF headquarters right away. Anything else I can do for you?"

She shook her head.

"Sure? Dragons to slay? A diamond tiara?"

"You've done enough. Thank you."

"Enough for you, but what about me?"

"What about you?"

"I like this. It makes me feel ten feet tall making you look like you do right now. I think it may be addictive."

She swallowed. "You'll get over it."

"I'm not sure. We'll see." He pulled out his phone. "But evidently it's making you uneasy, so I'll go outside and make my call."

As soon as he walked out the door, she released the breath she hadn't known she was holding. Christ, she was actually shaking. The last thirty minutes had been too charged with emotion: anger, relief, bewilderment, joy.

And lust.

Don't dodge it. It was lust she had felt, lust for Logan. Strong and hot and basic.

He had felt it too.

But he hadn't pushed. He had stepped back and turned away.

And she had been disappointed. Stupid. God, that was stupid. A sexual involvement was the last thing she needed with a man like Logan. He was too strong and dominant and would interfere with her life.

But why would he interfere? They could be just ships that pass in the night. There was no way he would want any kind of commitment. She was really nothing to him.

Stop thinking about it. Stop thinking about him.

She got to her feet and moved toward the back porch. Monty was lying next to Maggie as usual but looked up and lazily wagged his tail.

"Some friend you are." She knelt beside them. "Here Logan and I have been working to get you out from under Madden, and you're in here making eyes at Maggie."

Beautiful. Love.

"How do you know? Maybe it's sex."

Love.

"Maybe." She stroked his head. "But you'll have to convince Maggie. She'll demand a commitment. She'll mate for life." But the bond between men and women wasn't as unshakable. A long time ago she had hated her mother's emotional instability and been determined to marry for life. But that was a child's dream. She had learned in a hard school that relationships between men and women were often casual and fleeting.

Love.

Not for her.

And not for Logan.

"I'll get right on it," Margaret said. "This is a good thing, John. I thought the pup belonged to her."

"So did I."

"Shall I stop the investigation into Madden's background?"

"No, I want to know everything I can about him."

"You sound grim."

"I feel grim. I want to hang him out to dry."

"Why?"

Because he was jealous as hell. Because he'd never had a stronger urge to destroy someone than at the moment he'd learned Madden had been Sarah's lover. "Why not? He's a sleazeball."

"You run into a lot of sleazeballs. You usually ignore them unless they get in your way."

"I'm not ignoring this one. I'm taking him down."

"Okay, okay. I'll try to have more information on him in a few days."

He hung up and dialed Galen's number.

"Where the hell is Rudzak?" he demanded when Galen picked up the phone.

"Hello to you too. Where are your manners, Logan?"

"Have you found Sanchez?"

"Last night. He didn't know where Rudzak was, but I persuaded him to make a few phone calls. He was told Rudzak had returned to the U.S. a few days ago."

"Where?"

"Destination unknown. But before he left he made a buy from a Russian dealer for a hell of a lot of explosives and detonators."

"Shit."

"He's through playing penny ante and it's a good bet he's going after his prime objective. We should be able to make a guess. Dodsworth?"

"Probably. But I've got seven factories and twenty-two research facilities in the U.S. I've increased the security on all of them and ATF is making regular checks."

"Not enough."

"I know that, dammit."

"But you're lucky. You have me flying to your aid even as we speak. I should be landing in San Francisco in a couple of hours. I'll go check out the plant in Silicon Valley tomorrow, since that's your largest facility, then Dodsworth. After that I'll tap my contacts and see if I can get a lead on Rudzak. If that meets with your approval, of course."

"And if it didn't, you'd do it anyway."

"What can I say? So I have an overabundance of initiative. How's the dog lady?"

"Fine."

"Do I detect a sour note? That was a distinct growl."

"I don't growl."

"Well, you might come to a better understanding with her if you did. She seems to have an affinity for animals. But I thought you've been on friendlier terms lately."

You are *an animal.*

Logan's hand tightened on the phone as Madden's words to Sarah came back to him. "Just find Rudzak. Fast."

"I'll find him." Galen hung up.

Logan shoved the phone into his pocket, his gaze on the sun setting behind the mountains. He should go in, find Sarah, and smooth over the ripples of discord he had stirred after Madden left. He'd bungled it badly. With Rudzak no longer a continent away, he must not be forced to leave Sarah.

He couldn't go back in the cabin. Not yet.

Damn Madden. With a few sentences he had blasted through Logan's composure and shocked him into losing control.

She fucks like a wild animal.

He closed his eyes. "Jesus." He could feel his body ready again even while fury and jealousy coursed through him.

She's the only woman I ever screwed who never said no.

What erotic games had she been willing to play?

Get control. This almost painful lust wasn't natural to him. Sex had always been an exquisite pleasure, not a driving obsession.

It wasn't obsession. He wouldn't let it be. He had reacted with instinctive arousal to Madden's words, but any man would have had the same response.

And as soon as he could get his body in check, he'd go back in the cabin and make Sarah forget that he'd made that slip.

"Something's happening," Bonnie said. "I don't like it, Mama."

Eve glanced away from the skull she was working on to look across the room. Bonnie was curled up at one end of the couch. The little girl was dressed in jeans and a T-shirt, as she always was when she appeared to Eve, her red hair wildly curly and her expression radiant and full of life. Eve's heart leaped with joy.

She quickly looked back at the skull. "Well, hello. I wondered if I was going to see you again." She changed the tab on the skull to a different depth. "I mean, dream of you again."

Bonnie chuckled. "Of course that's what you mean. You never give up, Mama. But someday you'll admit I'm who I say I am. You're already halfway there."

"To the funny farm? No, thank you."

"You know you're not crazy. Where are Joe and Jane?"

"They went to a matinee in town. Jane wanted to see some new Matt Damon movie. I had work to do, so I passed on it." She paused. "But I must have gotten sleepy and stretched out on that couch for a nap. Or you wouldn't be here."

Bonnie grinned. "Isn't it great how much work you got done on that skull while you were sound asleep?"

"Shut up, brat. I don't care what you say. You're

not a ghost, only a figment of my imagination. I created you, and as soon as I no longer need you, you'll fade. I'm already on the way. You haven't appeared for months." She kept her eyes on the skull. "I thought when Sarah found your body and we brought you home that maybe you'd moved on."

"And that made you happy?"

"Yes, of course." She closed her eyes. "No, I'm lying. I've missed you, baby."

"I've missed you too."

She cleared her throat. "Then why haven't you come to see me?"

"You were all confused about me. You know, for a smart woman, sometimes you don't think so clearly. I thought I'd stay away until you and Jane got everything straight."

"How diplomatic of you."

"I want things right for you, Mama. I would have stayed away longer, but I got worried." She fell silent a moment. "Something's going to happen."

"You said that before."

"Because it's true. Something bad."

"And I'm supposed to believe you?" Her hand was shaking as she placed another tab. "Joe? Jane?"

"I don't think so. Maybe. You know I can't see what's going to happen. I just get glimpses or feelings."

"A fine ghost you are. Get me all excited and then tell me you don't know any details."

"Sarah..."

"What?"

"There's darkness all around Sarah. Death. So much death."

211

"She just got back from Barat. There was plenty of death there."

Bonnie shook her head. "Something's going to happen."

"Then go visit her dreams."

"Mama."

"What can I do? Tell her my daughter who we just buried is worried about her?"

Bonnie nibbled at her lower lip. "It's not only her. Some of the darkness has to be near you or I wouldn't be able to feel it." She cocked her head, listening. "I have to go now. I hear Joe's car."

"I don't." Eve wiped her hands on a towel and moved toward the window. Joe's car was just turning the far curve in the road. "How do you do that?"

"There are some advantages to being a ghost. I love you, Mama."

"And I love you, baby." She turned her head. "But you can be very—" The end of the couch was empty. No small jean-clad form, no bright, mischievous face. No Bonnie.

She closed her eyes as disappointment surged through her. Most of the time dreaming of Bonnie brought her a sense of peace, but this time she had a nagging feeling of disquiet. Why?

Something's going to happen.

Darkness.

She had thought she had left darkness behind. These last months with Joe had been filled with joy and light. The only cloud had been Jane's attitude, and Eve had been sure that could be remedied. If there were something menacing coming, she wouldn't believe the fates would let it come to them.

She was whistling in the dark. When Bonnie had been murdered, she learned there was no justice in the world. She could only cling to the people she loved and hope.

Joe parked beside the cottage and he and Jane were getting out of the car. They were laughing and Eve suddenly felt better. She headed for the front door to meet them. She wasn't going to let her imagination depress or panic her. Bonnie was not a ghost, only a dream. She had no power to see danger on the horizon. Sarah was perfectly safe, and no darkness was near either Eve or the people she loved.

Darkness was falling, but Rudzak could still see the eager, loving look on Eve Duncan's face as she moved across the porch toward Joe Quinn and the child. It told him all he needed to know. It appeared Logan's affair with Eve Duncan was as dead as yesterday's news. Duncan had a new man and Logan wasn't one to accept the role of second fiddle.

Too bad.

He lowered the binoculars and turned to Duggan. "Start the motor. We can go now." He settled back in his seat as Duggan piloted the speedboat across the lake.

The dossier on Logan had told him that the relationship with Eve had faded, but Rudzak had had to see for himself. It would have been exquisite to destroy a woman Logan loved. However, he might reconsider Eve Duncan if nothing more interesting appeared on the horizon.

His fingers touched the ivory and jade comb he'd slipped into his pocket when he'd left the hotel that morning. He'd thought perhaps...

Not yet, Chen Li.

He would be glad to rid himself of the comb. It was one of the last gifts he'd given her and the memories were bitter.

"You shouldn't give this lovely thing to me." Even as Chen Li spoke, her forefinger ran delicately over the yellowed ivory teeth of the comb. "It's too expensive. John never says anything, but I think it makes him feel bad that he can't give me gifts like this."

"Logan isn't that selfish. You like it, don't you?"

"It's wonderful." She reluctantly handed it back to him. "But John's feelings are more important. You do understand, Martin?"

Fury tore through him. He turned away so she wouldn't see it. "Of course I understand." He moved toward the cabinet where she kept her treasures. "But it belongs to you. Suppose we just put the comb in the back of the case and not mention it to Logan? He'll probably not even notice it."

"I—I suppose that would be all right."

"I'm sure it will." He closed the case and smiled at her. "After all, he does want you to have the things that make you happy."

*"It's not things that make me happy, Martin.
John makes me happy."
"That's good. That's all I want."
And to see Logan dead.*

She had gone to the doctor the next week
and he diagnosed her with leukemia. After all
those years he had been cheated.

Logan had cheated him.

"Are we coming back?" Duggan asked.

"Maybe. But not right now."

"Where do we go from here?" Duggan
asked. "Sacramento? Dodsworth?"

"Patience," Rudzak answered. But Duggan
had no patience; in many ways he was like a
child.

"Dodsworth?" Duggan persisted.

"Eventually. But there are other things to
do first. I've waited a long time for Logan. I've
always found that anticipation can almost be
more rewarding than the act itself."

"For you," Duggan said sourly. "It seems
to me all that trouble we went through in
Phoenix was a waste of time."

He was really incredibly dense, Rudzak
thought with amazement. And stupidity was
dangerous. Already Rudzak had decided that
Duggan would not survive the blast he was so
eager to engineer.

But that was down the road, and Duggan's
usefulness was not plumbed fully yet. So keep
him on an even keel, don't show him the
scorn. Push the right buttons. With Duggan

215

it was his self-love and conceit. "I know it's difficult for a man of action like you to hold back," he said gently. "It's one of the qualities I admire in you. But give my way a try. I think you'll be surprised."

He watched the words work on Duggan.

Finally the man shrugged. "If you say so. I guess I'll go along with you."

"Thank you." Rudzak smiled brilliantly. "I promise this job will be the ultimate experience of your lifetime."

Eve called Sarah at nine-thirty that evening.

"Is everything okay?" Sarah asked. "How's Jane?"

"Not much better. Though you'd never guess if you didn't know her. She's just... quiet."

"And how are you?"

"Fine. I knew you'd be worrying, so I thought I'd give you a call."

"The offer is still open. I'm having a few problems right now, but they should be settled soon and I'd love to have Jane for a while."

"We're a family. We'll work it out."

Sarah shook her head. "You're so stubborn. It's not a crime to ask for help from a friend."

"We'll work it out. How's Monty?"

"In love. With a wolf."

"What?"

"Don't ask." But that gave her an idea. "Maggie, that's the wolf, has a fractured leg

216

and I could use help tending her. Jane is really good with animals."

Eve laughed. "And that's going to make me send Jane to the rescue? Only you would think a wounded animal is a perfectly good reason to send a child into a wolf's den."

"Hey, it's my den. The wolf is just a guest."

"No deal."

"Jane would love her. Maggie's not easy, but she has character. Come to think of it, she reminds me a little of Jane."

"Does she?"

"I can tell you're not convinced. Keep thinking about it and let me know."

"Take care of your own wolf." Eve hesitated. "How are things with you? What kind of problems? Besides the wolf."

"Isn't the wolf enough?"

"You're being evasive."

"Maybe a little." She looked at Logan sitting in his chair across the room. "But any problem I have isn't anything that won't go away. I'll call you in a week and see if you've changed your mind about sending me Jane. She really would like Maggie."

"That's what I'm afraid of. All I need is to have her heart broken when she has to leave your damn wolf." Another pause. "You're sure everything is under control with you? I've been uneasy about you lately."

"Why on earth?"

"I don't know. I just feel..."

"You're crazy. Nothing ever happens to me. Or, if it does, I always come out of it."

"Yeah, sure. Well, I suppose you wouldn't tell me anyway. But if you don't call me next week, I'm calling you. Give Monty a pat for me." She hung up.

"You tried to give away my job," Logan said as Sarah turned away from the phone. "And I thought I was doing pretty well with Maggie."

"You'll do." She sat down on the couch across from him. "But Eve would be better off with Jane here."

"So you'd throw me out. It's not a good idea. Not now."

"If you get rid of Rudzak, I could go on with my life."

"I'm trying. I have to find him first." His gaze narrowed on her face. "It hasn't been so bad having me here, has it?"

"No." She looked away. "But it's time for it to be over."

"Why now?"

You're sure everything is under control with you?

It was odd Eve had asked that question. For the first time in years, Sarah was feeling out of control. Hell, for the past two days she had done everything under the sun to keep herself busy just to avoid Logan.

"Why now?" Logan repeated.

She got to her feet. "I think I'll check on Maggie and then turn in."

"Aren't you going to tell me why Eve called?"

"She said she was uneasy about me."

"And you told her nothing could put you down."

"If you're going to eavesdrop, get it right.

218

Any number of things can put me down, I just usually manage to work out of them."

"I stand corrected. Why was she uneasy?"

"No reason. She doesn't know anything about Rudzak or that you're here. The situation with Jane probably has her on edge."

"Maybe." He thought about it. "But it's not like her. She's been through too much to let one worry carry over to another."

"You should know." She headed for the porch. "Since you lived with her for a year. Don't worry about Eve. It's Joe's job to take care of her now."

"For God's sake, I'm not worrying about Eve."

The harshness of his tone startled her, and she looked at him.

He held her gaze with an intentness that made her lose her breath. "I'm worried about you. Is that too much to believe?"

She breathed deeply to ease the sudden tightness in her chest. "Yes. I don't know... I mean...naturally, you'd feel concerned about Eve."

"Naturally."

"You care about her."

"Of course I do. That doesn't mean I can't feel anything for any— Where the hell are you going?"

"I told you, I'm going to bed."

"Look at me."

She didn't want to look at him. She was feeling the same mindless heat she'd felt that day Madden had come. "I don't want to talk anymore. Good night."

"Then don't talk. Listen." He was out of his chair and standing before her. "You know what we both want. If you refuse to take it, I'm not going to force you. But don't throw Eve between us. She has nothing to do with this."

He wasn't touching her, but he was so close, she could feel the heat of his body. She felt dizzy, tingling... She wanted to step closer. He was so big. What would it feel like to have that body against her own? The next moment she knew.

He inhaled sharply and went rigid. "What are you doing?"

She wasn't sure. The movement had been purely instinctive. "I don't know. I wanted... I think I made a mistake."

"You'd better make up your mind fast. I'll count to five."

How could she make up her mind when she was so dizzy she couldn't put two coherent thoughts together? "It probably shouldn't happen. We're not really compatible."

"The hell we're not." His hands dropped to her hips and he pressed her to him, rubbing in an undulating, catlike motion. "You can't be more compatible than that."

She bit her lower lip as a wave of sheer lust surged through her. "You'd try to control me. You're a manipulator. You like things your own way."

He kissed her. "Doesn't everyone? But I'm willing to negotiate, and I know better than to get in the way of your precious job."

"What about Taiwan? There are jobs I have to do alone and you'd—"

He kissed her again. "I promise."

"You said—you'd count—to five."

"I did. Internal clock." He stepped back and took her hand, pulling her toward the bedroom. "And it's still ticking. God, is it ticking. Want to hear it?" He put her hand on his heart. "If you're going to say no, it better be now."

She could feel the rapid thump of his heartbeat beneath her palm. It was sending shock waves through her with every beat. It filled her body. It filled the room. It filled the world.

"It's going to be good. Can't you feel it? Don't you—"

"Stop talking," she said unevenly. "I'm not going to say no. How the devil could I?" She followed him down on the bed and covered his mouth with her own.

"I really have to go check on Maggie." Sarah yawned and cuddled closer to Logan's naked body. "I should have done it hours ago."

"You were busy." He brushed a kiss on her forehead. "And you're going to be busy again in about...two minutes."

She chuckled. "Your internal clock again?"

"You bet. It's wound tight and ready to spring forward."

She reluctantly pushed him away and sat up. "Maggie."

"I'll do it." He swung out of bed. "You stay here. I don't think you've had much

221

practice at balancing duty and pleasure. I wouldn't want those weights to swing in the wrong direction."

She felt a ripple of heat go through her as she watched him walk naked across the room. The very first time she had seen him she thought he was beautiful as a cougar. He was muscular, big, strong, fit, as comfortable in this bedroom as he had been in the jungle.

He had swept her away with his bawdy eroticism and dynamic energy, totally surprising her. She had thought sex with him would be intense, overpowering, and it had been. But it had also been fun. If she had been over-powered, it had been by her own sexuality. Logan had not tried to dominate her. He had led, offered, tempted.

But wasn't that the height of power and manipulation? To seduce was a thousand times cleverer than to force, and Logan was the most seductive man she had ever met.

To hell with it. She didn't want to analyze what had happened. It was sex, not brain surgery. She had enjoyed her body and his. That was all. No harm had been done.

"Maggie's fine." Logan was coming back toward her. "I changed her bandage."

"You were quick. It usually takes me longer."

"I had incentive." He sat down on the side of the bed. "Scoot."

She moved over. "Is Monty okay?"

"If you call mooning at Maggie okay. I've never seen an animal more lovesick. She's leading him on a merry chase."

"She has to be careful. It's forever for her. Not that I'm defending her. Poor Monty is— What happened to your hand?"

"Nothing much." He looked down at his left hand. "Maggie nipped me a little. She barely broke the skin." He put his hand on her breast. "Not her fault. I was in too much of a hurry."

She felt a tingle of heat go through her. "Go wash and put antiseptic on it."

"Later." He moved over her and parted her legs. "The clock's ticking."

"Now." She pushed him away. "Never mind. I'll do it myself. I won't have you bleeding all over me."

"That's tender."

She got up and hurried across the room. "I'm not into kinky sex. Well, maybe I am a little, but blood doesn't turn me on."

"You say something like that and then expect me to be patient and keep my—"

"Hush." She came back a moment later with the medical bag. "It will take only a minute."

He watched her bent head as she swabbed the wound with alcohol. "This isn't necessary. I think you're only trying to torture me."

"It's a thought. Or maybe turnabout is only fair play. You cleaned up my knuckles after I decked Madden."

"But you weren't in the shape I am right now."

"Yes, I was. Not right away, but you were angry and I could sense..." She lifted her gaze. "What Madden said excited you. You looked at me and I could see you thinking about the things you'd like to do with me. And then I started thinking about them and I became excited too."

"Madden had nothing to do with this."

"Of course he did." She looked down again and began rubbing antiseptic on the cut. "Madden called me an animal. Was I animal enough for you, Logan?"

He said gruffly, "You were damn wonderful." He tilted her head so she could look into his eyes. "I wanted to kill Madden when he called you that, but there's nothing wrong with being an animal. Not if they're as clean and bold and beautiful as you are. And maybe Madden was the catalyst, but this would have happened eventually anyway. Remember?" he teased. "It's a guy thing. What else can you expect from a man who thinks about sex every ten minutes."

"Eight minutes," she said unevenly. "After tonight, I have an idea that magazine article was dead on the money."

"Tonight wasn't a fair test." He pulled her back into bed. "What do you expect me to think about when I'm making love to you?"

She looked away from him. "Turn out the light."

"I like to look at you."

She liked to look at him too. "Turn it out."

He did and pulled her into his arms. "If you didn't like it, why didn't you tell me before?"

She did like it. It was just easier to say

some things in the dark. "You said you were making love to me. But you're not making love to me, it's just sex. We both know that. You don't have to pretend anything else."

"Oh, I don't?"

"It's better not to confuse the issue. I know you couldn't love me any more than I could love you. We're like fire and water."

She could feel his muscles stiffen against her. "I...see."

"I'm not like Eve."

"No, you're not."

"And I'm sure I'm not like Chen Li."

"Not the slightest."

"So sex is enough." She buried her face in his shoulder. "I...like this. I like you. I thought—I'd like it to go on for a while. But it can't if we're not honest with each other."

"Well, no one could say you're not being honest enough." He was silent a moment. "Tell me, did you ever tell Madden you loved him?"

"What difference does—"

"Did you?"

"Yes."

"Anyone else?"

"No."

"That son of a bitch really did a number on you, didn't he?" He pressed her head into his shoulder. "Never mind. We've talked enough about Madden tonight to last me a lifetime. I just wanted to get the picture straight."

"You can't think I'm pining for that bastard?"

"Perish the thought. You're not scarred. I'm the one who's carrying all the baggage. Right?"

He didn't wait for an answer. His mouth covered hers and he moved over her. "Now shut up and let's have sex. I promise I won't make love to you. I wouldn't want you to think I'm dishonest."

He was angry, she realized. This time it was rougher, deeper, harder, and yet she found herself responding with a passion even stronger than before. It went on for a long time before he collapsed on top of her.

His chest labored as he struggled to get his breath. "Isn't it lucky this is just sex? It might damn well kill me if it was anything more serious."

It was almost ten o'clock when Sarah opened her eyes.

Monty.

She had to feed Monty and Maggie.

She usually fed them at seven, and she was surprised that Monty hadn't been pawing at the door.

Logan's arm was draped across her breasts and he was still asleep. One more minute wouldn't matter. She lay there, looking at him. It was pleasant seeing Logan with his defenses down. He looked younger, more vulnerable. It gave her a warm, cozy feeling to know he trusted her to see him like this.

Monty.

She carefully got out of bed. No need to wake Logan yet. She'd feed Monty and Maggie, shower, and maybe fix them breakfast. She grabbed her robe, gathered her clothes, and shut the bedroom door silently behind her.

Monty greeted her with reproachful eyes and a soft woo-woo when she came out on the porch.

"Don't give me that." She set his bowl of food down beside him. "I deserve a life too, you know. You're not the only one who needs a little companionship." But it hadn't been companionship, or her body would not have this delicious lethargy and sensitivity. She set Maggie's bowl down before her. "And you weren't very nice to Logan last night. I thought you'd stopped that snapping."

Maggie gave her an enigmatic look from silver eyes, then started to eat.

It had been her fault. Maggie was Sarah's responsibility and she had let Logan do her work. It had been easy to let Logan take over.

Much too easy. She frowned as she slowly rose to her feet. Wasn't it possible she would start unconsciously trying to please him?

There wasn't anything wrong with trying to please a man who was obviously trying to please her. She could guard her feelings and take the pleasure.

Guard her feelings? Where had that thought come from?

"No," she whispered.

Monty looked inquiringly at her.

She shook her head. "Not you, baby." She left the porch. That tiny ripple of panic had no reasonable basis. There were no feelings to guard except liking and respect. She didn't have to give up going to bed with Logan as long as she could keep her head straight and her life as independent as it always had been. That was the only sensible way to—

The phone rang.

Howling.

Logan's eyes flicked open.

It had to be Maggie.

And Sarah was no longer beside him.

He tossed the sheet aside. "Sarah! What's wrong with Maggie?"

No answer.

He went cold. "Christ." He ran out of the bedroom. "Sarah!"

She wasn't in the living room.

The porch.

No one was on the porch but Maggie. No Monty. No Sarah. Maggie gave him a baleful glance, then lifted her head and gave another mournful howl.

Where the devil was Sarah?

Don't panic. He doubted that she'd taken Monty for a run. He'd dress, go check to make sure the jeep was still there, and if it wasn't, he'd go after them.

He saw the note on the kitchen counter on his way to the bedroom.

Logan,
I got a call from Helen Peabody. They need Monty and me for a water-search job. It's local, so I should be back tonight or tomorrow. You take care of Maggie.
Sarah

Shit.

He punched in Franklin's number. "Sarah's left the cabin."

"I know. About thirty minutes ago."

"Did you have her followed?"

"You've got to be kidding. Galen told me he'd have my ass if we slipped up on this one. Smith's tailing her. She's on Highway 60 heading east. There's no one following her."

Relief surged through Logan. "Good. Tell Smith not to lose her." He hung up.

It could be all right. The call had come from Peabody, someone she knew and trusted.

And it could be a trap.

He dialed Margaret. "Get Helen Peabody, Tucson Search and Rescue, on the line. I need information. Make her cooperate any way you have to." He went into the bedroom and threw on his clothes. The phone rang as he was buttoning his shirt.

"Helen Peabody," Margaret said as she patched him through.

"I'm sorry to disturb you, Ms. Peabody, but I need your help."

"Certainly. How do you do, Mr. Logan? I want to thank you for your help in getting our group to Taiwan. And now Ms. Wilson said

Sarah had persuaded you to make a donation to our organization. I'm sure you're aware how desperately we need it."

"Sarah was very convincing. But she left before we were able to finalize the donation. I believe she talked to you before she ran out the door."

"I'm sorry, but Monty is the only dog in our group who does water search. I didn't like to bother Sarah since she just returned from Taiwan, but when Sergeant Chavez called, I gave in. It shouldn't take more than a day or two. But I could discuss the contribution with you. Actually, it's really my job. Sarah is in the field."

"I started the talks with her and I'd like to continue. But my time is at a premium right now. Perhaps I could reach her through this Sergeant Chavez? Do you know him personally?"

"Several of our group have worked with Richard in the past. He's with the Maricopa Sheriff's Department and works with the lake patrol. Nice guy. He was terribly concerned about those kids."

"What kids?"

"Haven't you seen the stories on TV? Three teenagers were picnicking in the Tonto Basin forest near Apache Lake and they disappeared. Search parties have been looking for them for the past two days. Thank God it's summer. It increases the chance of survival enormously."

"No, I didn't see the story." Sarah didn't

have a television set. "Is Sarah going directly to Apache Lake?"

"Yes, she's to meet Chavez at the rest stop."

"Can you give me his phone number?"

"Sure. But he's hard to reach. In emergency situations he's usually out on the trail or water with the search teams."

"I can try." He took down the number. "Thank you. I'll have Sarah get back to you about my donation." He hung up and called Margaret. "Get in touch with the Maricopa Sheriff's Department and check on Sergeant Richard Chavez. Make sure he's on the up-and-up. Then get me any information on the search going on at Apache Lake."

"Got it."

He hung up the phone.

Maggie was still howling.

Maybe she was hurting. He went to the porch and checked her bandage. It was fresh; Sarah must have changed it before she left. Maggie snapped and he barely eluded those powerful jaws. "I can't help it, dammit. I didn't send them away."

She glared at him and then raised her head and howled.

He got to his feet when the phone rang.

"Chavez checks out. Been with the patrol for fifteen years and has a chest full of commendations. He's working the Apache Lake case. Anything else?"

"Not right now." He hung up and sank down in his easy chair.

Everything looked okay. It was a valid case,

231

Chavez had checked out, no one was following Sarah but Smith.

Okay, hell. Just the fact that Sarah had not woken him to tell him she was going was significant. She had reasserted her independence and delicately thumbed her nose at him. It was a reaction he had half-expected, one he couldn't ignore. Now what was he going to do? The situation appeared safe and she was only doing her job. If he went after her, she would have grounds to claim he was interfering with her freedom.

Maggie howled.

And she had told him to take care of Maggie. He couldn't leave the wolf alone or under the care of someone Sarah didn't trust. Any other action would really blow any gains he'd made the previous night.

Maggie howled again.

He felt like howling too, in frustration, anger, and panic. What appeared smooth on the surface might be nasty underneath. He didn't know Smith. Was he sharp enough? And there were too many things Logan didn't know about the job Sarah was going on.

Just what the hell was a water search?

She was being followed.

Sarah glanced at the rearview mirror again. Black Toyota SUV. It was the same car she'd noticed behind her a few miles after she'd left the cabin. And he was closer. Her hands tightened on the steering wheel.

She was going through the last small town before she hit that twisting road down to the lake. Time to check out the SUV before she got to a more isolated area. She pulled into a busy Texaco station and got out of the car. "Stay, Monty."

She took six steps back to the road, directly in the path of traffic. The SUV screeched to a halt only a few feet from where she stood.

"Jesus." A sandy-haired man stuck his head out the window. "I almost hit you, lady."

She glanced over her shoulder at the service station. They were attracting enough attention. Several motorists had stopped pumping gas to watch them. "Who almost hit me?" She moved to the side of the car. "Who are you? And why are you following me?"

"I wasn't following you. I was—" He stopped and grinned. "Okay, I'm busted. I'm Henry Smith. Franklin sent me after you when you left the cabin."

"And who hired Franklin?"

"Galen. Who else?" He glanced over his shoulder. "Could I pull into the service station?"

"The other cars can go around you. This should take only a minute. Call Galen. I want to talk to him."

He dialed the number and handed her the phone when Galen answered. "Galen, do you know a Henry Smith?"

"Sarah?"

"Henry Smith—do you know him and what does he look like?"

He answered crisply, "Yes. Thirty-something,

233

light brown hair, brown eyes, small scar in the hollow of his throat. If you have any doubts, ask him where he got the scar. It was in San Salvador."

He did have a small round white scar in the hollow of his throat. "Where did you get that scar?"

"San Salvador, 1994."

"It's him. Thanks, Galen."

"Sarah, what are you doing? Logan called me and—"

"I'm doing my job." She hung up and handed the phone back to Smith. "Sorry. Actually, I expected one of you to follow me. I don't take much stock in this threat Logan seems so sure of, but it would have been dumb of me not to be careful."

"No problem. I'm glad you're on your guard. But you could have told us you were going to Apache Lake."

"How did you know I was?"

"Logan. He called Franklin and told him where you were headed."

She was relieved Logan hadn't come himself. It seemed he had taken her words seriously. "I'm supposed to meet Sergeant Chavez in the rest stop at the lake. If you're going to keep an eye on me, stay out of my way and let me do my job."

He touched his forehead in a casual salute. "You won't even know I'm around."

"You don't have to take it that far." She turned and moved back toward her car. "Just don't get in my way."

"Ms. Patrick? I'm Richard Chavez." The man in the brown Maricopa Sheriff's Department uniform got out of the 4x4 Tahoe patrol vehicle as she walked toward him. "It's good of you to come." He handed her his badge and photo ID as he glanced at Monty. "Hi, boy, I've heard a lot about you. Helen says you're a wonder dog. Can I pet him?"

"Sure." She checked the ID, glanced at the corresponding ID in the patrol vehicle, then returned the badge. "But let him stretch his legs first. It's been a long trip. Go, Monty."

He bounded out of the jeep and tore around the parking lot.

"He's a beauty." Chavez's admiring gaze followed the dog. "I've got a mutt I adopted from the pound. Lots of character, but no one could say she's any beauty queen. Not that I'd want any other dog."

"Hey, everyone says mutts are the brightest. And I wish more people adopted from the pounds." She looked at the forest beyond the rest area. "When were the kids seen last?"

"Three days ago. They came up here camping. Josh Nolden called his father on his cell phone and said they'd be back before midnight. They never showed. We found their campsite about ten miles from here but no sign of them." He rubbed the back of his neck. "Late yesterday we found tire marks just beyond those pines near the lake."

"You think the car may have gone into the lake?"

"We don't know. We hope to God not. But

235

the incline is steep along there and the water's deep. If they went off the bank, they could have skidded right down into the water."

"Wouldn't there be tire marks on the incline?"

He shook his head. "Shale."

"Have you sent out divers?"

"Not yet. Not until we have more to go on." He made a face. "A water search can take days, weeks."

"I know." And it became a nightmare for the friends and relatives of the victims. "Where are the tire marks?"

"I'll take you. It's about a mile through the forest to the lake. I have a speedboat tied a short distance from the last place we saw the tracks."

She put on her utility belt. "Monty."

Monty bounded over to her and she put his leash on him. "Time to get to work, boy."

"Do you need the leash? He seems very obedient."

"He is." She followed him down the trail and into the forest. "But that doesn't mean he won't jump out of the boat and try to rescue them if he finds them."

"Even if they're dead?"

"Monty doesn't give up. He's an optimist. He doesn't want to believe it."

Chavez sighed. "Neither do I. Those kids are only sixteen and seventeen. The Nolden boy's an honor student, going to MIT this fall. Jenny Denkins goes to the same high school as my daughter. They know each other."

"Don't tell me about them."

"Why not?"

Because it broke her heart. "It's hard enough to try to find a stranger. It's worse to have a picture in your mind."

He looked at her in understanding. "Maybe you and your dog are a lot alike. I think you might jump in the water too if we find the bodies."

"Not anymore. The first couple of times I did a water search I was tempted. There's something terrible about someone's life ending underwater. You want to bring them up out of that darkness."

"But you're tougher now?"

"No, but I have to control myself for Monty. My job is to find them. Someone else can bring them to the surface."

"Like me."

"Like you. But I won't be here when you do. I'm taking Monty home if we locate— What's wrong?"

Chavez had stopped and was looking over his shoulder. He shrugged. "Nothing. A goose went over my grave."

"What?"

"I had a funny feeling in the back of my neck." His gaze raked the trees around them. "Like something's watching us."

She scanned the trees. She couldn't see anything and, unlike Chavez, she didn't sense anything threatening.

"Sorry. It's probably nothing." He shook his head. "There are bears up here, you know. And

237

they like to roam near the rest stops and pick up food from the trash barrels."

More likely Henry Smith was keeping his promise to keep out of sight. "Or it could be my friend who followed me here. I told him not to interfere."

"Someone followed you? Why?"

"He's a little overprotective. It's a long story, and you wouldn't be interested."

"The heck I wouldn't." His expression was sober. "You've got to be careful of people following you around. A lot of women discover that overprotectiveness is a sign of a stalker."

"I'm not worried." Time to change the subject. She could see Chavez was getting protective himself. They had reached the top of the hill, and the lake was spread out before them. "Beautiful. I'd almost forgotten..."

"Have you ever been here before?"

"Years ago. My grandfather brought me. He loved it here." She looked down at the blue lake. It seemed impossible such still, serene beauty could hide the bodies of those children. The thought was incredibly sad. Just do your job and get out of here. "Where's the boat?"

Chavez pointed down the incline about fifty yards from where they were standing. "The last tracks we were able to trace were right here. But the shale is harder packed from here on, and they could have traveled for another mile or two." He started down the incline and reached back to take her hand. "Let me help you. This stuff's slippery."

His hand was warm and firm and it felt

good. She was still feeling a little chill from that first sight of the lake, and it was nice to have someone to hold on to. She looked back over her shoulder but could see no sign of their footprints on the rocks. She could understand what Chavez was up against in determining where the car went into the water.

"Did you hear something?" Chavez's gaze was following her own.

"No, just looking at the shale." She added teasingly, "No bear in sight."

"I thought I heard— It must have been our footsteps. This shale is damn noisy." Chavez helped her into the boat and Monty jumped in after her. "Where do you want to start?"

"You tell me." Her gaze went to a point at the far end of the lake. She could barely discern a few highway patrol cars and sheriff's vehicles and officers moving around. "Is that your command post?"

"Yep." He waved his hand at one of the officers and the man waved back. "The parents are there too. I'm glad we're a good distance away. I told the guys to keep them away from the lake so they wouldn't see you. Not that they'd know what you were doing with the dog anyway. Not many people have heard about dogs that can find cadavers underwater."

"Bodies, not cadavers. I hate that word. It dehumanizes." She shaded her eyes. "How far out could a car hit the water?"

"It depends on how fast the car was going." He pointed to a hill a few miles away. "If it bounced and went off that incline at a high speed, it could be thirty, forty feet out. If it went into the water here, it could be right underneath us."

"It's not right underneath us. Monty would tell me." She settled back in the boat. "But we'll start close to the shore."

"It's about time you got here." Logan came out of the cabin as Galen parked by the front door. "Hurry. I need to take your rental car."

"I've been exactly two and a half hours," Galen said as he got out of the car. "And that's extraordinary considering I was in Dodsworth when you called. Really, Logan, you can't yank me around all over the country if you expect me to find Rudzak."

"This is important."

"She's all right, you know. I told you she called me to verify Henry Smith's identity. She's not being stupid and Smith will watch her."

Logan got into the driver's seat. "I want to go myself."

"Then why didn't you? Why bring me here?"

He started the car. "Maggie."

"Maggie?"

"The wolf. Someone Sarah trusts has to take care of her."

"You want me to baby-sit a wolf? That's not in my job description."

"You don't have a job description. And if you had one, it would be censored. Maggie's on the back porch. I just changed her bandage, but if I'm not back in a few hours, check it again."

"You'd better be back. I'm not too enthusiastic about—"

Logan was gone.

Galen shook his head as he watched the taillights disappear. It wasn't like Logan to roar off in a panic when there was no clear-cut danger. But then, Rudzak had always been the exception to any rule with Logan. Ever since that time with Chen—

Galen jumped as a piercing howl broke the silence.

"Jesus." He turned and went into the cabin. Back porch, Logan had said.

Maggie lifted her head and snarled when he appeared in the doorway. What the hell had Logan gotten him into? Change a bandage? The wolf wouldn't let him near her.

He'd better find a way. "Hello." He moved slowly toward her. "Aren't you a beauty. It seems we've got to become each other's best friend." Maggie didn't take her malevolent gaze from him. "I don't blame you for not trusting me. I don't trust many people either." He sat down a short distance away and crossed his legs. "But we're probably a lot alike. So I'll just sit here and talk a bit to you."

241

The last rays of the setting sun were casting scarlet streaks over the lake and Monty still hadn't indicated a find.

"Does Monty need to go ashore again?" Chavez asked.

"I don't think so." Monty's concentration was so intense on water searches that he had to take frequent breaks to prevent burning out. "It's been only about forty minutes."

"It seems longer."

It seemed longer to her too. Time was dragging as the tension built.

"Should we go in and start again tomorrow?" Chavez asked.

"No, not unless we've covered all the territory. Darkness doesn't make any difference to Monty."

"I hoped you'd say that. I want to go back and tell those parents we searched the entire area and didn't find anything." He guided the boat out farther into the water. "I'll stay as long as you will. But are you sure Monty can tell if there's anyone under the water?"

"As sure as I can be," she said tersely. "If you didn't think Monty could do it, why did you send for me?"

"Sorry." He held up his hands. "I don't know much about the technicalities of water rescue. I just wanted to do what I could for those parents."

"I know." She rubbed the back of her neck.

242

"I guess I'm kind of tense. Maybe they're not in the lake. God, I hope not."

"But if they're here, Monty will find them? How does he do it?"

"The body of a drowning victim releases invisible skin particles. The particles have their own vapors and oil and gas secretions that are lighter than water and rise from any depth to the surface. The minute they come into contact with air, the particles form the narrowest point of a widening scent cone. Monty will recognize the cone and follow it back to the area of heaviest concentration."

"Incredible."

"Training. Monty and I spent an entire summer learning how to locate underwater victims. We were both pretty waterlogged by the time we got it right." She patted Monty's head. "He is pretty incredible. His ability to pick up a scent is fifty-eight times greater than any human's and his sensitivity to particular molecules may be thousands of times greater."

"Impressive. Then, if he doesn't find a scent, we can assume they're not here?"

She shook her head. "If there's heavy algae, it could trap the scent. Layers of cold water can do the same thing. There are other factors that can interfere, but Monty's been able to locate the—"

Monty barked.

"Shit." So much for hoping those kids were safe.

Monty began running back and forth in

the boat, his head down, pointing at the water.

"He's found something." Her hand tightened on the leash. "Cut the motor and let the boat drift." When Chavez obeyed, she sat still, watching. Monty was excited, but he hadn't found the source yet. "Start the motor, but keep it very slow. Go first to the right and then to the left."

When they'd turned left and gone a few yards, Monty went crazy. He strained at the leash, trying to paw and nip at the water.

"Here." She swallowed to ease the tightness of her throat. "Throw out a buoy to mark the spot."

Mark the spot. Mark this spot so those parents could find their children. Lately it seemed as if she always had to just mark the spot and go on.

"Are you okay?"

Her gaze left the yellow buoy floating on the water to see Chavez staring at her sympathetically. "I'm fine." She smiled crookedly. "No, I'm lying. I was hoping I wouldn't find anything. Let's get out of here. I'm having trouble holding Monty."

"You warned me he'd try to jump in the water." He started the motor. "Do you need my help?"

"No. As soon as the excitement passes, he'll realize they're dead and he can't save them."

And neither could she.

"It doesn't have to be those kids," Chavez said. "Couldn't it be an animal or—"

"No, Monty knows the difference. It's at least one human being."

Monty had stopped fighting the leash and was looking back at the spot marked by the buoy.

Save.

"You can't save them, boy."

He was already realizing he couldn't save them, and she could sense the sadness.

Help.

"You did help."

Monty lifted his head and howled mournfully.

She stared at him in surprise. She was used to hearing him bark, even whimper, but he'd never given vent to that eerie sound before.

Maggie's influence?

He howled again.

"Christ," Chavez muttered. "He gives me the creeps."

"He's upset." She reached out and stroked Monty's head. "He'll be better soon."

"Sorry." Chavez grimaced. "Let him howl. I suppose we owe him a big debt."

"We'll know that when you get a scuba team out here."

"I'll put in a call right away." Chavez cut the motor as they neared the shore. He jumped out of the boat and guided it onto the bank. "Though I'd better tell them to report tomorrow morning. It's dark now, and trying to locate wreckage underwater can be dangerous enough in daylight."

"Will you tell the parents tonight?"

He shook his head as he helped her from the boat. "It won't hurt to give them one more night of hope. Hell, maybe your Monty is wrong. Maybe that million-dollar nose has a cold or something."

"I hope you're right." She nibbled at her lower lip as she urged Monty from the boat. His tail was tucked between his legs, and he lay down on the bank and stared out at the water. This wasn't good. She constantly had to fight to keep Monty from going into deep depression. Sometimes it took weeks to bring him out of it. She turned to Chavez. "Will you do me a favor?"

He looked at her inquiringly.

"Go hide in the woods."

"What?"

"Go hide and let Monty find you."

"I haven't got time for games. I have to go and make my report."

"Ten minutes. That's all I ask. It will help Monty. It's a form of therapy. A rescue dog gets terribly depressed when he finds only the dead. Monty needs to find someone alive."

"I shouldn't waste—" He looked down at Monty. "Poor mutt."

"Just ten minutes."

"Okay." He took out his phone. "I guess I can phone in a preliminary report while I'm hiding." He made a face. "Though you can bet I'm not telling anyone I'm playing hide-and-seek with a golden retriever. Do you need anything of mine to let him sniff?"

"Your cap will do. I'll give you five minutes'

head start. Just hide in the woods somewhere. But don't make it too easy."

He took off his black cap and handed it to her. "Ten minutes."

"Right. Thanks, Sergeant."

He smiled. "No problem. We wouldn't want him to have psychological problems." He started up the incline. "Jesus, what am I saying?"

She watched his shadowy figure disappear into the darkness. Nice guy. He had made the search as easy as possible, and not many officers would have been willing to go out of their way to accommodate a dog.

Monty whimpered, his gaze still on the water.

She knelt beside him and put her arms around his neck. "It's okay. You did good work today. In a few minutes we'll go find someone else and then we'll go home. You'll see Maggie. Won't that be nice?"

Monty nuzzled his head against her shoulder. At least he wasn't staring out at the water any longer. She held Chavez's cap beneath his nose. "Smell. He's lost. Soon we're going to have to go find him."

Gone?

"No, he's alive. Only lost."

She felt a little lost herself just then. Lost and discouraged and alone. She wanted to go back to the cabin and see Maggie and then curl up beside Logan and close out the world.

Logan. She had tried to shut out the thought of him all afternoon; only now and then had the memory of the night before filtered through. But now it would do no harm to think about him, and she needed warmth and passion to shake off the knowledge that those poor kids were—

Stop thinking about them. Take care of Monty and then leave and go home to Logan. She stood up and took out her flashlight from her utility belt. "One more sniff." She unhooked his leash and passed the cap beneath Monty's nose. "Find."

He bounded up the incline toward the road.

She caught up with him deep in the woods a few minutes later when he paused to scent the air. He was quivering, excited, his whole being concentrating on the job at hand.

Good. That's what you need. Forget death. Find life. She held out the hat, but he ignored it and turned and raced off to the south. He'd caught the cone.

She ran after him, her flashlight spearing the darkness ahead.

Bushes.

She ducked around them, but one branch caught her arm as she passed.

A gnarled fallen log.

Jump over it.

The ground on the other side of the log was muddy, and she slipped. She caught herself and ran on.

She could see Monty ahead, stretched out, in a dead run up the hill ahead. He reached

the top and stopped, his head lifted, silhouetted against the night sky. He looked back at
her and barked.

We've got you, Chavez.

A moment later Monty disappeared as he
tore down the other side of the hill.

Sarah stopped a moment to catch her breath.
She could afford a minute before she went down
to praise Monty. He'd be so proud and happy
that maybe he'd forget—

Someone was behind her.

She whirled around.

No one.

Nothing.

But someone was there.

Something is watching, Chavez had said.

She had laughed and made a joke about a
bear. She didn't feel like laughing now. The
fine hairs at the back of her neck were lifting.

"Smith?" It had to be Henry Smith. He
had said he was going to keep an eye on her.

No answer.

Her hand tightened on the flashlight, and
she forced herself to cast the beam slowly
over the terrain. Trees, shrubs, boulders. So
many places to hide. Anyone could be—

Monty howled.

He'd found Chavez. Relief surged through
her. She wasn't alone. She had Monty and
Chavez. She bolted up the hill and then down
the other side. She could see Monty now.
He was sitting near a pile of boulders, his
head lifted. Chavez must be behind the—

Monty howled again.

She skidded to a stop. It wasn't right. Monty always indicated a find by barking and running back to her. He shouldn't be sitting there, howling.

She moved forward slowly, her flashlight focused on the boulders. "Monty?"

He didn't move. His gaze was fastened on something hidden behind the boulders.

"Sergeant? He's found you. It's all right to come—"

Then she saw him.

His uniformed body was facedown on the ground.

And the hilt of a knife was sticking out of his back.

Monty edged closer. *Help.*

She couldn't help Chavez, she realized, sick. That knife had been driven through his body, pinning him to the ground. Who could have—

A twig cracked on the path behind her.

Her heart leaped to her throat.

Something is watching.

"Monty!" She flew down the hill, past the boulders. "Monty, come!"

Running footsteps behind her.

Knife. Knife in the back. Knife tearing through flesh.

All she had as a weapon was the flashlight.

Monty was running ahead of her down the path.

Suffocating darkness. Where was she going? It didn't matter. Follow Monty.

Footsteps pounding behind her.

Faster. Go faster.

A break in the trees up ahead. She could see light.

The rest stop. Relief tore through her as Monty stopped and looked back at her, waiting.

"Go." She spurted ahead and out on the concrete tarmac. A car she recognized was parked beside the building. Henry Smith's car, and he was sitting behind the wheel.

Thank God.

She glanced over her shoulder as she ran toward Smith's car.

No one.

But someone was there. She knew it. She could feel it.

She pounded on the window of the car as Monty bounded excitedly around her.

Smith didn't look at her. Why the hell didn't he—

Because there was a small round hole in his temple.

She backed away from the car.

Dead. Dead. Dead.

Smith dead. Chavez dead.

And someone was back there in the woods, watching, coming closer.

"Sarah."

She whirled and threw her flashlight at the man coming toward her.

Logan grunted as the flashlight struck him in the chest. "Dammit, that hurt. Why couldn't you—"

"Logan." She threw herself into his arms. "Dead. They're all—" She couldn't stop shaking. "And he's out there. He was running

251

after—" She tore out of his arms. "We have to get out of the light. I thought I was safe. He has a knife.... But Smith was shot. He must have a gun too."

"Easy," Logan said. "No one's going to hurt you."

"The hell they're not." Logan. No one must hurt Logan. She couldn't bear it if— She pulled him toward the building. "Get inside."

He only moved to stand in front of her. "It's safe." His gaze raked the woods surrounding them. "Look up the road."

Headlights. Two Sheriff's Department patrol cars were coming toward them.

She went limp with relief.

"I called them when I started down that screwed-up road. I wanted to be able to find you without scouring the entire lake area. They said they'd meet me here." He turned to face her. "Now talk to me. Slowly and clearly. Who's dead?"

Her knees felt as if they wouldn't hold her. She leaned back against the fender of the car. "Chavez. And Smith. He's in the car. I thought he was the one following me. He said no one but him had followed me from the ranch, but there must have been—"

"Shh, just a minute." He went around the car, took out a handkerchief, then carefully opened the driver's door and looked inside. "Christ." He slammed the door and turned back to her. "And Chavez?"

"In the woods. Behind some boulders. My fault. I sent him out there alone."

"Show me."

"I don't know if I can find it." She rubbed her temple. "But Monty can." Poor Monty, he would hate going back to Chavez's body. She had promised him life and brought him only more death. "If it's safe for him. I'm not going to have some crazy loon shooting at my dog."

"He's not crazy. And when he sees all those troopers, he'll leave as quickly as he can."

"How do you know? You think it's Rudzak, don't you?"

"Don't you?"

She didn't know what she thought. She was finding it difficult to think at all. But evidently the question didn't need answering, because Logan was walking away from her toward the patrol cars that had just pulled into the parking lot.

Monty stopped ten yards from the boulders and wouldn't go nearer. She didn't force him. She had no desire to see that bloodstained knife again.

She gestured with her flashlight. "There he is."

Logan and the four troopers moved closer, scanning the area with their flashlights before they took each step. She knew they were afraid of destroying evidence, but it seemed to take them forever to cover those last few yards.

Please. Get it over with and let's go home.

She averted her gaze, but she could still hear the murmur of their voices as they knelt beside Chavez's body.

"Sarah." Logan was back beside her. "Lieutenant Carmichael wants you."

"Why should I—"

"Just come, okay?"

"No, it's not okay." But she started for the boulders anyway. "Stay, Monty."

"Walk on the rocks so you won't disturb the—"

"I know." She was standing beside Chavez's body, staring over it at Lieutenant Carmichael. "You wanted me?"

"We can't move the body, but his head is turned to one side." He motioned for her to kneel down beside him. "Look at him."

She didn't want to look at him. She did anyway. His eyes and mouth were open. Death must have come suddenly and—

She stiffened in shock. "It's not Chavez."

"You're sure?"

"Of course I'm sure." She stared dazedly into the heavy features of the dead man. "It's not Chavez."

"Thank you." He motioned to Logan, who lifted her to her feet. "You can take her back to the rest stop now. But don't leave until after we've questioned her."

She stood there staring down at the dead man.

"Come on, Sarah." Logan gently nudged her up the hill toward Monty.

"It's not Chavez. I thought I'd sent him

254

straight into the hands of that murderer. But it's not Chavez."

Logan was silent. Too silent.

"What is it?"

"It was Chavez, Sarah."

"No."

"Those policemen knew him, worked with him every day. It was Chavez." His hand tightened on her elbow. "And he's been dead for a long time. Rigor mortis has started to set in."

She stared at him in bewilderment. "I spent the entire afternoon with Chavez. He was with—" She drew a deep breath as realization hit her. "Rudzak?"

"What did he look like?"

"Tall, forty-something. Fine features, gray eyes, white hair." She looked at him. "Rudzak?"

He nodded.

"But I...liked him."

"Everyone likes Rudzak. It's one of the things he does best. I'm sure Chavez liked him too. The lieutenant thinks Chavez was forced to call Helen Peabody this morning to request you to come here and then was murdered. He wasn't seen at the command post after ten this morning."

She shook her head. "But he waved at one of the troopers on the other bank and the officer waved back."

"How close were you?"

He was right. The officer had been too far away to realize the man he was waving at wasn't Chavez. My God, the boldness of the man. "Smith. I told him about Henry Smith when he said he thought we were being followed, but he couldn't have killed him. We were together on the lake."

"Did he use his telephone?"

She thought back and then nodded. "At least once. When we went ashore to give Monty one of his breaks. I thought he was reporting in to the command center. You believe he called someone to kill Smith?"

"I don't doubt it."

She shivered. "I was alone with him all afternoon. If he'd wanted to kill me, he could have done it anytime. Why didn't he do it? And why lead me to Chavez?"

"I don't know. Cat and mouse? Maybe he didn't intend to kill you. Maybe he just wanted to show me he could do it."

"This is all about you, isn't it?"

"You mean it's all my fault. Hell yes, do you think I'd deny it? I don't blame you for being angry."

"I am angry." She had been frightened and stunned, but now those emotions were being supplanted by pure rage. "That son of a bitch. He used me. And manipulated me."

"Rudzak has always prided himself on being able to push all the right buttons."

"And was killing that poor officer one of the buttons he pushed?"

Logan nodded.

"He's got to be crazy."

"I'm not sure he's insane. I think he was born with something missing. He has no concept of right or wrong as we know it. What benefits Rudzak is right, what gets in his way is wrong."

"A sociopath."

"You can't pigeonhole Rudzak that easily." They had reached the rest stop, and his hand tightened on her arm when he saw the forensic team going over Smith's car. "Why don't we go inside? You don't want to see this."

He was right. She didn't need to see another dead body, and neither did Monty. She headed for the building. "How long do we have to stay here?"

"The lieutenant wants to talk to you and take a statement, but I'll see if he can send someone to the cabin to do the formal statement. You're not classified as a suspect."

She hadn't thought she would be. "And what am I classified as?"

"Witness." He shrugged. "Or maybe... victim."

She remembered the terror and helplessness she had felt as she ran through the woods. She had felt like a victim then, and the memory filled her with anger. "The hell I am."

They weren't permitted to leave the rest stop for another four hours; by then Sarah was almost as drained as Monty.

"I'll drive," Logan said as he got into her jeep. "You rest."

"I can do it. You have your own car to—"

"It's Galen's rental car. He'll arrange to have

257

it picked up." He started the jeep. "Stop arguing and climb in. You know I'm in better shape emotionally right now. You wouldn't want to crack up on that ugly road and hurt Monty."

She hesitated and then got into the passenger seat.

"The one irresistible argument," he murmured. "Lean back and close your eyes."

She didn't feel like closing her eyes. She was numb with exhaustion, but her mind wouldn't stop working. Her gaze focused on the winding road ahead as the jeep slowly crept up the incline. "How'd you get Galen's rental car?"

"I phoned him to come and wolf-sit and then took his car."

"Galen's at the ranch?" So many things had happened that she'd forgotten about Maggie. "You shouldn't have left Maggie. I told you to take care—"

"Shut up," he said roughly. "There was no way I wasn't going to come after you. And you know Galen will be able to care for Maggie."

Yes, Galen would be capable of doing anything he wanted to do. "I suppose she'll be okay."

"Better than you. She has a keen sense of self-preservation."

"She walked into a trap too, like me with Rudzak. He knew I had to try to find those kids."

"And if you got another call from Helen Peabody, you'd go traipsing off again."

"Yes."

Logan muttered a curse beneath his breath. "Stupid."

"I wasn't stupid," she said, stung. "I got a call to do my job, and it seemed a legitimate search. How was I to know Rudzak would take advantage of those kids' disappearance to set a trap? He would have had to plan everything ahead with Chavez, the call from Hel— Oh, God." She closed her eyes. "The kids. Maybe he didn't just take advantage of circumstances. Could he have killed them, Logan?"

"Yes."

She opened her eyes and turned to look at him. "He'd kill three innocent kids just to set me up?"

"I think it's likely. He's very precise about his planning. He wouldn't want the kids to show up and spoil everything after he'd gone to so much trouble."

"I feel sick." The image of a yellow buoy floating on the water came back to her. "The lake..."

"Lieutenant Carmichael told me he was sending a scuba team out to the buoy. I asked him to call me if he found out anything."

"Kids...And you say he's not insane."

"He doesn't enjoy killing, he just does it when it benefits him." He smiled grimly. "Though I may be the exception to the rule. He'd definitely enjoy killing me."

"I hope they don't find the kids," she whispered. "Dear Jesus, I hope he didn't kill them to draw me here."

He covered her hand clenched on her lap. "So do I, Sarah."

Logan's phone rang when they were only a few miles from the ranch. "Yes, Lieutenant."

She tensed, watching his expression, but she couldn't tell what Carmichael was saying to him.

He hung up. "There's no trace of Rudzak. They think he's gotten away."

"What about the teenagers?"

"They found them under the buoy." He looked straight ahead. "They haven't gotten them out of the car yet, but the scuba divers say all three were bound with rope."

She felt as if she'd been stabbed.

"Say something."

She shook her head. What could she say? She just wanted to curl up and make the world go away.

"None of this is your fault, dammit."

"I know."

"Then stop looking like—"

"I can't help how I look." Her hands clenched into fists. "Were they alive when they went into the water? No, they couldn't know that yet, could they?"

"No."

"No one could be that terrible. To tie them up and then—"

"Don't let your imagination run wild. It might not have been that way."

"But it could have been." She leaned her head

against the window. "I don't want to talk anymore, Logan."

"Then don't talk, but don't think either, dammit."

"I'll try," she whispered.

He muttered a curse and jammed his foot on the accelerator. A few minutes later he drew up before the cabin. She jumped out of the jeep and started for the front door.

"Wait a minute." Logan came around the car. "You dropped something."

She shook her head.

"I saw you kick something out of the car. It must have been on the floorboards." He knelt in the dirt.

"What is it?" she asked dully.

"Nothing. Go inside."

He had something in his hand. "What is it, dammit?"

"A comb." He held out his hand and revealed the delicate ivory and jade comb. "A present from Rudzak."

She shuddered. "Do you suppose it belonged to one of the kids?"

"No, it belonged to Chen Li."

"Why would he—" She stared at him. "You expected it?"

"I didn't expect it, but I'm not surprised. Go on to bed, we'll talk about it later."

"You bet we will." But she couldn't cope with anything more just then. Her nerves were shredded. She turned and went inside the house.

"Hi." Galen came out of the back porch. "It's

261

about time you came home. I was beginning to feel like a— You look like hell."

"I'm tired. I'm going to bed." Monty. She had to take care of Monty. But Monty was already heading for the back porch and Maggie. "Good night, Galen." She closed the door of the bedroom behind her.

She threw off her clothes, crawled into bed, and drew up the covers. The sheets smelled of Logan and their intimacy, she realized dimly. Sex and life and a joy those kids would never experience.

"Move over." Logan slipped naked in bed beside her and pulled her into his arms.

"I don't want you here."

"Tough. You've got me." He brushed his lips on her temple. "My God, have you got me. Now relax. I don't want to do anything more than comfort you."

"I just want to go to sleep."

"And have nightmares?" He pushed her head into the hollow of his shoulder. "Talk it out."

"What do you want me to say? That three kids died because some maniac wanted to draw me into his damn web."

"That's not your fault. I thought we agreed that I was to blame for everything."

"I did what he wanted. He analyzed me like some Machiavellian shrink and then decided to kill innocent kids because that would make me do what he wanted. And he was right. He called and I came."

"What else could you have done? You went

262

there to— Stop crying. No, don't stop. It's probably good for you. It's just hell for me."

"It doesn't feel good for me. It hurts."

"That's because you don't do enough of it. You're out of practice. When's the last time you cried? When your grandfather died?"

"No, I promised him I'd be strong. It was when I found Monty at that police department in Italy."

"I should have known."

"Is Monty all right?"

"Monty's with Maggie."

"That's right, I forgot. But he usually senses when I'm sad and comes and sleeps by my bed."

"The poor mutt's hormones are raging. You'll have to make do with me."

"I'm glad he has Maggie. Maybe it will distract him from what happened tonight."

"It's you we're trying to distract."

"It shouldn't have happened. I try so hard to find the living and bring closure to the dead. It's what I do, what I am. And he used that and killed those kids." She was shaking. "He twisted everything I am and made it ugly and—"

"Shh."

"You just told me to talk."

"That's when you were making sense. There's nothing ugly or twisted about you. You're clean and beautiful and straight as an arrow. Ask me, I'm an expert on twisted and ugly. I've been there."

She shook her head.

"You don't believe me? It's true. I've done

263

things that—" He stroked her hair. "You don't want to hear about me."

She did want to hear about him. It was important, she realized. When she had seen Logan at the rest stop, she had known then that everything concerning him was vitally important to her. If he died... She didn't want to think about that now. She was too confused and numb. She just wanted to be held by Logan and pretend the nightmare at Apache Lake had never happened.

"Go to sleep now," he said. "I'll stay awake and be here for you if you have a nightmare."

Had he read her mind? Did he know what a rare gift he offered her? Never in her life had she ever had anyone to keep the nightmares at bay....

"Is she asleep?" Galen asked as Logan came out of the bedroom.

"Right now. I've got to get back. I promised I'd stay with her."

"She looked like hell."

"She went through hell." He went to the sink and got a glass of water. "Henry Smith is dead. Rudzak killed him."

Galen stiffened. "Why didn't you tell me right away? Franklin has been trying to reach him since you returned with Sarah."

"I'm telling you now. You couldn't do anything about it and she needed me." He drank the water. "Or someone."

"It was a trap?"

"Yes, and Rudzak used the death of three teenage kids to spring it. Do you know how that makes her feel?"

Galen's lips tightened. "I know how it makes me feel."

"Then make sure Dodsworth is ready. Or find Rudzak. He could have killed her tonight."

"But you came just in the nick of time?"

"No, I would have been too late if Rudzak had wanted to kill her. He didn't want her dead...yet."

"Then what was his little trap all about?"

"To let me know he could do it and to find out how high she was on his list of the things I value."

"And did he find that out?"

"Probably. If he was watching us. He's always been able to read me."

Galen lifted a brow. "And is she high enough on the list to be worth his while?"

"He struck pay dirt." Logan put the glass down and turned away. "So we've got to find the son of a bitch before he kills her. Because next time he'll do it."

Sarah was sleeping deeply, like a child after a hard day.

Logan stood staring down at her.

Tenderness. Protectiveness. Love. Passion. Fear.

She wasn't the first woman in his life. He had felt all these emotions before. But not like this. Not with this single-minded intensity and desperation. When had admiration and friendship become obsession?

It didn't matter. It was here, it had come. And Rudzak knew it had come.

Sarah stirred and whimpered something in her sleep.

Nightmares? He had promised to keep the nightmares away.

He slipped into bed beside her and drew her into his arms. She felt soft and womanly, but he knew how strong she was. Strong and stubborn and yet terribly vulnerable and guarded. It was a wonder he had even gotten into her bed. It would be a super-human task making her accept any other relationship. He would have to be careful not to rush her.

She whimpered again, and he brushed his lips across her brow.

"Shh, it's okay. I'm here. I'll never let anything hurt you." He drew her closer and whispered the words he knew she'd never believe if she was awake. "I'll always be here, Sarah."

Logan was still beside her when Sarah woke the next morning. His eyes were open and he was obviously wideawake.

"Good morning." He planted a kiss on her forehead and sat up in bed. "You hit the shower while I go and see about breakfast."

"What time is it?"

"Nearly noon."

"I have to feed Monty and Maggie."

"Already done." He stood up. "I left you long enough to take care of Monty, and Galen had already fed Maggie. You'll be glad to know that Monty wouldn't let him feed him."

"But he let you feed him again."

"Don't be mad at him. I'm special. We've gone through a lot together. Santo Camaro, Taiwan, and then last night. It's natural that—" He stopped as he saw her expression change. "Don't think about it right now. Get your shower and something to eat." He grabbed his robe at the foot of the bed and left the room.

Easy to say, she thought as she slowly sat up in bed. How could she help thinking about those poor kids? The events of yesterday were rushing back to her with every sickening detail, clear and dagger sharp.

Like the knife in Chavez's back.

She shuddered as a chill iced through her. Five lives wasted for no reason other than the desire to draw her to Apache Lake. How could anyone do that?

But he had done it. And he had gotten away with it.

Suddenly the chill was gone, replaced by burning anger.

Son of a bitch. Son of a bitch. Son of a bitch.

No way, you bastard.

Sarah, dressed in khaki shorts and a T-shirt, walked out of the bathroom twenty minutes later.

Galen looked up from the stove at her. "I still have to make the gravy and biscuits."

"Where's Logan? I thought he was going to cook breakfast."

"Get real." His expression was pained. "Much as I'd like to have Logan wait on me, there's no way I'd sacrifice my digestive system. Over the years I've become accustomed to fine cuisine."

"So where is Logan?"

"Outside with Monty."

"I thought Monty would be with Maggie."

"He's sulking. He doesn't like the rapport I've developed with his lady friend."

"What?"

"He's afraid Maggie likes me best. She totally ignored him when I was changing her bandage and feeding her. Anyone could see she's besotted with me." He shook his head as he added a flour mixture to the hot skillet, then he winked at her. "Just joking. It took me a long time to get her to stop howling while you two were gone. I think she's in a snit and playing hard to get with him. Of course, I could be wrong. My modesty gets in the way at times, and I—" He broke off, studying her. "You look better than you did last night but still pretty grim."

"I feel pretty grim."

"Then go talk to Logan. I need calm and good thoughts to reach sublimity in cooking."

"Did Logan tell you that Smith had been killed?"

"Oh, yes, and I had some grim thoughts myself." He stirred the gravy. "But after I put some wheels in motion, I felt much better."

"What wheels?"

"Determining and then verifying who was the logical person with Rudzak at Apache Lake. It's always necessary to be sure before action is taken." He opened the oven to check on the biscuits. "It was almost certainly Carl Duggan."

"How can you be sure?"

"I have great contacts. Everybody loves me. Did I mention that?"

"I got the gist. And what action are you planning on taking?"

He said softly, "Why, an eye for an eye. What else?"

She had a sudden memory of him running through the jungle, as much a predator as Maggie ever could be. She didn't find the idea repulsive. It would be a clean kill and well deserved. Not like Rudzak, who—

"You're thinking bad thoughts again." He clucked reprovingly. "I told you I couldn't tolerate that. Go out and talk to Logan. I'll call you when breakfast is ready."

Logan was leaning against the fence, talking on his phone. He lifted his hand in greeting but kept on talking. Monty was lying at his feet until he saw Sarah, and then he leaped up and bounded toward her, his fluffy tail wagging his whole body in joyful greeting.

"Now you're happy to see me," she murmured as she crouched to pet him. "Where were you last night, when I needed you?"

But she had not really needed him. Logan had been there, holding her. Maybe Monty had derived the same comfort from being with Maggie.

"Is breakfast ready?" Logan had hung up his phone and was watching her and Monty.

"Not yet. I was disturbing Galen and he sent me to you."

"I'm surprised. It takes a lot to disturb Galen. But I'm glad he has his priorities straight."

"Who were you talking to?"

"Lieutenant Carmichael. He's sending someone to take your statement this afternoon."

"Any word on Rudzak?"

"No."

She hadn't thought there would be. "What about the kids? How did they die?"

He shook his head. "You don't want to know."

"The hell I don't."

"One was shot. The others drowned. They were alive when they went into the water."

She flinched. "Christ."

"I told you that you didn't want to know."

"I had to know." She closed her eyes and held tight to Monty. "I have to know everything."

"Why? So you can tear yourself apart?" he said roughly.

"Because Rudzak hasn't been real to me. I knew he had killed those people in Colombia, but I couldn't really make the connection from him to me or my life." She opened her lids and stared at him with tear-wet eyes. "I'm making the connection now, Logan."

"And it's killing you."

"No, that would mean that Rudzak had won. I won't let that happen. I won't let him hurt me." She rose to her feet. "And I won't let him hurt anyone else. Not ever."

His gaze narrowed on her face. "What does that mean?"

"It means I'm going to find him before he kills anyone again."

"And then what?"

"You tell me. You said Rudzak was smart. Even if he's caught, it doesn't mean he'd get convicted. And if he was convicted, he got out of prison once. He could do it again, couldn't he?"

"It would be more difficult."

"But he could do it."

"Hell, yes, he could do it. What are you getting at, Sarah?"

"You know what I'm getting at." Her voice was shaking with rage. "Galen believes in an eye for an eye. You do too."

"But you don't. It's not your nature."

"How do you know? I've never been this angry before."

"You were angry when Madden took Monty away and you didn't kill him."

"Monty didn't die. I was able to save him.

Rudzak didn't give me the chance to save those kids. He killed them and then he took me to that spot and let Monty find them. He told me how sorry he was, and all the time he'd put them in that car and sent them—"

"You're taking this personally, but it was me he was really aiming at."

"You're damn right I'm taking this personally. I don't care if he meant to get at you through me. He used me and he used those kids and Chavez and Smith. He smiled and told me about the dog he'd adopted from the pound, and I liked him. He played me like a—"

"Shh." He was standing before her, his hands on her shoulders. "You're scaring me to death, and I'm choosing the wrong words to try to reason with you."

"How are you going to reason with me? Are you going to tell me I should just forget about that—"

"I'm trying to tell you that this is my battle, not yours. I'll find a way to get Rudzak."

"You haven't found him yet."

"And you're going to?"

"I'll find him." Her hands clenched into fists. "That's what I do. I find people. I'll search him out."

"That's what I'm afraid of." His hands tightened briefly on her shoulders and then dropped away. "I'm not going to be able to talk you out of it, am I?"

She shook her head.

"Then I suppose I'd better make the best of it." He stepped back. "If there is a best. I trust you don't intend to leave me out of this entirely?"

"How could I? I need you."

"That's comforting...barely."

"I don't intend to be comforting. You're the one who knows everything about Rudzak. Now I want to know what you know."

"Can we wait until after breakfast?"

"No."

"Okay." He led her toward the bench against the wall. "Sit down and fire away."

"Why did Rudzak put that comb in my car?"

"Is that going to help you find him?"

"Maybe. It will help me to know him and what he might do."

He was silent a moment. "He wanted to show me that he was the one who had killed those kids and that he could have killed you too. He gave the comb and several other ancient Egyptian artifacts to Chen Li, and now he's using them as a kind of signature when he makes a kill."

"What kind of signature?"

"A symbolic death gift. Egyptian rulers had their treasures entombed with them, and he wants to honor Chen Li's passing with other deaths." His lips twisted. "And make a stab at hurting me at the same time."

"Then all this is about Chen Li? Were they lovers?"

"No, they were half brother and sister."

She stared at him in shock. "And you had him put in prison?"

"Yes."

"For God's sake, why?"

"He killed Chen Li."

"What?"

"He went into her hospital room and he broke her neck. He called it a mercy killing."

"And what did you call it?"

"Murder. She was in remission and the remission could have lasted." His lips tightened. "He didn't give her that chance."

"Did he know she was in remission?"

"I told him. He didn't believe me. He didn't want to believe me. He'd lost her and he didn't want her to live if he couldn't have her."

"Lost her?"

"He loved her. He wanted to go to bed with her."

She gasped.

"That's why he tried to draw her into the Egyptian mystique. It was common then to go to bed with close relatives. He wooed her like a lover and never took a wrong step. But I think she guessed it toward the end and he sensed her revulsion. He couldn't accept it, so she had to die."

"And you sent him to prison?"

"If I'd caught him before he ran off to Bangkok, I would have killed him. Instead, I told the authorities in Bangkok when and where they could find the drugs he'd smuggled into the country. Then I bribed the judge at his trial to give him a life sentence in one of the worst prisons in the world. Galen assured me that even the cockroaches bailed out of that place after they got a look around." His smile was chilling. "That made me very happy."

"Rudzak smuggled drugs?"

"His father owned an import-export house in Tokyo. Rudzak began by taking advantage of his father's contacts to do a little art smuggling. That's where Galen met him and introduced him to me. We did a few runs together and he brought us home to meet his family...and Chen Li."

"You were a smuggler too?"

"I told you my life hasn't been squeaky clean. I was broke and trying to make a stake. I stopped when I married Chen Li. Rudzak told me he was quitting too, but he just shifted his focus. Galen came to me two years later and told me Rudzak had started smuggling drugs throughout Asia. It was much more profitable but a hell of a lot more dangerous. I knew it would kill Chen Li if she found out, so I tried to convince him to quit. He assured me he'd do it right after the next run."

"But he didn't."

Logan shook his head. "He was making money hand over fist and there was no way he'd stop. So I turned a blind eye and just tried to protect Chen Li. Everything I did at that time was aimed at protecting Chen Li. I'd just found out that she had cancer and I was searching desperately for a cure for her. I was so young, I didn't believe anything could beat me."

No, Logan wouldn't believe anything could beat him, she thought. And as a younger man he must have been even more willful and determined to get his own way.

"So now you know what a bastard Rudzak is and you have a better picture of me too. Why don't you bow out and let me go after him?"

She shook her head.

"You're being a fool," he said roughly. "You're not equipped to go up against him. He's studied you. He knows your weakness."

"What weakness?"

"Humanity. If you're needed, you'll go to help. Just as you did at Apache Lake."

"And what am I supposed to do? Just sit here?"

"Would that be so bad? It won't be for long. He's evidently done his homework and he'll be on the move now. Things will be moving fast."

"What homework?"

"We think he's found out about Dodsworth. Galen planted a man at the courthouse and he says someone's been nosing around the records."

"Dodsworth?"

"That's my medical research facility in North Dakota. It's been doing less sensitive work than Santo Camaro. As soon as Bassett gets his notes in order, he'll be going up there to complete the project with that team."

"You never explained how Rudzak found out about Santo Camaro. If it was top secret, how did he do it?"

"Money. He zeroed in on someone and bribed him for information."

"Who?"

"Castleton."

She stiffened in shock. "Castleton? Are you sure?"

"I'm sure."

She thought about her meeting with Castleton and couldn't recall anything suspicious about him. But looking back and knowing Logan as she did now, she could see there had been something in his attitude that wasn't quite right. "You knew that evening we arrived."

"Yes."

"And you let him go?"

He didn't answer for a moment. "No."

After all she'd learned about Logan, she wasn't even surprised. "Because you were afraid he'd tell Rudzak about Monty and me and spoil the surprise attack?"

"Partly. But I'd have done it anyway. He'd betrayed those people at the facility. He was responsible for their deaths. An eye for an eye. Remember?"

She slowly nodded. "Then that's how Rudzak knows about Dodsworth?"

"What Castleton knew, Rudzak knows. The first thing I did was increase the security in all my plants and research facilities."

"All of them? But you think he'll target Dodsworth."

"Probably. But who's to say that's the only one he'll pick? I can't take a chance. Besides, we know he bought enough explosives to blow up a small town."

"Explosives," she whispered.

"You were at Oklahoma City. You know what explosives can do."

She knew very well. She had helped take out those pitiful babies from the wreckage. "You can't let it happen. Why haven't you notified ATF?"

"I have notified them and the FBI."

"Did you tell them about Dodsworth?" She could see the answer in his face. "You didn't tell them."

"Not yet."

"Call them."

"No one will be hurt at Dodsworth."

"How can you say that?" She could still see the tragedy at Oklahoma City before her. "You just said Rudzak has explosives."

He shook his head. "It's the first time we've had an inkling where Rudzak may strike. We may have a chance to trap him."

"It's too big a risk. Let ATF trap him."

"There can't be an obvious official presence at Dodsworth if I want to draw him. He'd regard my security people as a challenge, not a deterrent. But security is as tight as a drum there. No one could get through."

"Call them."

"Not yet. Not until I'm sure it's necessary. Not until I'm certain we can't stop him. Trust me. I'll act if I have to."

"How many people do you have in that installation?"

"Fifty-seven."

"And do they know what danger they're in?"

"Yes. I told the head of the project to tell everyone what happened at Santo Camaro and that they might be next. I gave them the option of staying or leaving. Six left. The rest stayed."

"You should shut down the facility."

"Rudzak would just change his target." He stood up. "If you want ATF called, do it yourself."

"I will."

"But be sure you're ready to accept the responsibility of another Kai Chi."

She could feel the blood drain from her face. "Kai Chi?"

"That was Rudzak. A tribute to Chen Li. Do you want another Kai Chi or do you want a chance to catch the bastard?"

"Kai Chi." She stared at him in horror. "Why didn't you tell me?"

"Because I knew you'd look at me as you're doing now and run to the opposite end of the earth. You don't understand anyone who would kill five hundred people to make a sick statement."

"Do you?"

"No, but I'm part of the problem, and every time you look at me, you'll see Kai Chi."

"Please, call ATF," she whispered. "You saw the baby who died in Taiwan. It's nothing compared to what a bomb did to the children in Oklahoma."

He was silent for a moment, a multitude of emotions crossing his face. Then he shook his head. "I'll give you anything else in the whole world, but I can't give you this, Sarah. I have to have a chance of catching him."

"It's wrong, Logan."

"Then make the call. No one's stopping you." He started into the house. "But think long and hard about it. And remember Kai Chi. It could happen again."

No one was stopping her? The hell no one was stopping her.

Oklahoma City. Oh, God, she couldn't stand to be responsible for another disaster like that.

Kai Chi.

If Logan was right, could she bear being responsible for the death of even more people than those at Dodsworth?

She had to have an answer and soon.

Monty whimpered and put his head on her knee.

"It's okay." She stroked his head. "Go on back to Maggie."

He didn't move. He was there giving her comfort and companionship as Logan had done the night before. But in the morning Logan had offered nothing except loneliness and despair.

Sarah tried to ignore the pain. Stop feeling sorry for yourself. She had told him she expected nothing but sexual pleasure. It was too bad she had let him slip beneath her defenses. But it would be okay. She had been alone most of her life and she had made out fine.

He asked her to trust him. Could she? Because of the way she felt about him, or because she truly believed the risk was worthwhile? She had always thought for herself, but she had never been as emotionally involved as she was with Logan.

When she had come out to speak to him, everything seemed simple. She was filled with rage against Rudzak and determination to find and punish him for the atrocity at Apache Lake. Now an even greater atrocity was looming at Dodsworth and nothing was simple anymore.

Nothing but the fact that whatever decision she was about to make could be the wrong one.

"My biscuits and gravy are ruined," Galen told her when she walked into the cabin an hour later. "And Logan wouldn't eat either. But out of the kindness of my heart, I'll make you both a new batch. You'll have to wait though. Perfection takes time."

"I'm not hungry." She looked at Logan sitting in a chair at the table. "Something's sticking in my throat."

Logan met her gaze. "I don't doubt it. The question is whether you'll be able to swallow it."

"I'm going to try. I don't see any other solution." She crossed her arms across her chest. "I'll wait awhile before notifying ATF about

Dodsworth. But the minute I see any danger to the facility, I'm going to blow the whistle and I won't let you convince me otherwise."

"I didn't think you would."

"And I'm not willing to sit here, twiddling my thumbs, until I hear Rudzak's blown it to kingdom come. You said you think Rudzak's ready to move. I want to go to Dodsworth and be there before he decides to set his explosives."

"I told you, the target might not be Dodsworth."

"But it's your passion and he knows it. You don't think he'd pass that up."

"No."

"And you on site would be another reason for him to zero in on it."

"Yes."

"And evidently he also wants to target me. Right?"

"You couldn't be more right." His mouth lifted in a crooked smile. "Or more terrifying."

"Then the multiple targets should draw him." She turned to Galen. "You're sure the security at Dodsworth is unbreakable."

Galen nodded. "I'd set up shop there and I value my neck more than I do any of those scientists. Science may save the world, but where would it be without charm and fine cuisine?" He glanced at Logan. "It seems plans are escalating. We were planning on waiting a bit."

"I don't want to wait," Sarah said. "I want Rudzak now."

Logan nodded. "I'd hoped to keep you out of it."

"Rudzak doesn't want to keep me out of it."

"Then why give him what he wants? Stay here and be safe."

"Makes sense to me," Galen agreed.

"When do we go to Dodsworth?" Sarah said.

Logan sighed. "When Bassett is ready to join the team up there. I think Rudzak will want to eliminate all hope of success for the project with one roll of the dice. He can't do that if Bassett is left alive."

"And you said Bassett will be ready to go within a week?"

Logan nodded.

"Good. Then I have plans to make myself." She went into the bedroom and shut the door.

"So much for keeping her out of it," Galen said. "I'll try to take care of her at Dodsworth, but I can't promise you anything if she goes off on her own the way she did at Apache Lake. You can't protect someone if they don't want to be protected."

"I know."

"And I detected a coolness in her attitude that may make things more difficult."

"Can you blame her? I'm surprised she doesn't want to cut my throat. I had to tell her about Kai Chi or she would have gone off on her own after Rudzak."

"True." Galen turned back to the stove. "But I'd stop brooding about how she feels and go in there and see what she's doing. If she says she's making plans, I don't think you want any of them to surprise you." He looked down at the gravy congealing in the frypan. "Pity. The two of you have spoiled everything. It was going to be a masterpiece of a breakfast."

"What are you doing?"

Sarah looked up to see Logan standing in the doorway. "What does it look like?" She threw a load of underwear into the duffel she had set on the bed. "I'm packing. I want to be ready when Bassett is ready."

"We won't have to walk out the door the minute he does."

"I know." She tossed a cardigan and two pairs of jeans into the duffel. "But I'll go crazy if I don't do something. You and Rudzak may have all the patience in the world, but I don't. This isn't some kind of contest to me."

"It's not to me either. You're not being fair, Sarah."

"Maybe not. Ask me if I care."

"You care. That's the problem. You care too much." He crossed the room and stood next to her. "It's playing hell with my plans, but I wouldn't have it any other way."

He was too close. She could feel the heat of his body. She took a step away and went back to the bureau. "I care about those people at Dodsworth. Not about you."

"I never meant anything else," he said quietly. "I know I'm not in your good books right now. It will be different once this is over. I'll make it different."

She didn't answer.

"We have to work together, Sarah. You can't let your feelings get in the way."

That was exactly what she was trying to prevent. She had to keep him at a distance. She couldn't let the way she felt about him cloud her judgment. Not with all those lives in the balance. "I'll work with you." She met his gaze across the room. "But don't expect anything else from me. I can't give it to you."

"You will. As you said, I can be very patient."

"By the time this is over, you may have changed your mind."

"I won't change my mind."

Her hand closed tightly on the knob of the bureau drawer as he walked out and closed the door behind him. Finish packing. Don't think about him. Don't let him be important to you. Even if he seems to care about you now, how long can it last? You're too different from him.

And that's okay. She didn't want to change. She didn't want to be anyone but herself. She was a woman who could make decisions and run her own life to suit herself.

Don't think about him. Think about Rudzak and how to protect Dodsworth.

"You want me to come there?" Eve repeated. "Why?"

"Maggie. She's much better, but I need someone to take care of her while I'm gone."

285

"I thought it was a joke when you said you needed Jane to nurse your wolf."

"It was at the time. But not now. I need your help. Can you come?"

"Do you have to ask? You came when I needed you; you found my daughter. I'll be there on the next plane."

"Thank you. Will you have your mother take care of Jane and bring Joe?"

"I'll see if he can get away. But why should I bring Joe?"

"I'd feel better. I don't think there's any danger for you as long as we're not here, but I'd like to know Joe is with you."

"We? Who's with you?"

"Logan."

A pause. "Are you going to tell me what's happening?"

"As soon as you get here. But bring Joe if you can. Though I probably shouldn't tell you to do that. He's going to make you get right back on a plane to Atlanta as soon as I tell him about Rudzak." She rubbed her temple. "Well, maybe he should. We'll leave it up to him."

"You're being as clear as mud."

"That's what I'm wading in. I want you to know if you decide not to help me that it's okay. I'll understand and you mustn't feel obligated to—"

"Shut up. I'll call you when I find out when my plane will arrive in Phoenix." Eve hung up.

Sarah headed for the door to the living room. It was done. Now to find Galen.

But the living room was empty. "Galen!"

"Out here," he called from the back porch. "I've just fed Maggie."

"I called my friend Eve, and she's—" Her jaw dropped as she stopped in the doorway. Galen was sitting on the floor close to Maggie and her head was on his thigh. "That's a good way to lose a body part. One you may treasure highly."

"We understand each other." Galen stroked Maggie's head. "We talked it over and decided we're a lot alike. Isn't that right, Maggie?"

"How are you alike?"

"Same background. From the cage, to the wilds. Same instinct for survival." He winked. "And we're both so damn smart, it's enough to stun the senses."

"I'll brace myself against the shock. Will you please shift a few feet away from her? You may understand each other, but I'm the one who brought her home and I'm responsible for any damage she might do."

"If it makes you feel better." He carefully moved his leg from beneath Maggie's head so he wouldn't jar her, then continued to stroke her. "You do know that I have to leave this beauty and go to Dodsworth? My job is there now."

She nodded. "I called someone to take care of her. Eve Duncan and Joe Quinn are coming today."

"Indeed? It's going to be a bit cozy in this little cabin, isn't it?"

"I want to make sure you're not pulling your men away from here. I want Eve and Joe protected."

"I was going to send them to Dodsworth."

"Get someone else. Logan has plenty of money."

"Money can't buy training and the skill to—" He grinned. "What am I talking about? Of course it can. Isn't it lucky that I already have enough men at Dodsworth?"

"Then why were you giving me a hard time?"

"I felt obligated to try to get you to stay here. Logan does pay me, and it's what he wants."

"Where is Logan?"

"Out for a run with Monty. I think he needed to blow off a little steam after he left you."

She started to leave, then stopped. "You might call Franklin and tell him that I'm going to leave within the next fifteen minutes and head for Logan's house in Phoenix."

"Why?"

"I'll be closer to Bassett and I can wait there until he finishes his work. Logan appears to think he's important to Rudzak."

"You could wait here."

"It's also closer to the airport. I want to pick Eve and Joe up."

"Let one of my guys do it."

She shook her head. "I want to talk to her and Joe at the airport. They might decide to get right back on a plane."

"And if they don't, you'll bring them here?"

"No, I'll send them. As you pointed out, there's not much room here."

"Logan's going to be right on your heels."

"I'm not trying to run away from him. He can come with me if he likes. I'm going to have to go after him to pick up Monty anyway."

"I'm sure he'll be grateful."

He wouldn't be grateful. He'd be impatient and probably angry that she had taken the initiative.

Eve set down the phone after making her flight reservations and crossed over to the window to look out at the lake.

Joe was strolling along the bank with Jane at his side. He was looking down at her, listening intently to something she was saying. It was a bittersweet fact that Jane had grown closer to Joe since Bonnie had been found. But the slight estrangement might be for the best. Eve would overcome the problem with Jane and then they would be a true family.

Perhaps as soon as she got back from Phoenix the three of them would take a little trip together. In a vacation atmosphere Jane might talk more readily to her and they could get misconceptions ironed out.

After Phoenix. What was happening to Sarah and why was Logan with her?

Something bad is coming.

Her gaze lifted to the hill across the lake. "I hope not, baby. I hope not."

14

Sarah and Logan met Eve at the Phoenix airport that evening. Joe Quinn was not with her.

Eve held up her hand when Sarah opened her mouth to protest. "Jane is disturbed enough. I didn't want to take Joe away from her."

"Do you have luggage?" Logan asked.

Eve shook her head as she knelt to pet Monty. "I hoped I wouldn't need more than my carry-on." She looked at Sarah. "Will I?"

"I don't think so." Sarah frowned. "I wanted you to bring Joe. Did you tell him—"

"I told him you needed me to wolf-sit." She smiled as she rose to her feet. "After all, that's all I know. Right?" She started for the exit. "He didn't like the wolf bit, but he would really have been worried if I'd told him you wanted me to have a bodyguard. Joe's a little protective."

Logan snorted. "A little?"

"Maybe more than a little. That's not a bad thing." She glanced at Logan. "You're pretty protective yourself. I'm surprised you let Sarah get into a mess that—"

"I had no choice." Logan took her carry-on. "But she has one right now, and if you can talk her out of going to Dodsworth, I'll put you both on a plane to Atlanta."

"Dodsworth?"

"I'm not going to Atlanta." Sarah looked him in the eye. "And it's a dirty trick to try to use Eve to change my mind."

"Not nearly as dirty as what you're going to find at Dodsworth."

Eve said, "It would be nice if you'd let me know what's going on."

"I will." Logan swung open the door of Sarah's jeep. "I'm dropping Sarah off at the Phoenix house and I'll drive you to the cabin. There will be plenty of time to fill you in on the way."

"I'll drive her," Sarah said. "I brought her here. I should be the one to explain what's happening."

"Too bad. Joe's not here to ride shotgun, so I take over," Logan said. "And I want you under lock and key until I get back." His lips twisted. "You're the one who wanted to stay on top of Bassett. Maybe you can push him to finish a little faster."

"Eve's more important."

"Yes, she is." He started the jeep. "And I'll take good care of her. Do you doubt it?"

Sarah looked from one to the other. She could almost see the bond of memories and experiences that linked them together. She slowly shook her head. "No, you always did take good care of her."

"Then trust me to care for her now."

Her gaze shifted to Eve. "If you think there's any hint of danger after Logan tells you about Rudzak, I want you to go home. Don't stay. Okay?"

Eve smiled. "Don't worry, I'm staying clear of trouble these days. Life's dealt me a very good hand lately. I want to savor every play."

But Eve had come when Sarah had asked. "Remember that when Logan tells you about Dodsworth."

Fifteen minutes later Sarah stood outside the Phoenix house and watched Logan and Eve drive out the electronic gates. They were chatting casually as old friends...or lovers always did. She felt suddenly empty and alone. It was dumb to stand there, looking after them.

She would call Eve at the cabin and talk with her. Perhaps she'd call Joe too, and tell him what was going on. She'd make that judgment after she talked to Eve.

Another judgment. She didn't want to weigh lives and choices. She wasn't Solomon. She was just a search and rescue operator who tried to do the best she could. How had she gotten roped into—

"Thank heaven someone else is here to take over baby-sitting." Margaret marched toward her across the foyer. "I've got a thousand things to do, and I'm stuck with Bassett."

"Has he been a problem?"

"I guess not. He just doesn't know what's good for him and he won't listen to me."

"I'll help all I can."

"Well, at least a little. Logan placed the responsibility on me and I won't shirk it." Her gaze scanned Sarah's face. "Things not so good with you?"

Sarah shook her head.

"Well, then it's just as well that you're here. Nothing like regular meals and exercise to keep your nerves in check. I'll go dig Bassett out of his lab and we'll all go for a brisk walk around the grounds."

"I don't need—"

But Margaret was gone. Sarah shook her head resignedly. It seemed she was being established firmly under Margaret's wing. She should never have admitted anything was wrong.

Bassett came down the hall a few minutes later. "Hi, I'm glad you came back. It gets kind of lonely here."

It was the first time she'd seen him. He had been in his laboratory when Logan and Sarah had dropped off their suitcases. His hair was tousled and there were circles beneath his eyes. Evidently he'd been burning the midnight oil.

"I don't see how anyone could be lonely with Margaret around," she said.

"She's a cross between a mother and a dictator. She makes me eat, go for walks, and constantly interrupts my work."

"Good for her."

"But I could use some company who doesn't nag me twenty-four hours a day."

"Well, you shouldn't be lonely long. Logan says you're almost finished and should be heading for Dodsworth soon."

He went still. "Logan told you about Dodsworth?" A smile lit his face. "I'm glad. I didn't like closing you out after you helped me, but it was necessary. Artificial blood is a prime target for industrial espionage and—"

She held up her hand. "I've been over that with Logan. As long as there's no danger of anyone at Dodsworth being hurt, I'm not going to blow the whistle."

His smile faded. "We all knew what we were getting into when we took the job."

"You didn't know about Rudzak."

"No, I guess I didn't, but I'd still hire on to get in on the ground floor of this research."

"How close are you to completing your notes?"

"At least another five days. I'm working as hard as I can, but there are only so many hours in the day."

Her gaze narrowed on his face. "And you haven't spent very many of them sleeping."

"I told you, it's my dream. Maybe you can understand now that you know how important the project is."

"I do understand." She shook her head. "But you don't have to kill yourself."

"I'll survive. People are dying every day who could live if we meet our goal. It's worth a little exhaustion." He rubbed the back of his neck. "I try to take a walk every day to work out the kinks and clear my head. Want to come with me?"

"I thought that was Margaret's job. I don't want to hurt her feelings."

He made a face. "I guess she can come with us. I like to amble and she sets a pace like a Nazi drill sergeant."

"I'll come if you can wait until I give Monty some water."

"I'll wait. Maybe we'll even have a real conversation." He leaned against the doorjamb. "You know, I get a little lonesome with no one to talk to. My wife says I'm way too gregarious for a scientist." He chuckled. "Which means she thinks I'm a chatterbox. I tell her my work is so solitary that the floodgates just break open when I leave the lab."

"How is your wife?"

"Fine. I miss her. I call her every day, but it's not the same. She's taking our son to the Bahamas for a vacation this week. We went there on our honeymoon. I wish I were going with them. Do you know the scuba diving is fantastic off— I'm babbling, aren't I?"

"Well, you can babble all you please as soon as I get Monty his water. Neither one of us is a talker, but we're both good listeners."

"You say that as if your dog is human." Then he nodded. "Why not? He's part of your work and your work is your passion too."

"He's more than that. He's my friend."

"Lucky Monty," he said wistfully. "I haven't had much time for friends. I've barely had time to be a decent husband and father."

"You're young. You've got plenty of time." She motioned for Monty to precede her into the kitchen, then added grimly, "If you don't let Logan bulldoze you into another project like this one."

"Logan never bulldozes me. It's not his way."

"Not unless he thinks it's necessary." But she knew what he meant. Logan's usual way was charm and subtle maneuvering, which invariably got him what he wanted. Who should know better than she how powerful that spell could be? She had been caught and was still held fast by Logan.

"You're still angry with him? I hoped you'd realize what a great guy he is."

"I'm not angry." But she wanted to be. It would be so much easier if she didn't know Logan so well. But she'd seen his vulnerability, his humor and determination. Walking away from him would be difficult. What was she thinking? He would probably be the one to walk away from her. Their sleeping together meant nothing. Even now he was with a woman he'd had a relationship with not even a year ago. Who would be next year's woman?

"And I do admire him," she told Bassett. "I just don't think he's a hundred percent right a hundred percent of the time." She followed Monty into the kitchen. "I'll be back in a minute. I'll give Monty his drink and then we can get Margaret."

"If I didn't know you better, I'd swear you have no conscience, Logan," Eve said sternly. "You shouldn't have involved Sarah."

"You're preaching to the choir." Logan parked the car next to the cabin and turned off the ignition. "But it's too late now. I just have to do what I can to protect her."

"As long as you can also protect this Dodsworth. I wouldn't want that responsibility."

"Neither do I." His hands tightened on the steering wheel. "You know I'm no saint, Eve. I'm arrogant and selfish and more bullheaded than any man has a right to be. Years ago I made a mistake and let Rudzak live, and now I have to correct it. Dodsworth is the bait, and I have to run with it."

"If Sarah lets you."

"She'll let me. I'll make sure that security is so tight, she won't believe Rudzak has a chance."

She was silent a moment. "You said that Rudzak would target anyone close to you. Does that include me and my family?"

"I don't think that's likely. I've had two security guards watching your cottage since Rudzak surfaced, but it was only a precaution." His lips twisted in a wry smile. "He's not interested in past history."

"You'll always be my friend, Logan."

"I know, and that's enough for me." He paused. "Call Quinn and tell him to come. Sarah will feel better about it."

"What about you?"

"You'd probably all be safer here. You're under surveillance from the foothills and it's a clear view to the cabin. It's hard to guard that cottage in the woods. You found that out when you were dealing with that murderer who stalked you."

She shivered. "Rudzak couldn't be as clever as Dom."

"Don't bet on it. He fooled Sarah, and she's pretty canny."

"Yes." She frowned. "I'll think about it." She got out of the jeep and reached for her suitcase. "Don't get out. I'll introduce myself to Galen. I know you want to get back to Sarah. You seem worried about her."

"I am. All the time."

"But the guards at the Phoenix house are very—" She stopped, her gaze on his face. "My God."

He nodded. "No possibility that she's not a target." He said, mockingly, "Quinn would laugh. He always told me I didn't love you enough, that it had to be an obsession. I didn't understand then, but he was right, you know. It's an obsession."

"If anything happens to those people at Dodsworth, she'll hate you, Logan."

"I'll hate myself." He started the jeep. "Call her and tell her you're going to ask Quinn to come. She's worried enough about Dodsworth. She doesn't need to worry about you."

Logan's phone rang on the drive back to Phoenix.

"I met your Sarah," Rudzak said. "Did she tell you what an entertaining time we had together? She's an interesting woman. Not nearly as fascinating as Chen Li, but then, you never had the sophistication to appreciate her. It doesn't surprise me that you've formed an attachment to someone as blunt and straightforward as Sarah Patrick."

"She did a job for me. There's no attachment."

"It's too late to lie to me. I saw you together and I read you so well."

"You don't know jack. You haven't been around me for a long time. I'm not the man you knew all those years ago."

"You've matured, you're sharper, but the basics are still there. You become involved and you're pitifully sentimental when your sympathies are aroused. Look how unreasonable you became when I did what was best for Chen Li."

"I agree. It would have been far more reasonable to have broken your neck then. I'll have to do it now."

He laughed. "Then come and get me, Logan. Find me. I'm waiting for you. Oh, by the way, the comb wasn't for Sarah or anyone at Apache Lake. That was just a mere exercise, not worthy of Chen Li."

Logan stiffened. "Then why throw the comb in her jeep?"

"It wasn't for Sarah, Logan." He hung up.

15

"Where's Jane?" Eve fired the question at Logan as soon as he picked up the ringing phone the next morning. "You said they'd be safe. Damn you, where's Jane?"

"What?" Panic spiked through him. "What are you talking about?"

"I'm talking about Jane. Joe just called me and told me that Jane's missing."

"Missing from where?"

"My mother's house in Atlanta. Joe dropped her off there last night when I asked him to fly out here today. When my mother went into Jane's room to call her for breakfast, she was gone. Goddammit, you said they'd be safe."

"Was there any sign of forced entry?"

"No, I don't think so. Joe's on his way over there to talk to my mom and check out the house."

"Could she have run away? She's been upset lately."

"Not enough to run away."

That was Logan's impression too, but he'd been reaching. Any other explanation scared him shitless.

The comb wasn't for Sarah.

Rudzak's words had been clawing at him since the previous night.

Had it been for little Jane MacGuire?

"Why aren't you saying anything?" Eve demanded.

"I was thinking. Let me get off the phone and call Galen. He wouldn't have let Jane be dropped off without putting a guard on your mother's house."

"Then phone him and call me back." Eve's voice was uneven. "You get my Jane back, Logan. I won't lose another daughter." She hung up.

"What's wrong?" Sarah had come into the living room. "What about Jane?"

"She's disappeared from her grandmother's house." Logan was punching in Galen's number. "Eve's nearly frantic."

"Of course she is," Sarah said. "It must bring back Bonnie's kidnapping and all the horror that—"

"Galen, who the hell do you have in Atlanta? Jane MacGuire's missing."

"The kid? No way. I stationed two good men at her grandmother's last night. They would have reported anything wrong."

"Well, your two good men fouled up. She's missing. Call them and see what the hell they know." He hung up. "Galen didn't know anything about it. He said the house was guarded."

"Rudzak," Sarah whispered.

"I don't know."

"She's only a little girl, Logan." She shuddered. "But those kids at Apache Lake were just children, too, weren't they? He doesn't care."

"No, he doesn't care." His lips tightened. "But we shouldn't jump to conclusions."

"Why not? With that monster out there?" She reached for the phone. "I've got to call Eve."

"Not now."

"I brought her here. If she'd stayed with Jane, this might not have happened."

"And what are you going to say? That you're sorry? Is that going to make her feel better? Keep her line open in case someone needs to reach her."

"Like the police," she said dully. "Isn't that what they say when a child is missing?"

"Quinn is on the job, trying to find Jane. He'll be calling Eve as soon as he hears even a whisper." He paused. "It doesn't have to be Rudzak, Sarah."

"And this is just a coincidence? Isn't that what you told yourself about Kai Chi?"

He couldn't deny it. "Don't jump to conclusions."

She headed for the door. "Not until we find one of Chen Li's artifacts beside Jane's body?"

He was glad that she had left the room. He wasn't about to tell her what Rudzak had said, but she might have read something in his expression.

The comb wasn't for Sarah.

"Any news of the kid?" Margaret asked as she walked beside Sarah to the front door.

Sarah shook her head. "Galen's men swear they didn't see anyone near the house."

"That's good news."

"It only means Rudzak's smart. I can't wait any longer. I'm going to drive out to the cabin to see Eve."

"You can't do any good there."

"I can be there for her. For God's sake, it's almost dark and they found out she was gone this morning. I was hoping we'd hear something right away."

"Wait a little longer," Margaret coaxed. "We'll go for a stroll with Bassett, and if Logan hasn't found out anything by the time we return, you can scoot out of here and I'll cover for you with Logan."

"I don't need anyone to cover for me."

"Then you can cover for me for not doing my job and keeping your mind off Jane."

"Is that what Logan told you to do?"

Margaret shook her head as she opened the door. "Some jobs are implied. There's Bassett waiting already."

Sarah shrugged. Another fifteen minutes would do no harm. "Okay, once around the grounds."

"Super." Margaret passed Bassett at a fast clip and started for the back of the house. "Get the load off, Bassett. Get that circulation moving."

"Yes, ma'am." Bassett winked at Sarah as he followed Margaret. "Here I go again. The woman's the bane of my life." He sobered. "Logan told me about the little girl. Have you heard anything?"

Sarah shook her head as she fell into step with

303

him. "Galen flew to Atlanta this afternoon." And he and Joe should be meeting by now.

"She may be okay. Kids are funny. Maybe she's hiding or trying to make them worry about her."

"That's not Jane."

"Well, maybe her grandmother is making—"

"Hurry up." Margaret waved at a security guard standing by the front gate some distance away. "Hi, Booker. Did you ever see two worse wimps in your life than these two?"

The security guard grinned. "Do you really expect me to answer that?"

"Coward." Margaret started to turn onto the path leading around the house. "Come on, exercise isn't any good unless it raises your heart rate."

"Coming." Bassett's pace quickened. "Right behind you."

They weren't right behind her. Margaret actually was yards ahead of them. She turned and gave them a scornful wave. "I told you that you had to hustle to—" She stiffened, her gaze on the front gate. "Booker?"

The wolf was howling again. Eve felt like howling too.

Oh, God, let Jane be all right.

Go check on Maggie, make sure she's okay. It was something to do. She moved toward the back porch and stuck her head in the door. The wolf glared at her resentfully and raised her head to howl again.

304

"I can't help you," she whispered. "I can't bring them back."

And she couldn't help herself.

Or Jane.

Dammit, Logan, find her.

She stiffened as she heard a knock on the door.

She slowly moved across the room.

If they'd found her, they would have called immediately. People came in person to give you bad news. Policemen knocked on the door and said how sorry they were that your little girl was dead.

Bonnie.

No, this was Jane, and God wouldn't let it happen to her again. There had to be some universal law that forbade—

Another knock.

The wolf howled.

She leaned her forehead on the door for a moment. Face it. She stepped back and threw open the door.

Herb Booker was clinging to the gate, staring straight ahead. Blood was pouring from his shoulder. His whole body suddenly jerked.

"Christ, he's been shot." Bassett ran past Margaret down the driveway. "We've got to *help* him."

A shot? Panic surged through Sarah. "Bassett, stay away from the gates!"

"Drop to the ground." Margaret was already

running toward Bassett and the fallen Booker. "Stay low, Bassett."

"What the hell's happening? Booker's been—" Bassett spun around clutching his wrist.

Another shot.

And Sarah saw blood gushing from Margaret's chest as she slowly sank to her knees. "Sarah?" she whispered in disbelief.

Sarah screamed and ran toward her.

"Call security," Bassett said, dazed. He was clutching his wrist and blood was running through his fingers. "For God's sake, call—"

"Hit the ground and stay there," Sarah yelled at him. "You can't help. Monty, stay with him."

A bullet whistled by her cheek as she knelt beside Margaret, who had slumped to the ground. "Margaret?"

Margaret's eyes were staring straight ahead. "Stay...low..."

She was still giving orders, Sarah realized. Should she move her? What if the bullet shifted?

Help. She needed help.

She opened her mouth and screamed.

"I know you're going to be mad at me." Jane straightened her shoulders belligerently. "That's too bad. I'm here and I'm going to stay here. You can't just go away and not expect— Let me go. I can't breathe."

"Too bad." Eve's arms tightened around Jane's thin body. "I'm not letting go." She cleared her tight throat. "Well, not for a minute or two. Then I'm going to murder you."

"I knew you'd be mad. I would have told Joe or your mother, but I knew they would have stopped me from coming. They think I'm a kid."

"You are a kid, dammit."

Jane looked at her.

"Okay." Jane was no more a child than Eve had been at her age. They had both grown up on the streets where youth had been stolen from them. "Then you should have been adult enough not to worry me to death."

"You wouldn't have let me come." She stepped back. "And I'm here now. You should call Joe and tell him I'm here, shouldn't you?"

"Yes." She didn't want to move. She didn't want to stop looking at her daughter. "How did you get here?"

"I bought an electronic ticket on the Internet and charged it to your credit card. I owe you money."

"They let you on the airplane by yourself?"

"I managed. Is that the wolf howling? Where is she?"

"On the back porch. And how did you get here from the airport?"

"I hitchhiked." She held up her hand to stop Eve's protests. "I know it's dangerous. I picked an old man and his wife and they lectured me all the way here. They stayed outside in their truck until you opened the door. I want to see the wolf." She started toward the door Eve had indicated. "You call Joe and then you can yell at me later."

"Count on it." She headed for the phone. "And stay away from Maggie. She's crabby."

"Why?"

"I think she's lonely."

Jane looked at her over her shoulder. "That's a bad thing to be. It...hurts."

"Yes, it does."

Jane looked away. "Call Joe."

Another shot tore by Sarah's ear as she huddled over Margaret's body, both hands pressing above the wound.

"Sarah!" Logan was running toward her from the house with Juan Lopez behind him. "Get yourself and Margaret into the trees, dammit."

"I'm going to. Go take care of Bassett and Booker. They've both been shot."

"Lopez, call 911," Logan shouted.

There was a screech of tires outside the gate, and a dark Camaro tore down the street.

Lopez ran out the gate and stood looking after it. "Son of a bitch."

"Forget him. Call 911."

"Is she going to be okay?" Bassett was standing over Margaret, still clutching his wrist. "This shouldn't have happened. I thought we were safe here. Is she going to live?"

"She's going to be fine." Oh, God, she couldn't stop the blood. "Don't you dare fall asleep, Margaret. Stay with us."

· · ·

Eve walked to the back porch and stood beside Jane in the doorway. "I called Logan but couldn't get an answer. I left a message on his voice mail. You've caused him a world of trouble. I was able to get hold of Joe. He's hopping the next plane. He says he's going to scalp you. I told him I'd tie you to the stake for him."

"She's beautiful, isn't she?" Jane's gaze was fastened on the wolf. "But you're right, she's crabby. It's a good thing I'm here to take care of her."

"You?"

"Joe didn't like you being here with the wolf. I could tell. So I came to take care of her."

"And me?"

Jane's gaze shifted to Eve. "Sure. This is something I can do. I'm not Bonnie. I'll never be Bonnie to you. I don't think I'd want to be her. I talked to your mother about her, and Bonnie was so nice, I don't even know if I'd have liked her."

"You'd have liked her."

"Maybe. But I know I like you." She looked back at the wolf. "Maybe I even…love you."

"That's nice. I know I love you."

Jane nodded. "I went up on the hill and visited Bonnie's grave after you left yesterday afternoon."

Eve went still. "Why did you do that?"

"I don't know. I just did. And I decided it doesn't matter that you still love her. I'm

309

not nice like she was, but I can do things for you that she couldn't. She wouldn't have been able to take care of you like I can. I'm smart and I know the same things that you do. That's got to mean something."

"It means a great deal."

"So you're lucky to have me."

"Oh, yes."

Jane gave her a disparaging glance. "You're not going to cry?"

Eve shook her head. "I wouldn't think of it." She cleared her throat. "When you're only being sensible."

"Good. Crying would be silly." Jane walked toward the wolf. "Now show me what to do to take care of Maggie."

Sarah tensed as Logan walked into the hospital waiting room. "Is she going to live?"

"I don't know. They were able to get the bullet out, but she's in critical condition. It'll be touch and go for a while." He sat down and buried his face in his hands. "I just don't know."

She was silent a moment. "She's been with you a long time."

"Almost fifteen years." He raised his head to reveal a haggard face. "We've worked together for so long, she's like family. But I didn't think Rudzak— I thought she'd be safe."

"She was behind electric fences with security guards."

"It shouldn't have happened. I should have been more careful. I should have stopped her and Bassett from taking those walks."

"It was safe as long as they stayed away from the gates. That's the only place where there's a clear view to get a shot. You couldn't know that the shooter would target Booker first to draw us to the gates."

"That doesn't mean I'm not responsible. I should have—"

"Shut up, Logan." She took his hand and held it between hers. "You did the best you could. You're not a fortune-teller and you're sure not God. So stop blaming yourself."

He smiled with an effort. "Thanks for the sweet words."

"You want sweet?" She blinked the tears back. "Sorry. I can only be myself. If I could take this away from you, I would. At least Booker and Bassett are going to be okay. The doctor said Booker is being taken off the serious list, and Bassett's only got a nasty wound in the hand."

"He's pretty shaken up. He wants to finish the research at Dodsworth."

"He knows Dodsworth may not be safe either."

"He'd rather take his chances there. I tend to agree. Dodsworth is safer." He stood up. "I need to move. Do you want some coffee from the machine?"

She shook her head.

"I'm having Lopez pack your bag. Galen's going to pick you and Bassett up and take you to Dodsworth."

"Me?"

"I have to stay here, and I want you where Galen can protect you. He has to be at Dodsworth."

"Did it occur to you that I might want to stay with you?" she asked unevenly.

"It occurred to me. In spite of your lack of tender feelings for me." He gently touched her cheek. "But if you want to help me, you'll go to Dodsworth. I don't need to worry about you too."

"I don't want to—"

"What about all those people at Dodsworth? Have you forgotten you may have to blow the whistle on me?"

"I haven't forgotten."

"Then go and make sure Galen is doing his job. I'll be there as soon as Margaret takes a turn for the better."

Dammit, he was in pain and she didn't want to leave him. She wanted to hold him and get him through this horrible night as he had held her after Apache Lake.

"Rudzak is going to be at Dodsworth, Sarah. I couldn't be more sure. And I don't need you or want you here." He left the room.

She caught up with him halfway down the corridor. "Don't you dare try that bull with me." She spun him around, her arms around his waist, and she hugged him with fierce strength. "I won't let you. You do want me here. I know you care something about me and I could help you." Her arms fell away from him. "But I'm going to Dodsworth. To make sure nothing happens to those people so you won't end up feeling guilty for the rest of your miserable life." She stepped back. "I'm going to Bassett's room. Tell Galen to pick me up there."

The ivory mirror was in the shape of an ankh. An asp was intricately carved around the teakwood handle. It had been his last present to Chen Li.

It would be his last present to Logan.

"An ankh?" Chen Li held up the mirror. "It's the symbol of immortality, isn't it?"

"That's why I brought it to you. To show you that you'll live forever."

She made a face. "I don't feel immortal at the moment, Martin. Though I'm much better than I was last week. Maybe I am getting well after all."

She wasn't getting well. Sitting there in that chair by the window, she looked thin and weak and pale. She would never be the same Chen Li again. Death was stealing her from him just as Logan had stolen her. And Logan would keep her his until the very end, giving her hope and yet telling Rudzak that she was not well enough to see him. "Did you go to sleep early last night? Logan said I couldn't come in."

She looked away. "I was a little tired."

"The weariness will go away soon." He stepped behind her and put his hands on her shoulders. "This mirror is very special. It belonged to a high priest. It will make you live forever."

"Perhaps we should tell my doctors about it. They

313

could use a little help." She leaned forward and his hands fell away. She was trying to avoid his touch, he realized with incredulous fury. She was already lost to him.

But he could get her back. He could take her away from Logan.

"Let's try it," he said. "Look in the mirror."

"I don't like what I see in any mirror these days."

"But you should. You're beautiful."

"Yes, sure. That's what John says."

He didn't want to hear what Logan said. This moment was his alone. "Because it's true." He bent over her and put his hands on her nape. "You can see it in my eyes. Look in the mirror. If you won't look at your reflection, look at mine and you'll know that you'll live forever and always be as beautiful as you are to me at this moment. Lift the mirror."

She slowly lifted the mirror. "Why, Martin, what's wrong? There are tears in—"

The mirror fell from her hand as he snapped her neck with one violent twist.

"Good-bye, Chen Li." He tenderly kissed her cheek, then picked up the mirror. "Good-bye, my love."

He tucked the tissue paper carefully around the mirror and placed it in the box. He slipped the note he'd written on top of the mirror and closed the lid.

He addressed the box to Sarah Patrick at Dodsworth.

Had he heard something?

A door swinging shut?

Probably not. He'd been imagining sounds in this creaky old building all evening, Bill Ledwick thought. When you were as bored as he was, your imagination had a field day. He'd be glad to get back with the guys at the facility.

Better check the sound. Galen didn't like anyone taking anything for granted.

He got up from his chair and moved down the long, dark corridor.

Silence except for the soft thud of his rubber soles on the marble floor.

He paused at the glass door of the record room. He stepped to one side and threw open the door. He waited a minute and then reached in and flipped on the light.

No one was in the room.

Of course not. Imagination.

Check. Just to make sure.

He moved to the file cabinet across the room and pulled open the drawer. He knew exactly where the file was kept. He'd checked it often enough.

He opened the file folder.

Shit!

"I heard from my man at the courthouse," Galen said when he called Logan the next day. "The blueprints of the facility disappeared from the record department."

Logan was silent a moment. "I thought that would happen. Rudzak's not the type to rely on a truckload of dynamite parked near his target. No random hits for him. He wants to be sure of me."

"Then he should have had his hired gun shoot you instead of Margaret."

"That wouldn't have satisfied him. It's not a big enough statement. He wants to bury me at Dodsworth like I buried him in that prison. A final tribute to both him and Chen Li."

"How is Margaret doing?"

"Not out of danger, but better. They're going to let me see her in a few minutes. Her folks got in from San Francisco last night and they let her brothers visit her in intensive care." He paused. "How's Sarah?"

"A pain in my ass. She and Monty have been over every inch of the facility looking for cracks in my security. She knows emergency procedures better than my second-in-command, and I think she's memorized every corridor in the damn building."

"Did she find any cracks?"

There was a hesitation. "One. But it was more of a hairline fracture."

"So she's satisfied that Dodsworth's safe?"

"Yes, but now she doesn't see why Rudzak would persist in targeting it."

"Tell her about the blueprints."

"I'll tell her. She may still worry about all your other facilities."

"Your job is to keep her from worrying."

"Until she makes another one of her four A.M. inspection tours." His tone was distinctly sour. "I'd rather take care of Maggie. When are you coming to get her out of my hair?"

"I'll be there as soon as I can, but I assure you that Rudzak isn't going to start without me. No word from him?"

"Just the missing blueprints. That's a pretty decisive statement. Give Margaret my best." He hung up.

Logan slipped the phone in his pocket and headed for intensive care. It was no surprise that Sarah was giving Galen a hard time. She wouldn't care how much she liked someone if it got in the way of her job and, in this case, her job was to keep Dodsworth from becoming a disaster area.

"What are you doing here?" Margaret's voice was only a breath of sound, which he could barely hear from where he stood in the doorway.

He crossed the room and took her hand in his. "How are you feeling?"

"Like shit." She glared at him. "And mad. Why are you here moaning and groaning instead of going after the asshole who shot me? Did you think I was going to die?"

"The thought never occurred to me."

"Liar. But I'm not going to die and"—she had to pause to get her breath—"and I have enough problems with my brothers being overprotective. So get out of here."

He stood looking at her.

"Okay, okay, I promise I won't die, John."

She showed her teeth with tigerlike ferocity. "And instead of flowers, why don't you send me Rudzak's head?"

"I'll do my best."

"Good." She closed her eyes. "Now get out of here. I'm tired."

"Shall I call a nurse?"

"His head, John." She didn't open her eyes. "Stop standing there worrying and just get out of here and bring me his head."

"Yes, ma'am." He turned toward the door. "Right away, ma'am."

7:45 P.M.

"Joe got here yesterday," Eve told Sarah on the phone. "He's going to be here as long as you need me. Do you have any idea yet how long that will be?"

"I wish I did."

"No problem. I just like the idea of being home with my family."

"Jane is okay now?"

"No thanks to me. She worked it out for herself... I think."

"What do you mean?"

"It's funny how clear and simple everything is when you don't let baggage get in the way. What are you doing there at Dodsworth?"

"Keeping myself busy."

"Is the security as good as you hoped?"

"Better. And that bothers me. Why would Rudzak think he could take down this facility?"

318

"You're afraid he'll target another place?"

"I seem to be the only one. Galen and Logan think the stolen blueprints are cast-iron proof. I'm afraid it might be a red herring."

"Logan's nobody's fool."

"I know that. It's just—" She stopped, frustrated. "I'm afraid we're on the wrong track. It doesn't smell right."

Eve chuckled. "You sound like Monty on a search."

"Monty's usually right."

"I'm the last one to disagree. You should follow your instincts. I've got to go. Time to feed Maggie."

It was time to feed Monty too. "Come on, boy." Sarah hung up the phone and headed toward the cafeteria with Monty at her heels. She'd packed one of the kitchen cabinets with his food and vitamins, and she tried to feed him in the evening when he wasn't distracted by the constant attention of the scientists. Monty was already practically a mascot, and he'd rather have gotten belly rubs than eat.

Bassett was sitting at a table, and he looked up when Sarah came into the room. "Got time to sit down and have a cup of coffee with me?"

She shook her head. "I just came to feed Monty. I'm nervous enough without the caffeine."

"Are you? I feel a lot safer here." He got to his feet and followed Sarah and Monty into the kitchen. "Funny. I felt fine until that last day in Phoenix. Have you heard how Margaret's doing?"

"She's still alive."

"I complained a lot about her, but I really liked her."

"I know. How do you like your lab here?"

"Fine. They've assigned Hilda Rucker to work with me. She's brilliant." He wrinkled his nose as he looked down at his bandaged left hand. "And she's got two good hands to operate the computer. That's nothing to sneeze at." He finished his coffee in one swallow. "I'd better get back to the grind. Hilda's no Margaret, but I can't let her get ahead of me. Let me know about Margaret."

"I will."

Galen passed him at the kitchen door and gave him a casual nod before coming toward Sarah. "Logan's on his way. He just called and told me that Margaret had kicked him out. He should be here within a few hours."

"Good." She leaned down and put Monty's dinner before him. "Then she's better?"

"Well, it's clear she's functioning in her usual manner." He made a face. "I'm glad she's in Phoenix. I don't need another high-powered woman here."

"Yes you do. But you'll have to be satisfied with me. Speaking of high-powered females, I talked to Eve a little while ago. She thinks Maggie is either pouting or mourning. She won't stop howling."

"Then why don't you go home and take care of your wolf yourself?"

320

She gave him a sly glance. "Maybe I should send for Maggie and Eve, have them come here instead."

"Forget it." He headed for the door. "I'm out of here."

"Can't take the heat?" But he'd already gone.

The large kitchen was suddenly cavernous and lonely. Her smile faded as she leaned on the counter and watched Monty eat. Sparring with Galen was an outlet she badly needed. The tension was growing with every hour, and she needed it over.

Monty looked up at her. *Sad?*

She shook her head as she filled his water bowl. Not sad, uneasy. And lonely. It was strange how lonely you could feel when you're apart from one special individual. "Eat your dinner. You haven't eaten decently since we left the cabin."

Sad.

"This is our job. I had to take you away from Maggie."

Sad.

"Heaven save me from a lovesick—" Why was she blaming Monty, when she'd been mooning around herself only a few minutes before? "It's okay," she whispered as she reached down to scratch behind his ear. "I know it's bad, but we've got to go on. Now eat your dinn—"

"Sarah."

She turned to see Galen standing in the doorway. "Why did you come ba—" She stiffened. "What's wrong?"

321

"A package for you." He crossed the room and handed her a neatly wrapped box. "It just came. Special delivery."

All packages coming into the facility were X-rayed. "What is it?"

He shrugged. "I couldn't tell. Something weird. But it's not an explosive."

She slowly took off the wrap and opened the lid. The object inside was old, very old, the ivory yellowed by time, but the gold-sheeted mirror still shone. She felt her stomach clench. "Chen Li."

Galen stiffened. "I was afraid of that. Don't read the note. Maybe we'd better save it for Logan."

"It's addressed to me." She unfolded the paper.

Sarah,
 As I told Logan, the last gift wasn't for you. This one is far more fitting. Notice the asp? You can share it with Logan.
                                    Martin Rudzak

16

8:20 P.M.

Just one more charge to go.

Duggan carefully set the plastic explosive high in a cleft in the column so it wouldn't be visible.

Now get down.

Get out.

And watch the damn place blow.

10:05 P.M.

"Just what am I sharing with you?" Sarah asked as she and Galen watched Logan read the note. All the blinds were drawn in the first-floor conference room, and Monty lay a few feet from Sarah. "Is the mirror Chen Li's?"

"Probably. But I've never seen it. The nurses told me Rudzak was carrying a box when he went into Chen Li's hospital room the night he killed her."

"And what does it mean?"

"If it's the last thing he gave her, it means he's growing impatient. He wants to put an end to this." His hand tightened on the mirror. "Thank God. So do I."

So did Sarah, but the idea also terrified her. "Then is Dodsworth—"

323

Logan's phone rang. He listened to the caller for a moment. "Right. I understand." He hung up and turned to Galen. "Rudzak's going to move. Clear the building. How many people are working tonight?"

"Twelve."

"Get them out of here. Then tell your guys to do a tour and get out too."

"I'm on my way." Galen headed out of the room at a run.

"Shall I call the bomb squad and ATF?" Sarah asked.

"Galen will do it." He touched her cheek. "It's okay, Sarah. The building will be cleared before anything happens. We have a little time."

"How do you know? Is that what Rudzak told you on the phone? Then you can expect the liar to blow it in the next few minutes."

"Rudzak's been planning this a long time. There's no one more methodical. He's taking it step by step. Trust me. No one's going to get hurt."

"How can I trust you, when you never tell me anything? Why didn't you tell me about Rudzak saying that comb wasn't for me?"

"Why worry you? I was worried enough for both of us."

"Are there other things you haven't told me?" He didn't answer.

"Ever since I met you, I've been fighting your secrets. You didn't tell me about Kai Chi either."

"Don't do this to me now, Sarah."

"Why not? It's important. You always have to be the big, strong hero. Well, I'm tired of it. What about sharing? And treating me as a partner? I'm not fragile like Chen Li. You don't have to take care of—"

"Be quiet." He gripped her shoulders and shook her. "Don't throw Chen Li in my face."

"I don't have to. Dear God, Rudzak is making sure that neither one of us forgets her."

"Listen to me." He stared directly into her eyes. "I'm no longer the person who married Chen Li, but I'm grateful for what she gave me."

"I know you are. You and she were—"

"Dammit, shut up. You don't know anything. I love you. I want to spend my life with you. I've never felt like this about anyone else, and I'm not going to let anything happen to you." He kissed her hard. "And I'm going to take care of you whether you like it or not. You go out when the security team does."

She watched dazedly as he walked away from her. "The hell I will," she called after him. "Rudzak wants me here. He may not come if I leave."

He walked out the door without looking back.

"Where are you—" She ran after him, Monty at her heels, but Logan had vanished around the corner.

She had no intention of leaving, but there was no time for arguing. There were people to get out of the building.

"Come on, Monty. Let's get everyone out of here." Monty followed her as she walked quickly to the lab on the ground floor where Kevin Janus was working.

Her uneasiness was growing. The whole situation was like a puzzle with key pieces missing. It shouldn't be happening like this. It didn't smell right.

You sound like Monty on a search.

You should follow your instincts.

She had no choice. There was no time to do anything but rely on instinct.

Okay, put your uneasiness on the back burner. But try to find the cone, try to find the source.

Before it is too late.

10:35 P.M.

The building was emptying. The parking lot was almost deserted.

"You shouldn't have sent them the warning," Duggan told Rudzak as they sat in the car watching. "They're scattering like scared mice."

"And you prefer the mice caught in the trap." Rudzak lowered the binoculars. "I'm willing to let a few unimportant people scamper away. The mice that count are still inside, Duggan. Where did you set the charge?"

"Where you told me. In the basement lab. The drainage tunnel was right where the blueprint said it would be. I was in and out in fifteen minutes. But you should have had me put the charge on a timer. That would be a lot safer."

"I don't want it to be safe. I want to be there, looking at his face when I tell him what's coming." He smiled. "You can understand that. You get a thrill from pressing the trigger yourself."

"Not while I'm sitting on top of a pile of explosives."

"But you said I'd have no trouble getting out the drainage tunnel. In and out in fifteen minutes?"

Duggan nodded.

"And you have the switch in the trunk? Get it for me, will you, Duggan?"

"Sure." He got out of the car, and when he returned, he handed the switch over. "It's real sweet. And I made sure it wasn't hair trigger. I didn't want you blowing yourself up by accident."

"Thank you for your concern, Duggan." He leisurely got out of the driver's seat. "But I really don't want you to have to worry about me anymore."

Rudzak shot him in the head.

11:10 P.M.

Darkness.

Logan stopped in the doorway, tensing. He knew what was ahead in that darkness. When his eyes became accustomed to the blackness, he'd be able to see Rudzak. He could almost feel the waves of hate bombarding him from the depths of that room.

But the verbal threat didn't come from the darkness. It came from behind him.

"Go on." The barrel of a pistol was suddenly pressed against his spine. "Move, Logan."

11:45 P.M.

Four labs cleared. Three to go.

Sarah and Monty hurried down the hall.

Galen's men had already cleared the seven scientists out of the second-floor lab by the time she and Monty got there. Next stop—Hilda Rucker and Tom Bassett on the third floor.

She ran into Hilda Rucker on the stairs. The gray-haired woman was carrying a boxful of files. "I know. They told me to get out and I will be in two minutes."

"You stopped to grab those files?"

"Do you think I want my work blown to smithereens?"

Logan was right. These people were as committed to the project as he was. "Where's Bassett?"

"Right behind me. He came back to the lab just after Galen's men left and I told him about the evacuation. He was dumping computer disks into his briefcase when I left."

"And probably throwing files into boxes like you did. I'd better get him out of there right now." She continued up the stairs.

She'd get Bassett out and then—

Get Bassett out.

Protect Bassett.

She stopped short.

Sweet Jesus.

Her phone rang as she started up again.

"Get out of there, Sarah," Galen said as soon as she picked up.

"Damn you, Galen. You and Logan both knew, didn't you?"

Silence and then, "Get out of there, Sarah."

"Go to hell." She hung up and took the rest of the stairs two at a time with Monty at her heels.

Protect Bassett.

Keep Bassett safe.

"Bassett!"

He came out of the lab carrying his brief-case. "Sarah, I was just going to call you. I ran into Logan a few minutes ago and he wants you to come with me to—" He stopped as he saw her expression. "I see. It's not going to be as easy as I thought, is it? You're a very smart lady. I was afraid you might figure it out. Too bad you did."

"You're the Judas, aren't you? Rudzak had you planted from the beginning. He wanted us to rescue you. He wanted us to get you out of Santo Camaro so that he could use you to set up Dodsworth." And set up Logan. Her heart stopped. "Where's Logan? It was you who called him, wasn't it?"

He nodded. "I told him I'd received a threat from Rudzak and asked him to meet at the base-

329

ment lab. Naturally, he came." He smiled. "We all know how Rudzak's targeted me in the past." He took a gun out of his jacket pocket. "But Rudzak also wants you with Logan, so I'll have to oblige."

"How much did he pay you?"

"More than Castleton. Even though Castleton brought me on board. I deserved it. Rudzak suddenly got impatient so he gave me an excuse to leave Phoenix right away. The bastard didn't tell me he was going to shoot me too." He motioned with the gun. "We'd better get going. Rudzak doesn't want to blow this building without you, but he may get edgy. I don't want to be here if he does."

She didn't move.

"Should I shoot your dog first?"

"No!" She started down the steps. "If I agree to go with you, is it all right if I send Monty to Galen?"

"You're afraid he'll be blown up?"

"There's no reason for him to be hurt." She stopped and turned to face him. "Let him go."

He shrugged. "It doesn't matter. I don't want to deal with him anyway. Send him away."

"Monty! Go to—" She launched herself up the stairs and dove low, grabbing Bassett's gun hand. "Monty!"

Monty buried his teeth in Bassett's wrist as Sarah grabbed his bandaged hand and pushed the fingers back.

He screamed in agony and dropped the gun. She scooped it up and hit him in the face with the butt. Blood spurted from his gashed lip. "Bastard." She hit him again with the gun. "Son of a bitch."

He doubled over in pain.

"Sarah!"

She saw Galen running toward them. She told Monty, "Release."

Monty reluctantly let go of Bassett's wrist.

"Excuse me." Galen stepped in front of her and gave Bassett a lethal chop on the carotid artery. "We don't want him interfering. My, that felt good." He looked down at Monty. "I never thought I'd see that ball of fluff on the attack."

"He doesn't like guns pointed at me."

"Maybe I shouldn't have worried so much when I ran into Hilda Rucker at the front door and she told me you were going to see Bassett. You and Monty seem to have everything under control."

"Nothing's under control." She started down the steps. "Logan's in the basement lab. If you didn't know already."

"I knew."

"And you and Logan knew all about Bassett."

"Not at first. We only suspected. But we confirmed when we found out that his calls to his wife were being forwarded to another number."

"That's why no matter how tight the security, you knew Rudzak would strike here. He had someone on the inside feeding him information about security checks and opening all the doors."

331

"Yes, that's what tipped you off, wasn't it? I knew it bothered you."

"Then why the hell didn't someone tell me?"

"Sarah, you're many things, but deceitful isn't one of them. You'd never have been able to look Bassett in the face and pretend you didn't know."

"So Logan is down there alone with Rudzak."

"You can't go down there, Sarah. That's what Rudzak wants."

"Watch me."

Galen's hand closed on her shoulder. "I promised Logan that I'd get you out of here."

"Then you lied through your teeth, because I won't—"

Darkness.

12:05 A.M.

"You're being very docile, Logan," Rudzak said. "I wonder why."

"It could be the gun in your hand."

"Yes, that would have a dampening effect. Then there's the fact that your feet and hands are tied up. And you're lying on the floor like an animal ready for slaughter."

"Or it could be that this building is crawling with security men and one of them will come bursting in here any minute and butcher you." Logan smiled. "I'm visualizing that possibility with great pleasure."

"I'd kill you first." He smiled back. "But

that's not going to happen. I've planned this too well. We'll just wait for your Sarah and then begin. I'm hoping the blast won't kill you immediately, but it probably will. If the blast doesn't kill you, then you'll still be crushed. I had Duggan plant the explosives at the top of those columns. The girders holding up this section of the building will topple like dominos."

"Another tribute to Chen Li."

"The last one."

"No, you'll be the last one. They'll catch you and send you back to prison. You'll die there."

Rudzak shook his head. "I'll get away from here the same way I got in—through an old trapdoor leading to a drainage tunnel beneath the building. I have a plane waiting for me at a small airport outside town. I'll be gone before anyone bothers to look for me. They'll be too busy trying to dig your body out of the wreckage."

"Don't count on it. Galen's smart and he's my friend."

"I was very tempted to include Galen in my plans, but it wasn't practical. Perhaps I'll have a chance at him later." He checked his watch. "Bassett is being very slow."

"Maybe he's tipped his hand. Sarah's not stupid."

"No, but Bassett says she likes him, and it's hard to suspect people you like." He smiled again. "You liked Bassett too, didn't you?"

"Wouldn't he have been here already if something hadn't gone wrong? Galen was ordered to clear the building. That would include Bassett. If Bassett objected, it would have sent up a red flare. Galen's not like Sarah, he suspects everyone."

Rudzak frowned. "You're trying to make me uneasy. Are you willing to give up your final moments to save the woman?"

Logan didn't answer.

"Maybe you are. You always were a fool." His frown cleared. "I'll wait a little longer. It may be worth it."

"Good." Push him, make him uncertain, make him uneasy. And hope Galen managed to get Sarah out of the facility. "Every minute you spend here will make it easier for Galen to catch you."

Rudzak hesitated and then shook his head. "We'll wait."

Five minutes.

Ten minutes.

Logan was staring at him. Where was his fear? Rudzak had wanted him afraid. Would he be afraid at that final moment?

And where was Bassett?

"He's not coming." Logan was reading his expression. "But Galen will come. He should be wondering now where I am."

Rudzak made a decision. "I don't need Sarah Patrick. I can always get her later." He walked over to Logan. "And I will get her, Logan. Think about that when those columns come crashing down." He opened his duffel bag. "I have a present for you. I was going to make the mirror my final gift, but I changed my mind. I decided that this should be the final resting place for all my other gifts to Chen Li." He pulled out a large teakwood box. "So I put the other six treasures I gave her in this box and a little something else besides." He opened the lid to reveal four sticks of dynamite beneath the artifacts.

Logan stiffened. "I hate to pun, but isn't that overkill?"

A response at last. Logan was trying to hide it, but the shock was clear.

"When I'm in the drainage tunnel, I'll blow the charges Duggan set in here. But that's a little unimaginative for me. So I want you to watch this fuse creep closer and closer." He placed the box beside one of the columns nearest Logan and unwound the fuse as he made his way across the lab toward the door. He stopped there and leaned down to light the fuse. "It's a slow-burning fuse. You won't know which one of the charges will take you out first, Duggan's or mine. You have about three minutes. Lie there and count the seconds." He took a last look at Logan. Logan's expression was grim, but he still didn't see fear, he realized in frustration. "Good-bye, Logan, you're going to die."

"If I do, then Chen Li will welcome me. I did all I could to save her. She wouldn't welcome you, Rudzak. You murdered her. She'd hate your guts."

"You lie. I *saved* her." He slammed the door and ran down the steps. Moments later he was in the drainage pipe.

• • •

Shit.

Logan stared at the bright glow of the burning fuse.

Think. Don't panic.

Don't panic when the damn lab might fall down on top of him any minute? His heart was pounding so hard, it felt ready to jump out of his chest.

Find a safer spot.

He started crawling across the floor.

Rudzak's footsteps echoed as he ran down the drainage tunnel.

What Logan said wasn't true. Chen Li would never hate him. It was Logan, not Chen Li, who thought that everything Rudzak and she had together was ugly and strange.

Another two minutes and it would be safe for him to press the switch. Logan would die.

And the memory of Logan and Chen Li together would die with him. Then Rudzak would remember only Chen Li, the way she had been before Logan had come along.

One minute.

He reached in his pocket and took out the switch. One more minute, Chen Li.

He ran faster.

Only a little while longer, Chen Li.

Soon, beloved.

Soon...

• • •

Sarah opened her eyes to black sky and trees overhead. She was lying on grass and Monty's head was on her arm.

And Galen was towering above her, talking to someone.

He must have felt her gaze on him, because he looked down. "Sorry." His tone was tense. "I had to get you out of there."

She vaguely remembered his hand on her shoulder. A pinprick... "You drugged me."

"Only the lightest sedative, or you'd still be out."

"You drugged— Logan!" She sat upright.

"I think Logan's fine."

"You think?" She looked around her. Grass. Men. A concrete drainage pipe. "Where are we?"

"Outside the facility."

"And Logan's still inside?"

"It's been only ten minutes."

"With Rudzak." She scrambled to her knees. "Why haven't you gone after him?"

"We're waiting."

"Waiting?"

He nodded at the drainage pipe. "That was the way Rudzak got into the facility."

"Then go after him, dammit."

"Logan told us to wait."

"What do you mean? He's going to blow—"

The earth shook beneath her before she heard the blast.

The drainage pipe erupted into a fireball of flying concrete and smoke.

"*No!*" She was on her feet and running toward the drainage pipe.

Galen tackled her before she reached it. "Sarah, it's okay. This is what Logan wanted."

She gazed at him in horror. "He wanted to be blown to bits? Are you crazy?"

"Logan's not suicidal. It wasn't the facility that blew, it was the drainage pipe. We knew about the explosives planted in the basement lab and we moved them to the pipe. Rudzak should have been in the pipe when he pressed the switch."

Hope surged through her. "The lab didn't blow?"

"No, just the drainage tunnel."

"You knew Rudzak was coming through that pipe, but you didn't call the police."

Galen was silent a moment. "Logan didn't want him caught and put in a jail somewhere. He wanted him dead. He made the mistake before of not killing him. He wasn't going to do it this time."

"So he made himself bait? What if Rudzak killed him before he left the lab?"

"Logan didn't think that's what he had in—"

"What if Logan was wrong?" She was starting to shake. "How can anyone guess what that son of a—"

Another explosion rocked the earth.

Sarah stared in shock at the building. The

smoke was clearing to reveal that not only the drainage pipe had been blown. She whispered, "Is it the lab?"

Galen was cursing. It was answer enough.

12:55 A.M.

The firemen were blowing out the drainage pipe, trying to clear it of dust and lethal gases. Sarah's nails dug into the palms of her hands as she watched them.

"It shouldn't have happened," Galen said. "My guys aren't careless. They wouldn't have missed any of the charges in that lab."

"Well, it did happen," she said dully. "And Logan will be lucky if he's not underneath a ton of wreckage. Even if he's alive, I don't know how the hell anyone's going to get to him. That corner of the building collapsed."

Monty pressed closer to her legs and looked up at her. *Find?*

She reached down and stroked his head. *Find?*

Yes, keep hope alive even if she was scared to death. So, stop standing there, shaking. There might be a way. Sweet Jesus, she hoped there was a way. "Find." She started toward the fire department rescue command post with Monty trotting after her.

"Where are you going?" Galen called.

"To do my job."

• • •

Christ, it was dark.

Monty was crawling ahead of her through the rubble in the drainage pipe. She could barely see him, but he was crawling steadily. He knew where he was going, he had the cone.

But that didn't mean Logan was alive.

Don't think about that. When they got through this pipe, they'd find Logan and he'd be alive. Repeat it like a mantra.

He is alive.

He is alive.

He is alive.

She could hardly breathe. She checked the monitor she wore around her neck. No lethal gases. It must be the concrete dust...and fear.

Digging her elbows into the rubble, she slowly made her way forward.

"Okay, Sarah?" It was Donner at the command post, speaking through her wire.

No, it wasn't okay. She was terrified. But she said, "No problem. There are more air pockets than I thought there'd be. And I haven't found any weak spots I wasn't able to shore up."

"That doesn't mean you won't. Don't be a hot dog. You should get out of there and let us go in."

She couldn't do that, not when she knew they'd be forced to take precautions that would eat up time. Logan's time. "No problem," she repeated.

Monty gave a low moan.

She knew that sound. Oh, God, he'd found something.

And it wasn't alive.

"I can't talk anymore, Donner. I hear Monty...."

She crawled until she saw Monty standing still.

Standing next to a body crushed beneath slabs of concrete.

Dead.

Please, Jesus. Let Monty be wrong.

Let Logan have a spark of life so she could save him.

She crawled closer.

Blood. She was crawling through blood.

"Easy, boy. Move just a little. I've got to help him."

Monty whimpered and shifted to one side.

Her flashlight speared the darkness, and her stomach wrenched. Blood. So much blood.

Puddled around the head.

Oh, God, not Logan.

Rudzak.

Eyes wide open, blood on his white hair, on his face and throat.

Dead.

Not Logan.

The relief was so strong, it made her light-headed.

"Find, Monty."

He looked at her, confused. Then he started down the pipe again.

Five minutes.

Ten minutes.

Darkness.

Dust.

Monty barked.

"Logan!"

No answer.

But she could see Monty ahead of her, and there had been eagerness in his bark.

"Logan! You answer me!"

"Sarah, what the hell are you doing down here?"

She almost fainted. She had to close her eyes for a moment before she could speak. "What do you think I'm doing? I'm rescuing you."

"Then get out of here and tell Galen to dig me out."

"Stop giving me orders. Where are you? I can't see you."

"I can't see you either, but I can hear you. I'm behind one of the collapsed columns in the lab."

"How many collapsed?"

"Two, one is still holding."

She wriggled closer to the sound of his voice. "There's a blockage."

"That's what I told you."

"But I think I can wriggle around it."

"Stay where you are."

"Shut up. Are you hurt?"

"A few cuts and bruises."

"Better than you deserve." She squeezed into the blocked passage. Monty whimpered eagerly and tried to come after her. "No, boy, you found him. Good boy. Now go tell Galen and Donner."

"*You* go tell Galen," Logan said.

"Go, Monty."

Monty looked at her uncertainly.

"Go."

He turned and started crawling back through the tunnel.

She spoke into her wire. "I've found Logan. I think he's okay. I've sent Monty to show you the way back." She switched off her wire, then turned the flashlight on Logan. "Now, where are these cuts and bruises that— You liar." She crawled closer to where he was lying. "It's broken?"

"I suspect."

"Anything else?"

"Isn't that enough?"

"Yes." Her hand trembled as she took out her first aid pack and got a good look at his arm. She cut the ropes binding him and then opened her pack. "It's not a compound fracture. I'm surprised because you never do things simple, do you?"

"The pot calling the kettle black."

"It could have been your idiotic head."

"That occurred to me. I didn't expect Rudzak to set a surprise charge before he left. I thought I had everything covered. I had the blueprints changed before he stole them to make the basement lab seem the perfect target. I knew he'd choose to—"

"Shut up and grit your teeth." She splinted the arm and then bound it. "Okay. It's done."

"I'm very...glad."

"So am I." She sat looking at him. "But I'll break your other arm if you ever try to keep anything from me again."

"It was necessary."

"Bull. Even if you didn't know about the second charge, you had to blow that pipe, didn't you? You had to take a chance that could—"

"I couldn't let him live. Not after Kai Chi. I just hope I got him."

"You did. Monty found him before we got here."

"Thank God."

"I thought he was you. I thought you were dead." She lay down beside him, not touching him. "I don't want you ever scaring me like this again."

"I think you could call this an extraordinary circumstance."

"I don't care what you call it. It's not going to happen. I don't want you hurt or broken or dead."

"Neither do I."

"Then you should take better care of yourself. You can't expect Monty and me to come after you whenever you get into trouble."

"I'll keep that in mind."

"Because we'll have to do it. We won't have a choice."

"Why not?"

She was silent a moment. "Because we...love you."

He stiffened. "You do?"

"Not that you deserve it. But that doesn't

seem to make a difference. We're stuck with you."

"My God, what a romantic declaration. I'm not sure whether it's you or Monty who's—"

"It's me. Monty has more sense." She moistened her lips. "And I don't care how many women you've loved in the past. Because I'm going to be the best and the last. We match. We could have a great marriage. I'll work at it and make you work at it until we have something that's really special."

"Are you asking for my hand in marriage?"

"No, I'm telling you that you should marry me because you're not going to find anyone who's better for you and I'm not going to let you go for the next hundred years or so."

"You don't have to be so argumentative." He cleared his throat. "I believe I made the first confession of affection. I could wish you hadn't chosen this hole in the ground in which to reply."

"I had to get it out."

"Could you at least take my hand?"

"No, I might hurt you. You broke your damn arm."

"I'll suffer."

She reached out and carefully linked her fingers with his. She whispered, "I do love you, Logan. I never thought I could love anyone like this. I hope you know it's not going to go away."

"I'll resign myself." He leaned his head on her shoulder and his weight felt dear and solid and wonderfully right. "There's only one other thing I want to know. It's of supreme importance."

"What?"

"Do you love me as much as you do your dog?"

EPILOGUE

They heard the wolf howl as soon as they got out of the jeep.

"Thank heavens." Eve had flung open the front door of the cabin and stared at them now in exasperation. "I never want to hear another wolf for the rest of my life. I may even cancel my subscription to *National Geographic*. I was tempted to give the animal a sedative just so we could get some sleep."

"Sorry." Sarah looked sheepish. "We'll take over. Where are Joe and Jane?"

"Out for a run. I think they wanted to get away from Maggie."

"That bad?"

"That bad." Eve glanced at Logan. "That cast on your arm may come in handy."

Maggie howled.

Monty barked joyously and disappeared into the house.

"You'd better monitor that encounter," Eve told Sarah. "She's very bad tempered. He may get his throat sliced."

"I think it will be okay," Sarah said. "She usually tolerates him. But we'll take a look."

"What are you going to do with her?"

"That's a big question," Logan said. "Do you think she'd like California?"

"No." Sarah frowned. "You can't take her out of the state. The authorities wouldn't permit it."

"I think I can guarantee that they'll cut us some slack."

"Even if you pull strings, what are we going to do? Let her roam among all those mansions on the seventeen-mile strip? She's better off here."

"And risk having your rancher friends shoot her?"

"No, of course not." She sighed. "It's just that Monty…"

"I know," Logan said. "He's got a problem." He tilted his head. "What's that?"

Sarah heard it too, a cross between a growl and a warble.

"Monty?" No, that wasn't Monty. She strode quickly to the back porch. "What's happen—"

Monty was on his back with his feet in the air. He gave an ecstatic woo-woo of a yodel.

Maggie growled in disgust but continued to lick Monty's face.

"I'd say that absence definitely made the heart grow fonder," Logan murmured. "That's more than toleration. Unless you want to turn Monty loose to roam with her, I believe we have to find a domestic solution. I can see a second generation on the horizon."

"Good luck," Eve said. "You'll need it."

"I'm not worried about luck." Sarah's gaze shifted from Maggie and Monty, and she smiled into Logan's eyes. "If we don't have it, we'll make it. Isn't that right, Logan?"

"I plead the Fifth Amendment. You've already accused me of blatant manipulation, and I've had enough problems convincing you to take a chance on me. If I rouse your suspicions, you might take your dog and head for the hills."

"What would you do then?"

"Go after you. Maggie and I would track you down. We both know what we want and we wouldn't give up. You told me that once Maggie committed, she'd mate for life."

"And what about you?"

He smiled. "Try me."